What Readers About *Paper*

D1538412

"I could hardly put it down. The history was quite a reminder."
– Marianne Mitchell

"Charming. Poignantly describes the twists and turns of life."
– Ariadne Voulgaris

"Wonderfully written and engaging." – Richard Sutz

"This book is a gem. Your characters spring to life
and I felt I knew them intimately." – Wink Blair

"Thought if I put it down the action would go on without me."
–Alvin Dattner

"Characters remained with me a long time. Only book I passed along to
both my mother and daughter." – Dorothy Bron

"My Book Club will love this!" – Rachel Thomas

"I was emotionally pulled into the lives of Paulina, Sarah and Mimi. Great
three-dimensional characters!" – Kim Hollenback

"I recommend this to everyone. Fosters great discussion!"
– Susan Brooks

"My heart strings were pulled to the breaking point."
– Daras Kirsh

"Loved these women!" – Janet Welk

"Weaves history, romance and adventure into a tapestry of family.
Magnificent creative piece." – Lee Robert

"One of the best books I've read this year! I learned so much."
– Gloria Robinson

"Truly evokes the times." – Virginia Nosky

"Have already passed my copy along to friends." – Tamara Gold

"Bravo! What a good story!" – Marcia Roth

"A real page turner. What a movie this would make!"
– Maxine and Bob Hyde

What Readers Are Saying
About *Paper Children* continued...

"Just finished Paper Children and loved it! The story is mine. It was expressed so well through dynamic characters reminiscent of my family." – Sandi Greenberg

"Riveting. Well researched. A must!" – Sharon Halliday

"An enjoyable way to learn history." – Roz Fischer

"I was touched, moved, totally absorbed." – Kathie Kelly

"Inspirational and clever! Every woman should read this book." – Elena Zee

"This compelling story progressed so quickly I couldn't put it down. A solid history lesson!" – Patricia Ternes

"I enjoyed reading about a real family, one that will live in my memory forever." – Abraham Lebos

"The twists of fate kept me holding my breath. This novel paints a fascinating view of Polish Jews and a vivid portrait of the aftermath of WWII." – Anya Achtenberg, author and poet

"Very sensitive description of characters. Bravo!" – Edith Kunz, author

"Well-researched novel about our shared history." – Vicki Cabot, *Phoenix Jewish News*

"The relationships between the three main characters are realistic, emotional and beautifully articulated. Fine's evocative metaphors and 360-degree descriptions allow the reader to see, smell, hear and feel each scene. She's an excellent writer and Paper Children is a must read." – Jenna Lee Dillon, *Trends*

"I indulged myself—finishing Paper Children in two days. Marcia Fine captured the deep essence of marriage, the way women have to suck back for survival and tradition. It's a gripping, elegant foray into a fleeting correspondence that sheds light on a time humanity should never, never forget. She's a writer worth following." – Renee Rivers, Associate Fiction Editor, *Hayden's Ferry Review*

Paper Children

An Immigrant's Legacy

···

Marcia Fine

For Tricia and Cody,

Another slice of history —

So wonderful to connect again!

xxt.

Marcia

7/18

Santa Fe

Other Novels by Marcia Fine

Gossip.com
Boomerang - When Life Comes Back to Bite You

The Blind Eye
First Prize Arizona Authors Association

Stressed in Scottsdale
First Prize Satire/Humor, Arizona Publishing Association
Silver, Living Now Awards
Honorable Mention, Arizona Author's Association

Paper Children
Finalist:
USA Book News Book of the Year,
Foreward, Book of the Year,
Eric Hoffer Award

For Lillian

Cover and interior design: Kim Appis
Photography: SMF Photography
Family Photographs: Marcia Fine

www.marciafine.com
www.paperchildren.com

Cataloging Publication Data Doctors
ISBN – 978-0-9826952-2-7
Library of Congress catalog card number: 2007927731
Scottsdale, Arizona
www.Limagepress.com
1. Historical fiction 2. Holocaust 3. Immigrants 4. Women's Issues
5. Poland 6. Florida 7. Displaced Persons Camps

Scottsdale, Arizona
 www.Limagepress.com

Paper Children

An Immigrant's Legacy

·•·

Marcia Fine

L'IMAGE PRESS

Scottsdale, Arizona

Preface

I had it in my mind to write about my grandmother's life since I was a small child. I adored her strange accent, wistful ways and interest in clothes. She told me tales of her life in Poland, her family and friends, the life she lost.

In my twenties I recorded these stories with their unusual places and incredible details. When I look back I realize she was the original story teller in the family. I never wanted to lose her voice and expressions. Before she passed she gave me piles of onionskin letters written in Polish, Yiddish and High German. It took me another thirty years before I knew their secrets.

Although many of the facts in this novel about her life and my grandfather's are true, including the prescience of gypsies, it is a work of fiction. Other family members and dialogue are fictionalized. Every attempt has been made at historical accuracy including visiting sites mentioned in New York, Miami and Poland.

I encourage others to learn their family history before the generation of immigrants and their wonderful stories pass. Their anecdotes are priceless.

The photograph on the cover is a photograph taken in Warsaw of Paulina in her early twenties.

PROLOGUE

Warsaw, Poland
September 1910

"Miss Paulina, what are you doing? You know your mama doesn't allow you in the kitchen. A boiling pot could fall on you." The servant shook her head, her mouth corners turned down in disapproval.

"I'm hungry. No, I'm thirsty." I played with a button in the pocket of my pinafore.

"Miss Paulina, if you want something you're to pull the tapestry cord and we bring it to you," said Magda, the cook, taking charge. She spoke to me in country Polish, not the language my parents used to converse. She wiped her mouth with the back of her hand and pushed her chair away from the table. The small warts on her chin reminded me of a witch from Hansel and Gretel. With a bustle to the stove she stirred the cholent, her large rear wide beneath the fabric of her dress.

"Yes, I know, but I want to see what you do down here." I shifted in my new shoes hand-made by Mr. Weiner.

"Come in, come in," urged Yadwiga, the youngest, offering me a chair at the barren table. "It's almost time for dinner, but I'll find you a rugelach." The rolled cookies filled with nuts, cinnamon or bits of chocolate were my favorite. "What about a glass of milk?"

Yadwiga, moved to a large pine cabinet, opening the doors to reveal shelves filled with tablecloths, napkins, aprons, table runners and vases, large and small in silver and glass. The Sabbath candlesticks, trays, and silverware in lined felt drawers remained locked in cabinets. Yadwiga's taut calves above her rolled cotton stockings bulged as she reached for a higher shelf.

A white linen placemat trimmed with lace appeared in front of me. Yadwiga smoothed it with her hand, the blunt fingernails clean but short. Magda placed a folded cloth napkin with a glass of milk on the placemat. Magda's large hands, a piece of gauze wrapped around a finger where she must have cut herself chopping vegetables, looked rough and red.

Yadwiga said, "You're thin so I know your mama will be pleased you're eating something." She turned to Magda. "See how blue the veins are on her arms?"

Yadwiga placed two rugelach on a white Rosenthal plate, edged in gold, and brought them to the table. I nibbled them like a winter squirrel, savoring every bite. The flavor of the sweetened dough satisfied me as I looked around the kitchen, absorbing the strange utensils, shiny copper pots hanging from a rack above the stove, metal trays, cookie sheets, large wooden spoons and two iron sinks. The steam from the cholent rose in wet clouds, the aroma enveloping the room. Yadwiga sat across from me, pleased at every bite I took. She said I reminded her of the younger sister she left in her village.

A sharp rap from the back door interrupted my reverie. I never went out that way, but I knew there was a concrete porch and beyond that, stairs to the back alley, a fence, and a place for refuse.

Magda bustled to look through the pane of glass across the top of the door. "Quickly," she hissed, her hands signaling a beckoning motion, "the gypsies are here."

Gypsies? A thrill of excitement raced through me.

The others stood up to search their pockets for coins. "I can't find any change. I'll have to look in my room," said Yadwiga as she rushed out the door.

Hard footsteps echoed on the tile floor in the hallway outside the kitchen. "Ladies," my mother's voice said to the group huddled near the back door. I bowed my head in a child's effort to hide.

With her heavy gait she marched over to the table and asked me, "What are you doing here? I've told you to leave the help alone."

Too frightened to answer, I stared at her black lace-up shoes on the black and white tiles. My eyes moved upward past her navy skirt to glasses that hung from a chain around her neck. I searched Magda's face for help. She shrugged her shoulders.

My mother, not as stern as she appeared, admonished them for allowing me to be in the kitchen. Yadwiga sidled in and stood near the stove, her hands in her pockets clinking coins. When my mother looked at her, she stopped toying with the change and turned to stir the cholent.

My mother addressed me, "You are not to be down here. Come with me."

She turned to Magda and said, "You know better than this." Her soft hand with pretty rings encircled my upper arm. "Paulina, your piano lesson starts soon." Afraid to resist, I said nothing. I blinked, worried I wouldn't be able to finish my rugelach.

Yadwiga came to my defense, eyes cast downward. "May she drink her milk? She's so thin."

My mother looked at me, her hand grasped around my slim arm, and dropped her grip. The pressure of her hand left the white material of my blouse bunched. "All right. This time only. But if I catch her down here again, you're all fired."

An urgent knock came from the back door again.

The faces of the servants froze. My mother's strides covered the kitchen floor in moments. She looked out the door.

"What are they doing here?"

No one answered. The servants focused on a speck of schmutz

on the wall or the pot on the stove, anything not to look at my mother.

"Fine. I don't know who's responsible, but I don't want them near our home. They're dangerous. Magda, send them away."

Magda moved toward the door and opened it a slice. I couldn't hear what she said, but the motion of her hand made the dark hair disappear.

My mother exited the kitchen and swiped a rugelach from the jar on the sideboard, her navy taffeta skirt swishing by us.

I stared into my milk. No one said anything, but I knew they wanted to talk about my mother's intrusion.

A frantic knock hammered the door.

Magda looked through the door window while Yadwiga ran to check the hallway.

Magda said, "Hurry. They're back."

In haste the servants pulled sweaters and shawls from iron hooks on the wall. I stayed at the table watching the cluster of women gather around the door. I imagined a dark head below them on the steps peeking through the hazy glass.

I left the table and ventured toward the group to put my arms around Yadwiga's waist. A dark, older gypsy, spiders of gray running through her untamed hair, stood ready to read fortunes. Her lined face, beautiful with age, had the longest, darkest eyelashes I had ever seen. The fringe of the ruby shawl wrapped around her shoulders, swayed in the breeze. I watched her gold hoop earrings move as she spoke in a strange accent that was probably Romanian because that's where gypsies lived when they weren't traveling.

My mother had warned me, my hand held tight, when we passed overloaded wagons with gypsies and their furniture, "Be careful. They steal possessions and children."

"Why?"

"They have no jobs. They don't live anyplace. And they never bathe." Their lilting songs accompanied by soulful instruments fascinated me. My mother said I asked too many questions.

"Open your palm for me," the gypsy woman said to Yadwiga who pushed to the front of the gathering. The others watched from the side. Magda stood behind them, her stirring spoon held high above their heads, in case she had to run back to the steaming cholent.

The gypsy's two gold teeth glittered as she began to stroke Yadwiga's outstretched hand for inspiration. I cowered behind her skirt. What an act of defiance to be so close.

The gypsy's eyes closed for a moment, then opened. She said in a low voice, "A young man desires you. He wants to take you to exotic places. You will have many babies."

Yadwiga giggled and covered her mouth.

I smelled something other than the cholent and fresh pumpernickel. As it wafted to my nostrils I realized it was the gypsy, her strong perfume and body odor twisting into a pungent mixture with the cool fall air.

As each servant took her turn, I became bolder. I stood next to them without clinging, able to observe not only the head gypsy, but the group at the bottom of the steps. A father, his head wrapped in a dirty turban, leaned against a painted wagon, pulling at black whiskers on his face. A young woman of Yadwiga's age, her ruby velvet skirt patched in places, wore an embroidered vest. Three small children with dirty faces and no shoes, played near refuse in barrels. No shoes! My mother would kill me.

When the palms had all been read and the gypsy paid her coins, Magda attempted to close the door. The gypsy's frayed slipper stopped her.

"What about her?" the gypsy asked, her chin thrust toward me.

Magda stepped aside to look behind her.

"No, her mother wouldn't like it." The cook's wide hips took up most of the doorway. "Thank you. That's all for today."

"But, madam," said the gold-toothed gypsy, her voice crackling a bit, "I want to read her palm." A crooked finger pointed at me.

I shook my head, no.

"Come, Miss Paulina, let's find out your future," she said as she stroked my hair.

"No. I don't have any coins." Fear sailed through my body.

"I'll pay," said Yadwiga.

Yadwiga dived into the front pocket of her apron for money and dropped it into the outstretched palm, designed with calluses and torn skin. I loosened my hands from her waist, curling them into fists at my side.

Yadwiga pushed me toward the open door. Without a wool scarf the air sucked the moisture from my throat. An unwashed odor wafted into my nostrils, like my own feet when I'd worn shoes too long.

"And, now yours, sweet one," she said smiling at me. Her black eyes locked into mine. She looked like a Brothers' Grimm witch from the tales my older brothers read to me at bedtime. I uncurled my fingers. When the old woman smoothed my palm, her rough fingers felt strange. Dark places under her nails gave me chills as I remembered Mama's warning about gypsies.

The wrinkled woman squinted at me. "You will marry a man much older." She stared at my small palm, her odor stronger as she forced me to take a step closer, pulling my wrist. She glanced back at one of the barefoot children who began to cry. "You will move to America."

America? Who would want to go there?

"When you leave you will never see your family again."

I pulled my hand away and turned back toward the warm kitchen.

Book One

Paulina
October, 1920

Chapter One

Paulina

October, 1920 ∞ Warsaw, Poland

Gustav loved me more than I loved him when we became engaged. My family thought it was the right thing to do; after all, I was twenty with few suitors. My friend, Yula whom I met through our piano teacher, Madame Selinski, introduced him to me. Yula, a gifted violinist a few years older than me, was engaged to an older man of twenty-nine. Her fiancé, Solomon, a tailor from a privileged family, had ten people sewing fine silk, wool and gabardine suits for men in his own shop. Gustav, a casual friend of his, said he fell in love with me when he saw my pale eyes, the color of lilacs.

The engagement party held in our home made the society pages. I wore a gown of blueberry taffeta and sapphire earrings, a gift from my father. Gustav and his family showered me with gifts—a silver evening bag for the opera, a ruby ring, Belgian lace. For the first six months we were engaged, Gustav came on Sundays with his family. We sat in the parlor, the women balancing drinks on their laps, perched forward in the chairs, feet planted on the floor. I was shy so I played the piano, mostly Chopin. Once we played a duet together. We said little to one another. He looked down when I looked at him, the peach fuzz of his mustache sweet on his lip. He was being trained in his family's haberdashery business and I was trained to be a lady.

Yet, we had a conflict as his confidence grew in the second half of the year. The wedding date needed to be set and I was not anxious. Gustav became demanding, telling me what to do. "Order the invitations. Book the staff. Pick wines. After we're married, no more music lessons." I wasn't ready. Used to the freedom in my home with parents who trusted me, something inside me didn't like his domineering manner.

One Saturday evening after the *Shabbat* meal, Yula and her fiancé, Solomon, Gustav and I went to a reading of Isaac Peretz's works. Excited about the prospect of hearing the gifted Yiddish writer who blended Jewish folklore and Hasidic tradition, I begged my parents to let me go. I wasn't allowed to be with Gustav alone, but they felt Yula was old enough to chaperone me. I pulled my lamb's wool coat with the mink collar and cuffs closer to me as we walked down the cobblestone streets, the light breath of a breeze in our hair.

Afterward we stopped for drinks at a popular café near the Volta River. In the darkness lit with table candles I noticed a few soldiers nearby after we were seated. One of them, a handsome man, caught my eye and nodded to me. I turned back to our group without acknowledgement. We didn't mix with Gentiles.

While we sipped sherry and sat laughing at one of Solomon's stories about a fat man who insisted his pants be made in a smaller size, the soldier appeared at my side.

"Would the young lady like to dance?" he asked, his speech slurred from too many beers.

I did nothing to encourage him. Horrified, I shook my head. Gustav stood up.

"She's engaged to me," he said, his chest pumped out. The soldier was taller and impressive in his uniform.

"I asked the lady to dance," he repeated in a louder voice.

"And I told you she can't," said Gustav.

"Aw, leave them alone," yelled one of his cohorts. "They're a bunch of Yids."

Solomon's chair scraped the floor as he stood up to join Gustav. "I don't think you should make trouble because the lady doesn't want to dance." At least as tall as the soldier he said, "Nor should you call us derogatory names."

I pulled on Gustav's sleeve. "Let's go. Don't make trouble."

He pushed me away. "I'm not going to let someone intimidate me into leaving," he snarled. He turned to the soldier. "What did your friend call us?"

Maybe I knew what ordinary Poles thought of us, but I rarely encountered it. My mother said they were jealous of our wealth.

I stood up. "It's time to go, anyway. My father will be expecting me."

When I saw the soldier's arm pull back to hit Gustav in the face, I screamed. The sound of flesh pressing into bone made my stomach turn. I reached for Yula's shoulder.

Gustav staggered backward, his eyes rolling in pain. He pulled himself upright and charged at the soldier, a bull with his head down. I grabbed for his arm as he moved past me, as though I could stop him. His jacket peeled off him and landed on the floor.

When the soldier hit Gustav again, blood spewed from his nose. Solomon punched another soldier, glasses shattering when a table turned over. A candle knocked off its base set the tablecloth on fire. Yula hit the flames with the bottom of her shoe.

As the rest of the soldiers involved themselves in the fray, I ran out the door, abandoning my silver evening purse. I looked over my shoulder and saw Gustav and Solomon punching with abandon, Yula screaming nearby.

I ran toward the street and luck gave me an empty carriage.

When we got to Bielanska Street I remembered the purse. It didn't matter. I had no money in it anyway. I knew my family would be asleep, the door left unlocked for me. The driver was not pleased he would have to return tomorrow for his fare but I promised him a big tip. I crept into the house and stole into my bed. Gustav was a fool. Was I ever going to marry him?

Asleep when the carriage driver arrived for his fare, I explained to my father and mother later that Gustav seemed ill-tempered.

Gustav came to call on me a few times during the next days, but I refused to see him. Yadwiga told me his eye was black-and-blue and scratches marred his smooth skin.

Yula stopped by. "He's sorry for the brawl. He loves you," she told me.

The next day I received a note on pastel paper, the handwriting in even strokes across the page.

> *My dearest Paulina,*
> *Forgive me for my desire to protect you in such a gross manner. I will not cause a scene again. I'm in love for the first time with a passion that rings in my ears. We must be together. Please do not let your beautiful face fade from my memory. I must see you.*
> *Gustav*

And so, I relented. We began to keep company again, but I didn't venture outside with him. My father said hooligans ruled the streets. Pressure began to build, especially when we sat in the parlor on Sundays with our families.

"Gustav's sister is to be married next year and we have a trip abroad planned," his mother told me one Sunday in December.

I knew I couldn't delay much longer. I thought if I waited my desire would grow, but so far I felt the same, complacent and resigned.

Finally, we set a date for six months in the future. Thrilled with the happy news, our families buzzed with plans. The wedding would take place in the basement *shul* of our building on a Saturday night at sundown, the end of the Sabbath.

One afternoon after the seamstress left, I contemplated my fate as a soon-to-be married woman. Would I still be able to spend time with my friends? I sat in the front balcony window that overlooked Bielanska Street, its cobblestones and concrete-poured sidewalks. Shoppers hurried with brown wrapped bundles, children played in the street, their balls elusive in the shadows, men wandered into a tavern across the street and the barber in his white jacket next door stood outside greeting people.

My father approached in step with a tall man who looked mature, maybe thirty, wearing an expensive overcoat, his hat brim pulled to a jaunty angle. His gait was one of confidence. They looked up and I waved, even smiling, a rare flirtation for me. Later, he would say he could see the depth of my blue eyes two floors above him.

My father invited the same gentleman, Nathan, to *Shabbat*, an elegant affair in our dining room with lace tablecloths, china and my mother's best silver. As the evening light faded we lit candles and recited the prayers over wine and bread. Nathan wore his dark hair combed to the side. With a straight Roman nose and strong dented chin, he had a handsome countenance. I could barely speak. He looked at me all through the blessing, his hand grazing mine as we passed the *challah*. There were hairs on his knuckles. A grown man, not a boy.

After supper he and my father made business plans in the library. With mutual interests in exports, my father's knowledge of languages and Nathan's burning desire for success, they forged an alliance. Later I heard my father tell my mother, "Even my sons don't have such a head for business."

When Nathan wasn't traveling he became a regular at our table. I can't deny the attraction to him, his manliness and his interest in me. My self-consciousness rendered me speechless at times because he looked at me with desire.

One night after supper, only a few months before my wedding, Nathan caught me in the foyer as he prepared to leave.

"Who is this Gustav you're engaged to? Why is he never around?"

I found myself defending his absence. "Gustav and I keep company on Sundays. We're to be married soon."

"Your father says he's a haberdasher. You're in love with this fellow? This is what you want? To be the wife of a man who makes hats?"

I backed away. I wasn't used to confrontations.

"My father says it is a good match."

Nathan made a noise with his lips. "Your father would say I'm a better match." He stepped closer in the darkness. "Would you like to cast your fate with an adventurer?"

My heart almost choked my throat. No longer intimidated I gave him a sly look. "And what does an adventurer do?"

"Fills your life with passion and excitement."

"I'm happy where I am. Right here in my papa's house." My palms reached back to touch the wall.

He tilted my chin toward him with one finger. "Break your engagement. Marry me. You can live here while I build a fortune. I can make you happy."

I turned and ran to my room, delighted with the knowledge that two men wanted me. What a child I was.

The next week my resolve not to marry Gustav strengthened.

I moped knowing it would be difficult to break it off, but I was bored already. Nathan arrived for Sabbath after traveling to Russia with a shipment of eyeglasses. He brought a bouquet of flowers for mother. We ate in silence, stealing looks at each other.

And then, my father announced to everyone Nathan would be my fiancé. Just like that.

"Maybe he will be a better match," my father told me later, knowing my unhappiness. Not quite as feckless as Gustav is what he meant. I adored my father who knew what was best.

I broke the engagement with a hand delivered letter that took me hours to write. Gustav and his family were furious and demanded their gifts back. I returned them all, except for the lost purse, with a note. I felt guilty not so much at the breaking of my agreement but with my delight at being free of Gustav and his oppressive family.

Did I have any say? Any choice? I suppose if I had objected my father might have listened, but what was the difference? Gustav or Nathan? I didn't know either of them. All I cared about was my life of music lessons and shopping and concerts and friends. I didn't want it to change.

After the engagement announcement Nathan joined my father in the import business: spices from Africa, linens from Belgium, delicacies from Germany, caviar from Russia.

Nathan spoke to me in Russian, a language I had studied, with words that were so expressive, romantic and mellifluous to my ears that I dreamed about his stories. I didn't know every word but our attempts at translation charmed me.

"In the beginning I started small," he told me. "The Russians have nothing and there's little manufacturing. My first shipment was a few bushels of pencils and paper from Warsaw in a cart. I sold them for triple what I paid for them. Next I found a bargain load of men's pants. They sold immediately. The past few years I have traveled all over Poland to buy goods. I rented entire trains filling cars with eyeglasses, fruit, underwear, brooms, towels, liquor. I buy with Polish zlotys. When I sell the goods I collect in rubles. Now with your father's backing I'll expand even more."

Nathan, twelve years my senior, was a man for my girlish dreams, a businessman who spoke in elegant Russian, the language of poets. Gustav faded with my girlhood.

The wedding with my family in attendance was held in the basement synagogue of our apartment house. No one from Nathan's side came. I wore my grandmother's veil, a beautiful piece of Belgian lace that trailed to the floor, covering my face. The day of the wedding I cried as I looked at myself in my mother's long oval mirror in my parents' grand bedroom.

"Papa, I don't know him. I'm afraid."

My mother held me to her bosom. Gustav, close to my age, seemed more appealing. We would both be innocents.

My father tried to allay my fears. "Don't worry, Paulina. You're living upstairs in a sunny apartment. Nathan's traveling with me on business so your mama will be here. And your brothers. Trust me, it's a good match. Someday your mother and I won't be here and he will take good care of you."

"But I don't like the way he eats."

"It's not important. Yes, I admit, he's a bit rough. Most Russians are. He carries terrible sadness of pogroms, Cossacks, hunger. One month his city of Slonim was in Poland, the next, Russia. Do you know what that means? New rulers, different money, persecution. You have to be smart to figure it out. His mother sent him to Warsaw with nothing, a child living on the streets at twelve years of age. Did you know he moved all ten of his brothers and sisters and his parents away under cover of darkness? Any man that takes care of his family that way will make a good provider. No more talk."

I moved away from my mother to sit down on her brocade lounge, her French perfume trailing away. My father leaned closer. "They were starving. He dug up potatoes with his fingers from a farmer's field to feed everyone. The oldest son accepts responsibility because the father studies the Talmud all day. Nathan's ambitious, smart and tough. It will be good." He patted my knee.

"Oh, Papa." I hugged him as I always did as a child. We were a close family and more affectionate than most.

My mother clucked as she checked the buttons on the back of my dress, then whispered in my ear, "We'll show him more refined ways."

"Are the potato-eating relatives coming?" I panicked. Coarse people at my wedding?

"No. They can't make it. Nathan left Russia for good when they conscripted him for the Army. Terrible what they do to Jewish boys who can't buy their way out, forcing them to eat *trefe*. He walked across the steppes to Poland."

"He's told me little of his background. Yet, I see he has belief in himself."

My father tapped the side of his head with two fingers. "He's got *sechel*."

I was so naïve. I thought, he's good looking and he carries himself well. We'll have beautiful children. But what did I have to do to get the children?

I turned to my mother. "What about tonight?"

She took my hand and kissed it. "It will be all right. Don't worry, Paulina."

And with that she led me downstairs to the waiting guests who included Yula, Solomon and all my relatives. Carlo, my favorite brother, winked at me. My oldest brother, Mendel, and his wife had a suite of rooms on the fourth floor. They sat in the front with their two children who kicked their little legs. They were like a brother and sister to me, adorable in their dress-up clothes. I was teaching Natasha the piano.

Only my middle brother, Itzak, was missing. With the sleeping sickness he dozed most of the days away in a stupor. I wasn't as close to him because of his illness. Boris, my father's valet and assistant, bathed and dressed him. My mother also fussed over Itzak, adjusting his clothes and combing his hair as though he was going to get up and go outside. I thought it a waste of time.

My mother handed me white roses imported from Holland. Nathan in a dark suit, a black *kipah* on the back of his head, waited under the *chuppa*, the canopy draped with a *tallit* prayer shawl to represent the home. The rabbi, his teeth yellowed like old piano keys, stood in front of us. His long black coat and beard swayed with the sing-song words that lulled my emotions. Nathan lifted the veil from my face and kissed me.

I was married.

That first night we slept together in the same bed in our new apartment decorated especially for us. It was a wedding gift from my parents along with a smaller, fully occupied building my father owned a few blocks away. Nathan was to collect the rents. After unpleasant heaving and breathing with his weight on top of me, I felt a little pain. I was surprised when it was over so quickly. He rolled off me, asleep in moments.

In the morning he checked the sheets for blood. It was there. My father and Nathan left for work together. I cried to my mother about my unhappy experience. I'm not sure what I expected, but it seemed so cold.

"Wait. It will get better," she told me.

"And if it doesn't?"

"Then you'll have to bear with it. It's a wife's duty."

Nathan liked it every day. I tried, but it was all for his pleasure.

He never stroked or kissed or held me, always in a rush. I don't know why. He'd only fall asleep afterward.

Of course I was pregnant in a few months. At first I didn't know what was wrong with me, tired all the time and nauseous when I looked at food. My mother knew right away.

"You're pregnant so fast? You couldn't wait a while? It doesn't look nice to be pregnant in such a short time."

"How could I have stopped him?" I asked, my eyes large with questions.

"Don't do it in the middle of the month. That's when you're the most fertile. Say you have a headache. Otherwise, you'll be pregnant every year." She sighed at me. "It's too late now."

The thought of feeling like this every year scared me. I turned away ashamed of myself.

The maids helped me, otherwise, I don't know how I would have managed. I slept late. Yadwiga brought a breakfast of tea and toast. I vomited anyway, spoiling the Belgian bedspread.

Nathan traveled often with my father to Berlin, Vienna, Paris and Brussels. When he was gone, I lived the life I had before I was married. As a woman with child I didn't go out much. I read. I practiced French with my cousin Malka. I played piano. If I wrapped myself in one of my mother's larger overcoats, Carlo and I could go for long walks, arm in arm through the beautiful parks that lined the Volta River. When the weather warmed, flowers bloomed in profusion and we attended outdoor concerts.

Our seamstress moved in for a few weeks to expand the waistlines on my skirts, make me dressing gowns and work on the family's wardrobe. I loved watching her sew in the attic aerie, head bent, her foot pumping the machine, the wild colors of thread in a basket next to her. Her son brought bolts of material that leaned in the corners of the tiny room, herringbones, velvet, wools, silks, tulle for petticoats, lace for collars, everything made-to-order.

Later in the winter the baby came, a boy we named Isaac after my mother's father. The *bris*, God's oldest covenant with the Jewish people, was on the eighth day to prove the baby could survive one Sabbath. When I couldn't bring forth any milk, Magda from the kitchen nursed him for me. It was her fifth child and my first.

The following year I was pregnant again. My mother let me know her disgust. "The servants have babies every year, not a lady. I told you what to do." I dropped my eyes and shook my head. He liked it.

Me? It didn't matter. I became used to it. The ordeal didn't take long. His body would slide on top of me then roll off to his side of the bed. He slept, tired from business and travel. Ambitious, he wanted an empire by forty.

The rest of the time my life remained a placid pastoral scene. I had a wet nurse for baby Isaac after Magda said it was too much. I checked on him throughout the day. She bathed him, took care of the messy part and I went for walks pushing his carriage, a linen cap on his head under the wool one that matched the sweater Mama knitted.

The second pregnancy was easier but the little girl died after a few days. I don't know why. Many women lost babies. I'm glad I didn't die because it was a long labor. Nathan and my father left the house after twelve hours. The midwife and the doctor tried to help, but she was fussy and small. When Magda went to her crib on the third day, she was lifeless.

The aftermath of the World War caused hardships for poor people but not us. We lived the same. I told Nathan the doctor did not want me to be pregnant so fast. I don't think he heard me. I woke up one morning with an acrid taste in my mouth. I made it to the washbowl in time but I knew. Pregnant again. I wasn't happy or sad, just part of the routine.

By that time my father had turned over many of the operations to Nathan for the import/export business. My father and my brother, Mendel, focused on the construction of apartments. Nathan approached my father with an idea while we sat in the library after dinner, the women reading or knitting, the men talking with a glass of sherry.

Nathan cleared his throat and placed his glass on the table next to him. He leaned forward in his chair. "I want to bring the business to America, a land of many opportunities. It's a safer place for my family. Europe is not a good place for Jews. Let's expand."

My father was startled, skeptical. He thought Nathan reckless. "Go to America with cowboys and Indians? A primitive, dirty place without culture, filled with the uneducated. Why are you paranoid?" My father sat back, his hands forming a pyramid. "Our families have lived in Poland since the fifteenth century. No one is going to harm us."

"Whenever there's a problem they always blame the Jews. We're always looking over our shoulder," said Nathan.

Nathan persisted, a stubborn, determined man who continued to pursue my father at every opportunity for financing to go to the United States. I whispered to my mother that my bed would be empty for a while.

My father relented. Early in the Spring of the following year Nathan left for an exploratory trip to the United States. It took two weeks to get there, he stayed for a month and then returned. He decided after his first trip that Jews needed *yarmulkes*, prayer books, *tallit*, *tefillin*, everything necessary for worship in the new country. He shipped trunks filled with religious articles.

After he left I learned I was pregnant again. By the time I delivered a little girl named Sarah in 1924, Nathan, who had traveled back and forth a few more times, was settled in New York

City. We sent him a telegram at his hotel. He didn't show much interest in the new baby in the letters he wrote to me. He was more excited about America and its possibilities. It didn't matter. I had my family around me.

Nathan returned with big plans and grand ideas. After long discussions in the library with closed doors, he convinced my father to back him with more inventory and money. Religious articles weren't enough. He spent months in preparation for his new venture. He haggled with local vendors over an inventory of nuts, spices, linens, flax, rope, shawls, caps and enameled Russian boxes, traveling to surrounding countries, shipping boxes to store, a whirlwind of activity.

I kissed Nathan goodbye with Isaac and Sarah at my side in the spring of 1925. Once again he took a train to London, then sailed to America. Nathan wrote to me on tissue-thin paper about the wonders of New York, the people and commerce. He stayed in a rooming house near Orchard Street. When he returned to Poland months later he brought gifts for me and the children and a signed contract to show my father. They were to import leather for shoes.

Nathan lacked patience when he returned. Isaac feared his occasional outbursts. He hid when he heard his father's loud footsteps preferring the company of Carlo. I did my best to please Nathan, but he remained distracted. He added numbers in his head, wrote notes that he stuffed into his pockets, talked to my father endlessly about business as though his heart burned with fire.

Nathan decided it was time for me to meet his family. We left the children with their grandparents and took a train to Bialystok. On our ride he shared his dreams and big ideas. He wanted to conquer the world. I listened with little understanding of his urgency. Life was comfortable. Why change anything?

Nathan wanted to move his family away from the Russian-

Polish border. With skirmishes as to whom owned the land, the money changed from rubles to zlotys every week. His parents, sweet unsophisticated people, couldn't deal with the worthless money, lack of goods and the fear of another pogrom.

When I met them they offered me a glass of tea and *mandel* bread, a hard cookie with almonds. The youngest girls, a set of twins named Goldie and Ruby stroked my fur collar and handed me wildflowers.

"You're the most beautiful woman I've ever seen," Goldie told me.

Nathan opened a cupboard and saw how little they had so we took the twins for a walk to the market. They chased behind us through the labyrinth of cobblestone streets. The country market, a series of wooden stalls, had fresh vegetables, chickens available for slaughter, and trinkets. I bought carved boxes and amber beads for my family, embroidered hankies for Magda and Yadwiga, ribbons for Goldie and Ruby. Nathan purchased food for his parents' table from the peasant women who gossiped among themselves, dressed in layers of clothes without coats. I was so uncomfortable. Later I saw him slip money to his mother when we returned to their small space of two rooms with a dirt floor.

While we talked one of Nathan's younger brothers ran into the tiny kitchen breathless. "A Russian is looking for you." He leaned against the wall in an effort to stop panting.

Panic spread across Nathan's face. "Who is he? What does he want?"

"I don't know. He said he has to talk to you. Tonight." He smiled revealing a gap in his mouth where a tooth was missing. "He gave me this," he said holding up a silver coin. "He wants to meet you at the inn."

Nathan, agitated that his slip from the czar might catch up with him, stood up. He paced the room from corner to corner, his hands behind his back. The Russian Army looked hard for deserters, killing them in front of their regiment. "Come on. Let's go," he said to me. "Those bastards can't do anything to me."

"We can't leave. There's no train. How do you know what he wants?" I asked, examining my lips in a small mirror from my purse.

It was the first time Nathan listened to me. He sat down.

"You're right. What can he do? I'm married to a Polish citizen," he said, looking at me.

We ate a lamb dinner at the inn and waited. A Russian military man in a khaki uniform, medals across his chest and high brown boots, approached us. He stared at me under the brim of his hat, his bushy mustache twitching when he spoke.

"Welcome," he said, pulling out a chair to join us.

Nathan's body tensed, the veins in his neck pulsing. The general offered Nathan a cigar that he accepted. He coughed at the new experience.

"In America everyone smokes," Nathan told the man.

The Russian leaned back in his chair. "I've heard about you, quite the businessman. You already know how to move products, deal with suppliers, watch for pilferers. I'll get to the point," he said putting his elbows on the table. He looked around and said in a low voice. "I want you to be the main distributor for vodka in Poland. I'll give you the entire territory." His fat fingers gripped the cigar he sucked.

"I can't. My wife and I are going to move to America."

I sat up straighter in my chair, readjusted my scarf. I am?

The man spit on the floor then pulled a piece of tobacco from his lip. "America? Barbarians. I'm offering you two hundred thousand zlotys and jobs for all your relatives."

"No, we're leaving Europe," Nathan said, his legs stretched out in front of his chair. He puffed and stopped to look at the cigar.

"Look, start the business for me. Stay a few years. Then take it to the United States. I understand they have a great thirst for our product. In the meantime, you'll make a lot of money."

"Double your offer and I'll consider it." Nathan's eyes took in the room to see if anyone was listening.

The Russian began to sputter. "That's robbery. What about my profit? And the bosses?"

"I'm sorry. It's an excellent offer but I can't accept." Nathan stood, shook the man's hand and turned to leave. "Call me when you're serious. This is for amateurs." Turning to me, he said, "Paulina, let's go."

I scrambled to grab my bag, coat and kidskin gloves.

"You're making a big mistake," the man called after us as Nathan guided me toward the door. "All right, I'll offer you a third more."

With our backs to him Nathan turned his head to the side, his scarf tucked into his coat. "Double or nothing. No one will be able to keep the hoodlums in line, but me."

Silence. We waited in the wooden doorway.

The man sighed and I heard the slap of his hand on the table. "You win. You've got an honest reputation and you're a businessman with a wolf's ambition. Four hundred thousand."

Nathan turned and returned to face him as the Russian stood. "I'll let you know my final decision in a few weeks," said Nathan.

Nathan looped his arm through mine, patting my hand as we strolled away from the inn toward his parents' home, toying with his cigar. My breath blew small vapor mists as we walked the deserted street, the moon shining on our faces, Nathan's profile potent in the dimness. I'd never heard a negotiation before but I knew my fate was forever tied to this man and his vision. I believed in his strength and decisiveness. Did this mean we would stay?

Chapter Two

Paulina

1925

After we returned to Warsaw, Nathan began to bring his brothers and sisters closer to us. Not to the city proper, but to smaller towns like Plock and Tykocin that were nearby. He traveled often, attending meetings, always on the verge of the next deal. Without a head for business I rarely understood what he was doing. The beautiful things life had to offer occupied me: music, art, books. If we were together, it was under the covers, a private time that I no longer dreaded but accepted.

One day Nathan, fully dressed and shaved, stood at the end of our bed. I was sitting up with a breakfast tray, my tea steaming hot in a china cup, a rose in a silver vase placed at the edge.

"Paulina, what are you doing today?"

I changed the subject because I knew he didn't approve of what I did with my time. I asked about the Russian we had met and his offer of vodka distribution in Poland.

"I'm not interested."

"Why not?" I was wary of the general, but I thought if Nathan was more engaged in Poland, he might be distracted from his passion to live in America.

"Who knows where he's getting the vodka? He might be setting me up. I don't want to deal with liquor or Russians."

"But why did you negotiate so hard?"

"Paulina, it's part of the game. I'm going to be a big shot in America. I was practicing."

He sounded exasperated and dismissed me with wave of his hand.

In six months Nathan left for America. A sigh draped itself over our house. At the time my brother, Carlo, was seeing a lovely woman, a violinist named Berta, who accompanied me to concerts and tea in the cafés. My parents and the staff watched the children.

Nathan wrote letters urging me to come to New York. They became repetitive.

> *My beautiful Paulina,*
> *Bring Isaac and Sarah. We'll have a third baby*
> *on American soil. He will be a citizen! This is*
> *the greatest country in the world. It's modern, the*
> *wave of what is to come. You will never know the*
> *breath of true freedom until you are in America.*
> *Your loving husband,*
> *Nathan*

The difficulty of traveling such a great distance with two small children overwhelmed me. After all, I had never done anything by myself, except maybe get dressed and I even had help with that. I was too afraid to contemplate such a trip. What would I do when I got there? I knew I didn't know how to manage a household, see to meals, take care of the children, let alone speak English. Also, I was pregnant again. When I bled a little, I said it was more. The doctor and my father forbade it.

And, as though I had jinxed myself, I lost the baby early, not so uncommon among the women I knew who lived in a cycle of pregnancy, miscarriages, pregnancy and births. I felt sad, but knew Nathan would return to give me another child. The doctor said I needed more rest for my weak constitution. I resumed my routine and included daily naps, waking late in the afternoon to the children's voices in the courtyard.

Nathan returned while the business prospered, showing me wads of dollars he brought with him. He worked with a slipper factory on the Lower East side, supplying the materials, importing leather from Eastern Europe, and selling the finished product in bulk to wholesalers. He even invested some profits in the American stock market, something I didn't understand.

In the meantime, the business he started with religious articles now included *tzdakeh* boxes for charity, *mezuzahs* for the door, rabbi's religious robes, black sealskin hats for the Orthodox, things Jewish people used and needed.

Nathan engaged his brother, Shemuel, to help. A tall, stoop-shouldered man with large eyes that seemed to pop from his head, Shemuel idolized his older brother, always ready to do Nathan's bidding. They were leaving in two weeks.

Alone in our bedroom we dressed for dinner. I stood with my back to Nathan as he buttoned my dress. He cursed as the fabric slipped in his fingers, a blue *peau de soie* that my father brought from Nice.

"Paulina, come with me. Leave the children. Take a look around in America. If you don't like it, you can come back," he urged, kissing my neck.

"I can't. It's too much for me." My nerves made me shake just thinking about such a big, new place without anything familiar. He turned me around to him, his face twisted with worry. I could tell he was trying to control his loud voice.

"How come Shemuel can make the trip and not you? My brother's an ignorant, country boy. You're an educated woman."

He moved closer to me, stroking my arms with his hands. "Besides, I want you there."

I turned my head away, not anxious to abandon my parents or home. Why should I leave what was comfortable for the possible hardships of the new? Silence filled the corners of the room as we finished dressing.

The next day my father called me into the library. He sat, legs crossed, a glass of sherry at his elbow, reading.

"Papa, I don't speak English, a difficult language at best." I knew I was pouting.

My father held up his book. "Paulina, Apollo Korzeniowski was a Polish patriot who directed our insurrection against Russian rule in 1863. Today his son is Joseph Conrad, one of the greatest writers in the English language. If he learned it, so can you."

"Oh, Papa. Who will help me? Nathan says people don't have servants. I've never cooked or cleaned." I folded my arms across my chest. "I don't want to go."

"My daughter, I love having you and my grandchildren under my roof. We're so attached to Isaac, who is beginning to read, and little Sarah, filled with affection." He placed his copy of *Heart of Darkness* on the table. My father, gentle yet firm, took my hands. "Nathan has spoken to me about encouraging you to join him. He's right. You must bind your own family together so there will be more generations. Yes, as much as it will pain me to have you leave, be with your husband."

I left the room without speaking. No was not a word I used with my father.

Angry and frustrated, on the day of his departure Nathan said goodbye to me in the foyer. "Paulina, get your affairs in order. You are moving to America." He picked up his valise and exited not even kissing me goodbye.

Secretly delighted that Nathan, Shemuel and boxes of inventory left without me, I smiled inside. My life went on as before, dinners with wine and laughter, concerts with friends, and strolls through Warsaw's gardens near the Vistula River with my family.

My parents, the children and I sat for portraits with the famed intellectual and photographer, Alter Kacyzne, who opened a studio a few blocks away on Bielanska Street. Dressed in our elegant style, we nodded to shopkeepers as we strolled. Some came to the door to watch us in our finery, like the barber next door who always stared as I passed. I looked away.

The following week I returned to Mister Kacyzne's studio with the children. We spent hours deciding which photographs we liked. I mailed the one with Isaac and Sarah in silk ribbon pajamas, candy cigarettes between their fingers, to Nathan, hand-tinted with reds, blues and greens.

After a long winter we welcomed the summer to warm our bones. The servants packed up the entire family for a holiday. We traveled, as we did every year, to the hot springs in Marienbad, a popular place for a respite. Opened since the early 1800s and famous for the cure, a parade of Kaisers and kings, the rich and sometimes famous, visited along with ordinary citizens like us. After an overnight train ride to Prague, we took another three-hour train ride. When we arrived, Yadwiga unpacked all our clothes and Magda set up our kitchen for kosher meals.

My mother said the springs were the only relief for her back. Neighbors from Warsaw greeted us as we walked the wooded paths, listening to the music of the waterfalls. We tasted chocolate wafers and sipped from porcelain Bechers, small vessels designed for the mineral-rich waters. Mendel's children played with mine in the shallow pools and fountains while Carlo rode horses with Berta.

Behind a pale-yellow colonnade that dominated the main square we dined every evening with other families in a cavernous barn painted the same buttery color. We feasted on blintzes with sour cream and fresh blueberries, *perogies* stuffed with potatoes, pickled herring in a brine of onions, fresh pumpernickel, *sacher* tortes with layers of chocolate and cream. Violinists played Smetana's symphonic poem from Bohemia over and over. The melody in a minor key swept a beautiful sadness over me, especially when I looked at other couples. Perhaps I did miss Nathan and his enthusiastic idealism. Maybe I would reconsider and visit him America.

When we returned another letter from Nathan waited for me.

> *Dearest Paulina,*
> *The business is prospering, but I cannot make a life here without you. A man needs a family. Your fears are ill-founded. The streets are not filled with gangsters, nor is English so difficult. I promise I will make you happy. Come to me.*
> *Yours,*
> *Nathan*

For another year he begged me until he wrote in the winter of 1928.

> *Dearest Paulina,*
> *I have been gone for four months. I am coming for you and the children. Eleven times I have made the trip to get you and each time you have refused me. Even my own brothers and sisters are starting to arrive. If you're not ready to come with me, I want a divorce. The twelfth time is the last. I am Nathan Korsakov. No one says no to me.*
> *Your husband*

A divorce? Who ever heard of such a thing? I cried, lying in bed for days while my mother mourned with me.

Finally, my father said, "Enough. You have to go."

A few weeks later Nathan returned, announcing in a proud voice that he was now a citizen of the United States of America. He was also the owner of a slipper manufacturing business in the boroughs and a warehouse in the city. As more immigrants arrived, they needed the religious articles of their faith. A thousand menorahs were shipped for Chanukah, five thousand *yarhrzeit* candles to commemorate the dead, ten thousand *mezuzahs* for doorposts and a thousand *siddurs*, daily prayer books. All needed packing and shipping.

"Slippers are very popular," Nathan told me with pride. "Everyone in the family needs a pair. Shemuel is watching our growing business. Come back with me. See what I've built."

When it was time to ready myself, I had cramps, sweats, headaches. I fainted in the downstairs hallway, too weak to begin the job of supervising the packing of a household.

Nathan's parting words reverberated around me, ones he spoke to me at the front door, light streaming through the beveled glass. "If you don't come next month, I will file for divorce. Eventually, the children will want to come and see America and they will leave you." He shook his head. "Such a wondrous place. I believe in it. Our future is there."

I turned my head away. After all, Nathan had threatened divorce before and nothing happened. He left, disgusted. Although I felt guilty at sending him on alone, I also felt satisfied that nothing had to change.

A few weeks after Nathan left, when the fireplaces were lit throughout the house to stave off the bitter winter winds, Yadwiga brought me a telegram. I turned it over in my hands. Not the usual letter with stamps that I saved for Isaac. I opened it with haste.

*Shemuel has run off with shiksa. Stop. All money
gone. Stop. Come immediately. Stop. I need you.*

Nathan had never needed me before. I had faith in his ability. Surely this was only a stumble. I ran to my father in tears.

"Paulina, you no longer have a choice. It is time to go to your husband. We'll help you," he told me, hugging me to his chest.

Over the next two weeks the entire household participated in my packing. Yadwiga sniffled as she folded my dressing gowns, silk and lace ensembles consisting of a slip and robe, hand-beading around the hems. My mother remained strong, busying herself with details of my wardrobe and the children's, checking straps, buckles, ornaments. She planned to stay behind, afraid emotion would overwhelm her. I sat at my dressing table with its taffeta skirt, brushing my new fashionable bob, one I had copied from pictures of flappers in America. My sterling silver hairbrush, comb and mirror were the last items I placed in my luggage.

My goodbye to Mama was excruciating. We sat on my bed and she held my hands. We couldn't speak. I was the only daughter and the baby. Daughters didn't leave to go so far away.

Finally, she spoke. "Paulina, be strong. Raise your children to follow our faith." Then her words caught. "And don't forget us." She began to sob and I cried, too.

I stood to go downstairs, knowing the servants lined up near the door to say farewell. I hugged and kissed my mother. She flung herself across my bed.

"What if I never see you again?" she sobbed.

I turned in the doorway. "Mama, you told me to be strong. Of course I'll see you again. I love you."

In those moments I emerged as a woman, my childhood fallen behind. What did she mean, be strong?

My father took us by train to London, continuing with us to

Southampton. We tried to buy first class tickets on a Cunard Line ship known as the "Grand Old Lady of the Atlantic," the fastest ship available, but they were sold out. Instead, I boarded the Mauretania, a former transport and hospital vessel from The Great War, a tired but elegant dowager, red banners streaming down the sides.

I swished up the majestic gangplank like a lady, a large hat hiding my face from an intermittent sun. My father inspected my stateroom, a two-bedroom suite with a bathroom, and stooped to kiss the children, their little arms around his neck. I watched his eyes well with tears. He straightened himself to his full height and gave me a small velvet bag.

"For you. For America." I slipped out a large pearl ring, a pair of emerald earrings and a large loose diamond. "In case. Hide it in the hem of your dress."

In case of what? Indians?

Papa's eyes remained watery. I didn't know what to say. The gypsies words that I wouldn't see my family again floated by me. It couldn't be true. The foghorn sounded as I clutched my father.

"Papa, I don't want to go. Don't make me go."

"Paulina, look at me." He tilted my chin toward him with his fingers. "You belong with your husband."

"What if I don't see you again? What if…" I bit my knuckle to stifle a sob building in my throat.

He hugged me, stroking my hair. "Mamala, we will see each other again. Don't talk nonsense."

The foghorn bellowed. My father kissed my cheeks for the last time and left.

I stayed in my stateroom, inconsolable for hours. Fears rattled around in my head, a ball of gripping aches—fear of New York, a big city where I didn't know my way, fear of not being able to communicate, fear of not having my family to help me. Maybe I was a spoiled, protected young woman, but I liked it that way. Finally, Sarah and Isaac pulled at me for dinner, still in their matching navy travel suits.

I splashed cold water on my eyes, straightened my dress, and dragged myself to the dining room, a large place with crystal chandeliers, striped silk chairs and uniformed waiters in white gloves.

I glanced around at the other well-dressed, regal people eating and laughing. A woman near the door wore a velvet hat with a large plume that tickled the bald gentleman's head next to her. I took the children's hands and marched in behind the host who seated us at a table with others who spoke Polish and French, one woman in a recently purchased gown from Paris with a fur capelet. At least we weren't traveling in steerage and arriving at Ellis Island like immigrants. I had heard stories about how they waited in line for hours.

Nathan said we'd disembark at the port because he was a businessman, a purveyor of goods.

Chapter Three

Paulina

New York City
April, 1929

Nathan, happy to see us for the first few hours, was mostly in a tirade about Shemuel running off with their secretary, an Irish girl who typed the billings.

"Where did they go?" I asked.

"How do I know?" he said throwing his hands in the air. "Maybe Canada. Her sister said Texas or beyond. They're gone with all our profits. If I find him, I'll kill him."

I stood outside the pocked door of our apartment, a silver *mezuzah* with a tiny version of the Ten Commandments scrolled inside and nailed to the doorjamb. In each of my hands a small one clung to mine, the children's pupils large in the dim hallway. Nathan bustled behind me with small train cases, bags of food, pillows, Sarah's cloth doll with a porcelain face. Our steamer trunks would be delivered later.

Nathan fumbled with the keys, dropping them once followed by a curse in English. When he threw open the door, it slammed against the wall. My life in New York began, a train switching tracks in a new direction.

I walked through the near empty rooms, my eyes filled with tears. I came for this? I ran my hand over the linoleum table trimmed with metal. So this was modern? How ugly.

Frost on the window blocked my view until I put my breath on it and made a clear space with my hand. Nothing. Another red brick apartment house with small, square windows. What was on them? No. People hung their clothes outside to dry, a blue blanket flapping in the breeze. I never saw such a thing. People's laundry. That's when it occurred to me I had no idea how to clean clothes.

"When do I meet the servants?" I asked Nathan.

He laughed. "In your dreams," he said taking off his black wool coat and hanging it on a hook near the door. "At least most of the snow has melted." With that he settled into a kitchen chair with a Yiddish newspaper.

In the weeks that followed we hardly saw Nathan. He left me in an apartment with two children, a few bottles of seltzer, un-made beds—a way station for two of his other brothers who arrived before me; his sister stayed in a rooming house—a dirty floor, dusty shades, and a room I'd never spent any time in before, the kitchen.

Our neighbor, Mrs. Dreichspun, also from Warsaw, helped me. Even though we didn't know each other, we found many people in common, including Gustav's family. He married after I did. Did I have regrets? Maybe, when I stood there in that kitchen looking at the stove. I couldn't boil water for a glass of tea. Mrs. Dreichspun took me to the kosher butcher, *a shochet*, the greengrocer, the fish woman and to register the children for school. Nathan gave me a small amount of money to buy dressers, a sofa, lamps, and a rug. The apartment looked better, but seemed shabby compared to what I had. I missed art on the walls, silver service, fine china, and servants. Oh, how I missed Yadwiga and Magda and a nurse for the children!

Finally, my containers and trunks arrived. Three men carried them up the stairs because they wouldn't fit into the lift. I became emotional as I unpacked a gilt-edged mirror, a large oil painting of a pastoral scene, a silk embroidered piano shawl, a set of Rosenthal china my parents gave us, piano music, linens with our initials, children's toys, compartments filled with hats and clothes, endless clothes.

The children learned English quickly, but I couldn't grasp the sounds. Polish is a Slavic language, similar to Russian. I knew the Latin alphabet and a phonetic language. English was impossible.

I took a class with other immigrants. The teacher, Miss Padilla, a serious woman with a plain face and a bun in her hair, wore long skirts. Her glasses hung from a chain around her neck. We had pencils. No pens, no ink, no inkwells. None of the elaborate writing utensils I remember from my schoolwork and my father's desk. I brought a leather bound book from Poland for notes.

I tried to understand what she wrote on the blackboard, sprays of chalk dispersing into the air. Pronunciation, the most difficult part for me. "*Blut.*"

"It's *blood,*" she'd repeat.

Blut. "Tongue between your lips for *th.*"

"*Dat.*"

"No, *that.*"

The other students, men, women, younger people, grandparents—all wanted to learn English, English for survival. They were not dressed as well as me with my calf boots, a cashmere coat draped across the back of my chair. It seemed like they learned it all so easily. How am I going to remember this? Why did I have to? I'd always have an accent. Oh, now money. Asking for change, shopping. How do I know what to buy?

Miss Padilla was patient, but not a great teacher. Too quiet to demand perfection and paid too little to ask for repetitions of words, she sighed at each of our errors. English, a language mangled by a polyglot of people—Italian, German, Lithuanian,

Yiddish, French, Polish, even Chinese-seemed impossible. How does anyone ever understand anyone?

Miss Padilla gave me a small book with common phrases in English and Polish on various topics. From the health page I memorized, "How do you do?" I tried to forget *Jak sie masz?* The choices weren't to my liking. Either I had to ask if someone was dying or say someone had a violent cold. *Ona ma silny katar.* I worked on the chapter about visiting. *Prosze siadac* meant "Pray take a seat." *Moze zechee pan zostac u nas na obiedzie?* Will you stay and take dinner with us? My favorite phrase, one that I repeated over and over was, "I cannot understand you unless you speak slowly." *Nie moge Pana rozumiec, jesli Pan nie mowi powoli.* The Polish never stopped roaming in my head.

In the apartment we spoke Polish or Yiddish if Nathan wasn't around. Yiddish, a hybrid of German invented by French settlers a thousand years ago, was *mameloshen*, my mother tongue. My father used it for business when he traveled because Jews from every country spoke it. Nathan insisted on English. He'd slam his hand on the kitchen table, rattling the plates. "Speak English in this house!"

I had to learn. It was very difficult. So many tenses: past, present, like my life. And vocabulary. So many words, even for things I'd never seen before, like a vacuum cleaner for *schmutz*, Yiddish for dirt. I remembered Yadwiga cleaning the hallway floors with rags on her feet, keeping time to a tune she hummed. I used Yiddish with the neighbors, but only my butchered English with Nathan.

Nathan said, "We're American now. When you learn English you'll understand why this is the greatest country in the world."

The chalk scratched the board.

During the week the city exploded with peddlers, their horses pulling carts piled with fresh fruits and vegetables from the lush soil of New Jersey. Taxis honked geese-like waking bundled babies in carriages, and an occasional fire truck added to the din. The smell of delis with their pickles soaked in barrels of brine, smoked white fish, herring and cured meats lured me inside. I bought salamis that hung from hooks in the window, wrapped in paper coating, and fresh pumpernickel bread.

People hurried everywhere, unsophisticated women in babushkas laden with shopping bags, their gait shifting with the weight of each step, and elegant women in furs who seemed to glide. Cops with white gloves stopped traffic so I could cross the jammed streets, their whistles screeching. The lure of endless shops distracted me—ones with beautiful clothes, shoes and hats with exquisite plumes that beckoned me from the windows.

With so many new things to learn, my life in Poland began to fade. On Friday nights we had Sabbath dinner before Nathan left for *shul*. I boiled chicken. Mrs. Dreichspun's face told me everything.

"Add an onion and some carrots. A little salt." What did I know about cooking?

Nathan walked to services on Saturday morning and returned in the late afternoon, his clothes musty from sitting inside all day. He took up smoking, waiting until the Sabbath was over to light up cigarettes while he read the newspaper. They smelled and filled up endless ashtrays.

At my suggestion not to smoke in the apartment, he said, "It's my house and I'll do what I want."

Later, I noticed he wasn't lighting them as often at home. Yet, the aroma hung in his clothes, invaded the velvet drapes and the brown stained his fingers. He also smoked cigars on occasion and chewed the ends. The children loved the empty boxes and paper rings, which he'd dole out if he was in good humor.

Mrs. Dreichspun, my refined friend with a daughter close to Sarah's age, came from affluence, too. She had been in America for five years. "Everyone starts over again here," she told me.

We shopped together with money Nathan gave me to run the household each week. I managed to save and buy a black wool suit off the rack. She showed me how to take it to a tailor to get an exact fit. Different than the clothes made to order for me. I used to pick the fabric and the style, a nip at the waist, a detachable collar, covered buttons. There were choices and fittings, endless discussions about wardrobe, boots, hats and kid gloves to co-ordinate, even whether my mother and I would have matching outfits. The clothes I outgrew went to the cousins upstairs, especially my favorite, Malka. What a different world I left.

In October, six months after my arrival, the stock market crashed. Nathan went crazy. He raged about the lack of regulation, the idiots in charge, corruption, and cancelled orders. We lost money on speculation and so did my father. Nathan had invested for him, too. He closed a warehouse, and brought home piles of slippers—leather, fake fur, cloth ones in red, blue and brown–for the children to sort and wrap with a rubber band. Isaac and Sarah sat for hours with mismatched slippers on the living room rug.

Mr. Dreichspun's boss jumped from a window of a high building. The business closed so Nathan hired him to hand deliver orders to surrounding areas. It was cheaper than packaging and mailing. Sad, he'd show up at our door looking haggard, his good suit shabby, to fill his sample case with the slippers the children had bunched together. Overnight his fedora changed to a working man's cap. At least it kept food on both families tables.

It was a terrible time. Nathan, with many others, lost money and his dignity. I thought about the offer to distribute vodka. Why did we come here? But, he was not one to jump out a window. He went back to pencils and sold them to men on the street who re-sold them. He stopped importing religious articles and concentrated on slippers and shoes.

"People are walking more," he told me. "They'll always need something comfortable for their feet."

Eventually, Nathan got back on his, but he worked many hours. He was gone every Sunday. I don't know what he did. There were deals, meetings, strangers in our home at all hours.

He came home late, showered without toweling off and climbed into bed. He still wanted me, but there were no words of endearment. His wet body pressed into me even if I pretended to sleep. He was a strong man, over six feet tall with enormous shoulders. There was no love in our coupling. Afterward, he would roll off me and snore, leaving my body damp with shower drops and sweat. Why wasn't he tired?

I awoke with headaches and rested on the sofa most of the day. Sarah brought me a cold, wet rag for my head. I no longer wore the silk nightgowns and robes that the seamstress had beaded with seed pearls and crystals. I packed them away in my trunk among taffeta sachets in shades of blue and lilac, each one with a handmade red rose crocheted of ribbons.

It pained me to go outside and see neighbors, their eyes vacant with grief, men from the *shul*, unshaven and sad, strangers in frayed cuffs standing in the chill of winter waiting on the sidewalks to sell an apple or a pencil or begging change for a cup of coffee or holding signs asking for work.

The Depression took its toll. Nathan became an angry man. Was it the loss of the promise of America? His dreams turned to resentments; he held grudges against people, our circumstances. Yet, he never gave up. He found a solution to every problem. He worked long days, doing most of his business as cash and carry. He'd sit in our bed in an undershirt counting the day's receipts, putting it in envelopes marked, groceries, payroll, taxes. He said there was never enough, but one time I saw him put bills into an envelope marked savings. He slid it under his side of the mattress. When I went to look for it, it was gone.

We struggled like millions of other people. I didn't know about deprivation, but I learned. Money for food. No extras. When I wrote to my parents of my cost-cutting measures, they told me to come home. Their life, even with some financial losses, had not changed.

Nathan, strong and smart, *schlepped* to the docks at dawn, bushels of slippers at his feet. He made deals with the drivers to fill half empty loads and send them to the mid-west. He bought inventory people defaulted on and marketed to local stores. Often, it ended up in our living room: piles of fabric remnants, jars of jam, fake fur hats, children's pajamas, boxes of buttons, umbrellas. Once we had stacks of wristwatches that didn't work. He kept making deals, shouting people into submission. So different from the genteel way my father conducted business, but we were never hungry.

Nathan found a small apartment building that was in receivership and bought it in early 1931. We moved closer to Central Park into a first floor apartment that was twice the size of where we had been living. The children had their own rooms. We rented six of the eight units so we could live rent-free. Two were left empty for his family. He had a plan. Of course he never discussed it with me.

Four more brothers of his ten siblings arrived. He'd paid for everyone's passage and it was their responsibility to bring over their wives. He bought a small laundry and cleaning business for Morris, the one closest in age to him, and put the others to work. He explained America to them so they wouldn't be greenhorns, and raided our house for linens and furniture. Who ever heard of so many people sleeping on mattresses on the floor? Everyone worked fifteen hours a day. I suppose I could have resented the extra guests, but I didn't, although I cooked for twenty some nights. I spoke Polish and Yiddish to them. His brothers were kind and they brought news and small gifts from my family.

One evening in March of 1933 I went to sleep with a cold, a mustard plaster glued to my chest. In the morning my dark, congested haze was interrupted by Nathan shouting, "Get up! President Roosevelt closed the banks. We've lost all our money."

"How do you know this? I asked, Sarah's body curling into my warmth beneath the covers.

"Mr. Dreichspun came over in is *gottkes*. You didn't hear him banging on the door?"

"What does this mean?" I asked peeling off the mustard plaster.

"It means I have to liquidate merchandise to raise cash," he said. He pulled clothes on over his pajamas. "It's not enough we lost money in Warsaw and the crash. Now this." His voice rose, fury spitting out the words. He threw a shoe against the wall.

"But, Nathan, I need money for food, the butcher, the children's shoes." I knew I was whining but my head pounded, an incessant drum. Sarah whimpered under my arm.

"Look in your brassiere. You always hide money there."

I sat up, surprised he knew where I kept money for treats.

He looked at me, level to my eyes. "You think I don't know you skim off a few dollars each week?" With that he left.

The banks re-opened and we recovered. By the end of 1934 the rest of his family had arrived. Everyone contributed to bringing over his parents. The youngest, twins in their teens named Goldie and Ruby, had been waiting in Krakow for a year. Nathan, filled with a fury, insisted everyone come to America. What drove him? I don't know. He became more agitated when he listened to news on the radio, ashes dropping from his cigarette, his expression glum at the kitchen table in a bathrobe with a glass of tea. He'd rant about a man who was head of the National Socialist party in Germany.

"Don't you see? The fact that President Hindenburg met with Hitler gives credence to his party," he said.

What did it have to do with me? I didn't understand half of it. I just knew it pushed him. My world was more immediate: shopping for all these people, translating, helping with papers, finding them work.

Goldie, my favorite sister-in-law, became my confidante and persuaded Nathan to do things for the children, like pay for dancing lessons for Sarah.

"Such nonsense," he would say, but I wanted them to have some of the things I remembered from my childhood. Goldie charmed him by telling him that he was the family hero.

Unfortunately, Goldie neglected her teeth. Ill with a toothache and high fever that stretched into days, I tried to take care of her. Chicken soup didn't improve her condition. I begged Nathan to give me money to take her to a dentist.

"Dentists! Doctors! They're for sissies," Nathan yelled, as he slammed down his newspaper. "Ach," he said, relenting.

I wrapped Goldie in a wool coat and guided her to the dentist's door. She was gone half the day.

When she returned, I asked, "How was it?"

"He gave me something to match my name." With a proud grin she revealed a shiny gold tooth in the front of her mouth. She thanked her brother for a sign she was rich, a real American.

I shook my head from side to side. How ostentatious, a Jewish gypsy. Shortly thereafter, two of my teeth rotted and had to be pulled. I did what Mrs. Dreichspun told me to do.

"Send the bill to my husband," I said with authority.

The dentist took the rest of my teeth, too. I didn't want any gold ones. I ordered white ones that came out every night and soaked in a glass of water next to my bed. In the beginning they hurt, shifting in my mouth, making my gums bleed.

Nathan said to me, "Stop clacking." I couldn't help it. It took months before I got used to them. "Tell the children to brush. You think I can pay for dental work for all these people?"

Nathan's parents lived with us in a back bedroom, small, scared people with traditions and superstitions I didn't understand. I wasn't used to country people. If anyone said something they thought would bring the evil eye upon our household, they'd say, "Poo, poo, poo" hitting their chest with their fist. My father-in-law studied Torah all day, swaying back and forth in dim light, his long, black coat moldy with sweat. Nathan's mother, her hair covered by an old wig in the Orthodox tradition, remained shell-shocked by America. No one ever saw her hair except her husband. They never learned English, changed their dress, or adapted to customs, remaining trapped in the *shetl* in Slonim.

When thunder rattled the windowpanes his parents crawled into the nearest hiding space. One afternoon, after a strong rain, I woke from a nap. I opened my hall closet to look for a towel and the two of them, dressed in black, were huddled underneath the bottom shelf. I screamed, my nerves shattered.

"They need to live someplace else," I told Nathan. He didn't object. They moved in with one of his sisters.

My parents begged me in their letters to come and visit. I approached Nathan one evening after dinner.

"I want to visit my family," I said, bold and determined.

"It's a bad idea," he said, not lifting his eyes from his newspaper.

"I want to know why it's a bad idea for me to see my family. They miss me and I, them." I waved the letters at him.

He placed the paper down on the table with a sigh. "Paulina, it's foolish to go such a great distance with children. Get the idea out of your head."

"You're afraid I won't come back, aren't you?" I asked, more brazen than I had ever been.

"That's ridiculous. No, you can't go. It's too much money."

"I promise I'll return in a month. I need to be with my parents, my brothers, my niece and nephew."

The tenor of his voice became louder. "What's the matter with you? Between recouping losses from my *schlmiel* brother who ran away, the stock market crash and establishing the rest of my family, I don't have time for nonsense. Am I providing for you?"

I left the room, refusing to be bullied.

The truth was he had little time for me or the children. I decided to go anyway and with the help of Mrs. Dreichspun sent my father a telegram. My father wired money to buy first class tickets.

Nathan agreed with reservation. He couldn't object once I had the money. He feared an escalation of war talk, but the reality was Germany and Poland signed a ten-year non-aggression pact in January of 1934. Poland was the first country to make a friendly agreement with Hitler. I couldn't understand what worried him.

"I miss my family. My parents haven't seen the children. It's time," I told him.

"You promise you'll return?" he asked, a hint of vulnerability in his tone.

"I promise. Just let me be with my mama and papa again. You have all your family here."

Finally, Nathan came home with tickets for Isaac, Sarah and me with the first breath of spring. He booked us on Cunard's White Star Britannic, the largest motor ship in the British Merchant Marine sailing to Liverpool. The Queen Mary wouldn't be ready for her maiden voyage until the fall.

I remember him telling me that afternoon with the sun breaking through the gray haze, "You've got an outside room decorated in art deco with full facilities. You're going cabin class."

Art deco was modern, but I was shocked. "Cabin class? My father sent money for first class."

"You're spoiled. This is the new way to travel. There is no first class. It's this and tourist. More affordable for everyone," he said with a smile, shoving his hands into his pockets.

He took the difference. I was furious, but didn't have the strength to argue with him. I would leave as soon as school ended in June.

I read and re-read my parents' letters. They were ecstatic I was coming and couldn't wait to see the children. Only three more months and I would be back in my wonderful Warsaw with its historical architecture, outdoor cafés, exquisite gardens, amphitheater concerts. My loving family waited for me. At night I tossed in restless sleep. I belonged there.

My dreams crashed when I found out I was pregnant in late April, weeks before I was to leave. I was sick every morning. I could barely manage the household, especially with extra people for dinner every night. I know the children felt neglected. I napped in the afternoon while the light faded outside. Nathan didn't come home until after nine o'clock. Who fed Isaac and Sarah? I don't know. They ate Saltines under the kitchen table. The radio played for hours as I drifted in and out of a hazy consciousness.

I felt better in early June so I planned for my trip. My parents and especially Carlo would be disappointed if I cancelled. They would be excited to see me pregnant. In preparation I created a flurry of activity cleaning the rugs, doing laundry, changing linens, ironing, and scrubbing pots, something I never thought I'd do. I had to make up for the days I was immobile. I cooked casseroles for Nathan, something new Mrs. Dreichspun showed me how to do. I folded and packed the children's clothing, put my hats in boxes, shopped for gifts for my parents and brothers and

Mendel's children.

One night in bed a week before the trip I felt something wet. When I touched the sheets with my fingertips and turned on the light, I saw blood. Nathan rushed me to the hospital. I lost the baby. Another life sucked away. I don't know why. God's will. Or maybe I didn't want it enough. Yes, I loved Isaac and Sarah, so high-spirited, but they antagonized Nathan.

When I came home from the hospital, I was weak. Mrs. Dreichspun took the children while I had my female trouble. The doctor said I was fragile and couldn't make a long trip. Nathan sent my parents a telegram with a message that the trip was not possible. I had no words to express my despair, but it felt like I was in a dark well hidden on the bottom. Sadness covered my soul.

I didn't get up or comb my hair or prepare food. I wanted to sleep. My parents wrote to me.

Dearest Paulina,
We are so filled with disappointment. The children are getting bigger. Will they remember us? Do they still speak Polish?
The most important thing is for you to be well.
Our Love to You,
Mama and Papa

It pushed me to take the children to a photographer for a sepia portrait so my parents could see what they looked like. I dressed them in their best clothes, suits with velvet collars, shiny shoes, clean socks. Isaac grew so quickly his pants were short. He sat in the photographer's ornate chair, crossing and uncrossing his ankles, while Sarah stood behind him. With Isaac's terrible *shpilkes*, he moved and fidgeted in a rhythm of motion, picking or pulling or touching himself or someone else in a constant whirl.

If Nathan was around it drove him crazy. He'd scream, "Stop it."

The children had to stand very still while the photographer hid under a black cloth. Twice he reprimanded Isaac for shifts of his body. He seemed incapable of not moving. I promised to reward them with something new, ice cream, if they would cooperate. Afterward, they loved the treat. A few weeks later I mailed the picture and a letter, my tears staining the paper. Nathan cashed in the tickets.

"I can bring over six more relatives in steerage," he said, his words stinging my soul.

It was a year before I got over the loss of the baby. I'd sit at the kitchen table, my chin in my hand, listening to *The Chase and Sanborn Hour* with Eddie Cantor. In time my spirits lifted.

When I came out of my malaise, Nathan took me to see the Empire State Building, the tallest structure in the world. It opened in 1929, but I hadn't been inside. We rode the elevator to the top. He was proud, as though he built it himself. Afterward, we visited the George Washington Bridge built in the same year. It connected New York to New Jersey across the Hudson River.

"A grand structure, an engineering feat," he told me. "Look what's happened since you've been sleeping." He spread his arm over the expanse. "This is the greatest country in the world."

Chapter Four

Paulina

New York City
June 1933

"Smoke Gets in Your Eyes" played on every radio station. I sang along, a sway in my step, amazed that my accent disappeared into the melody.

With all of Nathan's family settled in, I went with his sisters Goldie and Ruby to the movies and Vaudeville theatre. We told Nathan we were studying English. The twins worked in the garment district, contributing to their parents' upkeep. Goldie was keeping company with a young man she met at work. And, I was pregnant again.

In Germany, Hitler's party gained control. The letters from my parents said Warsaw was filled with refugees. In Germany there was a one-day boycott of all Jewish businesses. The Nazi leaders urged schools to expel Jews. What ridiculous ideas. My father said business was falling off, but he still controlled office and apartment buildings, construction projects, the import/export business and pawn shops. They begged me to visit as soon as I had the baby.

This time I rested more and gave birth in the hospital to a healthy little girl I named Rachel after my grandmother. Nathan, pleased with a new offspring, had a naming for her at the *shul*.

Sarah, thrilled with her new sister, showed her off to Isaac who ignored both of them.

Rachel, a happy baby, laughed and kept her blue eyes like mine. I knew my parents were anxious to see her. I booked passage for all of us again. This time I was going to see my family. Nothing would stop me.

I prepared with a new determination. One steamer trunk filled with three sets of children's clothes, another with mine, gifts for my parents, brothers, Mendel's wife and children, my favorite cousin, Malka, even Yadwiga. I wrapped cans of peaches, Bakelite bracelets, glossies of movie stars, leather wallets, blue and green eye shadows and silk stockings. We were leaving the day after school was over for the three months of summer. My parents planned a trip to Marienbad, the wonderful spa in Czechoslovakia we had visited before as a family.

Days before the ship was to sail Nathan and I took a walk after dinner in the calm summer air to discuss finances, the children and my departure. I think he still had insecurities that I wouldn't return. Of course I said I would, but the truth is I entertained the thought of staying there. Even though my life was in America, I missed my family. With cool spring weather fading like a disappearing sun, we left our jackets behind, greeted by the summer air.

The sidewalks clouded with steam after the rain and humidity clutched at us. Neighbors sat on stoops fanning themselves while children pushed balls on the sidewalks. Store awnings dripped moisture. I avoided the puddles in new shoes I bought for my journey, white spectator pumps with black trim.

In his shirt and vest Nathan strutted past store front delis, coffee shops, newsstands, laundries, bakeries where people slept in the back. His eye caught an orange and he kicked the rind, its sweet meat missing.

We passed a liquor store. He dismissed it with, "A dirty

business. You deal with *shikkers*, drunks. Too dangerous." The Russian in his shiny boots flicked across my mind.

He kicked the rind again. I hurried to keep up with his long strides. He wasn't one to stroll or make polite conversation, all business all the time. In my white cotton gloves and a hat with a veil, I thought I looked smart. My mother told me a lady never shows bare hands in the summer months. The help got freckles, not us. I reached for his elbow. Shouldn't he be proud to have a lovely woman on his arm?

"Nathan, I want to stop at Goldstein's to bring the children a little something. Sweets, maybe some *rugelach*."

"What?" Nathan wasn't listening. He sucked and twirled his cigar, small gray-black puffs sailed upward as he exhaled.

"Sweets."

"What?" Nathan checked his Timex, proud of his modern American timepiece, unlike the watch fobs immigrants carried. "What for? Children don't need sweets. We have enough problems with teeth in this—"

Across the street a woman's voice screamed, "Stop it. OhmiGod! Help me!"

I turned to see a large, burly man with greasy long hair hitting a barefooted woman in a flowered dress. He slapped her hard across the face. I heard the crack even at our distance. I'd never seen a man hit a woman. It shocked me.

She wailed, "Stop it. Help me, help me," her cries sounding weaker. With hands over her head, she created a lame defense against the rain of blows.

Nathan jerked my hand out of the crook of his arm, threw his cigar on the ground and raced across the street, dodging cars. A taxi honked in the dim light and a small child's cries pierced the heavy air. He broke through the crowd of onlookers.

Nathan stepped between the two people and pushed the

frantic woman aside. Without a word he reached for the man, grabbed his shirt, pulled him closer and punched him in the jaw. The man staggered backward, then recovered to retaliate. He bobbed forward, his arm held high.

I saw a gleam of steel flash, a pumping hand punctuated by moans of the crowd. I froze with fear. Nathan staggered backward and then fell to the sidewalk. The man hovered over him. I lifted my veil to get a better look, squinting as the streetlights blinked on. My hand clutched my mouth smearing red lipstick on my new gloves.

I dashed across the asphalt street through cars slowing down to view the commotion. The greasy man's eyes, crinkled with evil, caught mine. He dropped the bloodied knife, ran up the street past the liquor store and around the corner. Gone. Just like that.

A kid in a newsboy's cap took off his jacket and put it under Nathan's head. Someone unbuttoned his vest. Blood spread like a small lake on the front of his white shirt, then spilled onto the sidewalk. I felt helpless. A red-faced Irish cop on a horse broke up the knot of people with a shrill whistle.

"What happened here? Who did this?" he asked with his peculiar brogue.

The injured woman, her flowered dress ripped, sobbed on a doorstop. Like a battered bird without song, her head shook back and forth. A neighbor in a chenille bathrobe sat down, whispering in her ear for comfort.

The man from the barbershop took charge to explain. "We saw the knife," he said looking around at the nodding crowd for corroboration. "That bastard stabbed him three times." Nathan's eyes fluttered, then closed.

"Watch your language. You," said the cop as he pointed to the kid in the hat. "Call an ambulance." The boy took off in a scrambled run. The cop got down from his horse, took out a hankie and picked up the knife. "This the weapon?" People nodded. He wrapped it and placed it inside his pocket.

I stepped closer, my hand against my beating heart.

"Sir?" My voice echoed in my ears.

The officer looked at me. "Lady, you a relative?"

"Yes, I'm the wife," I said self-conscious of my accent.

He mumbled something under his breath. "Name? Address? Number?" He wrote down my answers on his notepad with a short pencil. "Your husband know the perpetrator?"

I didn't know the last word and asked him to repeat it.

When I still didn't get it, he asked, "Lady, did he know the guy who stabbed him?"

I shook my head. The officer's impatience intimidated me. He turned away to question the injured woman.

What if Nathan died? Alone with the children in this barbaric place? And, for what? Protecting a stranger? An Italian? I knew it was selfish to think of myself, but what about my trip? My parents? I pulled down my veil as though hiding my eyes could mask my panic.

The woman looked up at the officer, her lip swollen into a puffy piece of cotton candy. Her eyes, rimmed with red and black circles, filled me with a sense of tragedy. I moved out of the crowd to stare at Nathan and the bloodied sidewalk, the stain purple in the streetlight. I knelt down to touch his head.

It seemed like hours until the ambulance arrived. Finally, the nagging noise of the siren pulled closer. White jacketed orderlies lifted Nathan onto a stretcher and into the ambulance, his face gray, eyes closed. I clutched at him, then remembered his watch.

"Wait," I told the two men in white.

They looked at me in amazement and stopped. I unbuttoned his cuff. The glass face of the Timex was cracked. I pulled it from his wrist, the expandable band catching on his large knuckles. He must have fallen on it, the imprint of the watch molding its shape into his skin. I slipped it into my purse. I tried to climb into the back once he was loaded, my foot with its high heel almost on the fender.

They wouldn't let me go with him.

In the hospital the smell of disinfectant and ether burned my nose. A chest tube, a mask for oxygen and bandages covered Nathan. He didn't speak or respond to my voice. I sat there for hours, sick with worry. What would become of me if he died? Would I go home to my papa? What would my future be in America without him?

Did I love this man who took me so far away from my home? Yes, in a respectful way. Family meant everything to him. I was brought up to believe that, too, but he was willing to sacrifice. My father said a man had to be a good provider. Was I *in* love with him? I pondered this in the deathly silence of the ward, the nurses' rubber-soles squeaking while they shadowed the halls. Maybe. Not in the way I thought love would be—romantic and passionate, like the stories I read as a young girl, but in another way. He was my protector.

Yet, there were a few times when he came to me in the night where I wasn't indifferent. Times where he was gentle, vulnerable and I responded with excitement. One time when I waited without a nightgown, he came to me fresh-shaven. As our nude bodies coupled I lost control, a warm flush enveloping my body, tingling over me like warm salt spray. I cried afterward and he held me tight. We talked, facing each other on the pillows.

"What are you afraid of?" I asked.

"I have no fear," Nathan told me.

"What do you mean? Everyone is afraid of something."

"No, not me. At least not what normal people are afraid

of—whether I'll get sick or be able to support my family. I'm a businessman, a leader. People of power, people who command control, think about whether we will be respected or how much revenue can be generated by selling slippers or eye glass frames or buttons. Will the political climate in Europe effect shipments? What will be the Jews' fate if this clown Hitler's influence spread? That's what I think about."

Three nights later, as I held his calloused hand, gurgling noises came from his throat. A death rattle. I fled down the hall for the doctor. He ran back, the nurses and their starched white hats trailing behind him. They pushed me out of the way, pounding on his chest, shouting his name, fooling with a chest tube. I waited in the hall, my shoulder against the wall, biting an embroidered handkerchief from my mother. Was I crying for him or were my tears for the trip I knew I had to cancel?

"Your husband almost died," the doctor said as he exited the room. I began to sweat, then felt faint. He helped me to a chair. "He's tough, but this is going to be a long recovery. Some of the wounds are close to the heart."

I went home by streetcar, praying on the way. I couldn't lose him. I wasn't sure what to do, but I resolved to call his brothers and Mr. Dreichspun to run the business. Should I tell his parents?

I went to the hospital every day while Nathan improved, not an easy task. Finally, he could eat soft foods like eggs and pudding. I lied when he asked me if it was kosher. How could it be in a Catholic hospital? Consumed with guilt it was impossible for me to travel twenty blocks uptown with food every day from Brighton Beach *schlepping* a baby. The family helped but everyone worked long hours. The children were running wild.

Nathan came from the Pale of the Settlement where Jews were forced to live in poor villages called *shetls*. Not permitted to own land or live in cities, men became artisans, carpenters, tailors or shoemakers. His family had no money for an apprenticeship to one of the trades so his mother sent him to Warsaw at the age of twelve. She told him to bring home whatever he could earn. He traded his labor for pencils, sold the pencils and returned with money for his mother. He did that over and over again, the items and shipments growing. He supported everyone. Finally, on one of his trips home at eighteen, the czar notified him of his obligatory conscription of twenty-five years. It threatened his existence and his family's so he fled to Poland for good. Besides swearing allegiance to his oppressor it meant no kosher food. Was I doing the same thing by making him eat *trefe*? I brought leftovers from home.

The nuns were lovely to us. I brought Nathan his religious articles: *yarmulke*, *tallit*, a prayer shawl his father had given him for his *bar mitzvah*, and *tefillin*, leather straps he wrapped around his head and arms to focus on God. He mumbled his morning prayers at the window, dovenning, his body rhythmic with centuries of prayer. He noticed Jesus on the cross over his bed and said nothing.

As Nathan recovered he marched up and down the hospital corridors, unembarrassed that the back of his gown was open. He raged at whoever came to visit—Mr. Dreichspun, his brothers, employees—questioning them about inventory, shipments, deliveries. He added numbers in his head, as though he could stay in charge from a distance.

"What happened to the payments? What do you mean you collected half the deposit?" he barked at them. The objects of his anger stood stoop-shouldered like wretched dogs.

One morning as I readied myself for the hospital, Nathan walked in the front door with measured steps, weakened from his injury.

"I can't get any better in that place. Here you can take care of me. I can watch the business from home." He threw his hat across the room.

"But, what about the doctor? He said you wouldn't be ready to leave for two more weeks."

"Doctors. What do they know? I checked myself out." He undressed and put on a bathrobe. A rick-rack of scars tattooed across his chest. He climbed into bed and made me the nurse. "Paulina, bring me water. I need my glasses. Where's the newspaper? Turn on the radio. Cook me eggs," he shouted from our bedroom.

Three months passed, my trip postponed indefinitely. My heart longed to see my family. The greasy man who stabbed Nathan was never caught, disappearing into a vast city with thousands of people.

I spent long hours taking care of him. I felt relief only when he slept, a tyrant whose burning desire propelled him to be more. I'd sit for hours with the radio on and let my mind drift back to my idyllic life in Warsaw. Maybe I would go back to Poland to my papa's house where I would be safe.

Chapter Five

Paulina

August, 1933

Devastated that I canceled my trip to Warsaw, I moped for days. By the time Nathan fully recovered from his stabbing, our household had changed. Rachel, now colicky, sapped my strength. I spent nights walking her back and forth.

At first, when Nathan returned, the children were excited to see him. They jumped and bounced like monkeys leaping in their cages at the zoo. Then, after a few days, he noticed the messy apartment. I couldn't keep up with the dishes, the laundry, the shopping, the cooking, unmade beds.

Nathan, more impatient than ever, yelled at everyone. "Paulina, you're a slob. The kids are *momsers*. The relatives aren't running the business right. Where's Mr. Dreichspun? What happened to the shipments? Who's keeping the books?" The tirades went on for hours.

After his brother absconded with their money, he was suspicious of people stealing and free with accusations.

While Nathan languished the children had became wild. Isaac and Sarah wouldn't listen to me, and to be honest, I gave up. Summertime, without school, meant mischief.

When I was making my daily trek to the hospital, sometimes

coming home after dark, the children played games like hooligans in the street. Sarah would hide when it was time to help with the chores and Isaac lived outside. What did I know about raising and disciplining children? I had nannies and governesses in Poland. They even forgot most of their Polish and never learned much Yiddish. Both of them craved excitement, talking constantly in loud voices, their hands whipping through the air while they concocted another scheme. Isaac and his *shpilkes* made the atmosphere worse.

"Mother, get Papa to buy candy wholesale and then we'll sell it to our friends cheaper than the one-cent store. Or give us money. We'll take the subway to the picture shows."

Such *mishagos*, nonsense. They came home filthy, grimy lines of black circles around their necks, every bath a project. They fought me, running naked through the house, a smelly game of wills. Isaac, a ringleader with his gangly good looks and energy, would hang out the window and yell to his friends. He brought home creatures he found, bugs in a jar with holes on the top, a spider in a box, a green garter snake that got lost in the apartment. The confusion and chaos were too much for me.

One night after Nathan returned to work, he came home late. The early September chill meant summer was almost over and the children would go back to school soon. I was resting in bed, Rachel playing near me on the floor. Nathan, with a look of fury at the corners of his mouth, came in the bedroom holding Isaac and Sarah by the back of their collars. Sarah began to whimper. The children emitted a smell, animals in fear of a pursuer. Their eyes shone large in their dirty faces. Sarah's hair hung in oily strings around her face.

"Why are these children running in the street?" Nathan called them a Yiddish word for low life, the anger in his voice spitting out words.

I shrugged.

"Let me go!" screamed Isaac, his feet dancing for freedom from Nathan's iron grip. He struggled like a chicken before its neck gets twisted, lashing out at Nathan's hand. Nathan dropped them and reached for Isaac's hair. Nathan smacked him hard across the face. A spurt of blood dripped from his nose. Tears spilled into streams on his dirty face. My head dropped into my hands as I gasped. I couldn't move. Rachel crawled under the bed.

Sarah scampered away, ran into her room and slammed the door. Her sobs filled the apartment.

Isaac screamed bad words at Nathan. I didn't know what they were because they were in English—curse words, words from the street, terrible things. Nathan went crazy and started to chase him around the apartment. I hurried out of bed, putting on slippers, and stood in the doorway. As Isaac's wily body bumped a table, a lamp fell over, the bulb emitting sparks. I ran over and stomped on the carpet so it wouldn't catch fire. Isaac dashed into the vestibule and squeezed under a breakfront. Nathan, winded from his recovery, gave in. He leaned against the sofa breathing hard, pulling at the knot of his tie. I sat down and cried until my eyes, puffy red pillows, could not flow any more.

After that the children, even the baby, hid when Nathan came home. A few more violent episodes erupted over trivial incidents, a fresh answer or a slow response to do a chore. Or Isaac's incessant twitching. They screamed that they hated him. Sarah developed a stutter and had trouble beginning her words, which infuriated Nathan. In Europe children were to be seen, not heard, and did not talk back to their parents. Who expected such impudence? My head throbbed. I couldn't run a household or keep the children under control. I wanted to be dressed up and go to picture shows, museums, shop, read magazines, meet with friends.

Nathan said, "It's your fault, all this chaos." I didn't answer and he gave me the silent treatment, not speaking for days except for requests of food. Like the dangerous bears that growled in the Polish forests, he intimidated all of us. The air hung heavy in the apartment.

At my lowest moment I received a letter from my favorite brother, Carlo, saying if I wasn't able to come to Polyn, the word we used for Poland, he would visit me. I know my parents suggested it. They were concerned about my meager descriptions of life in America. Unmarried at thirty-seven, a point of great concern to my parents, maybe he would find a girl in America who wanted to live in Warsaw. With my brother Itzak ill, they wanted Carlo to have children, ones that didn't live on the other side of the ocean.

Carlo arrived in May, 1935, a year after a ten-year non-aggression pact was signed between Poland and Germany. It gave people a sense of security, especially after Germany's aggression in The Great War.

"See?" I told Nathan. "Everything will be all right."

Nathan urged my family to leave in short postscripts he added to my letters. "Hitler is a menace," he'd scrawl on the bottom. In one he mentioned Churchill's speech about Germany creating an air force.

Nathan looked at me, pen in hand. "They're gearing up for war. Anyone can see that. I don't trust those Nazis. Warsaw's going to be isolated. How many times does a country have to be conquered by its enemies traipsing through their corridor for them to see what's coming?"

I told myself Nathan was negative because he witnessed families destroyed by marauding Cossacks. My family was at the top echelon of society and did not see these things. Besides, if something needed to be done, my father had business connections and contacts among the titled aristocracy. He told stories of when his family had been court Jews, given special privileges and exempt from taxes, when they lived in palatial estates in the neighborhoods of Nowy Świat and Bankowy Square where they built fortunes. When I was growing up, our neighbors were entrepreneurs and bankers, not courtyard merchants from Żelazna Brama, the large open market, filled with workers and craftsmen. Hitler? I had other concerns than a former wallpaper hanger with *mashuga* ideas.

Carlo arrived on the maiden voyage of the Queen Mary to stay with us. At the dock, with its three stacks silhouetting the skyline, I spotted him, a head taller than anyone else. After he cleared customs I fell into his arms. Sophisticated, his hair combed straight back, he carried a camel-colored vicuna coat over his arm, a paisley silk ascot at his throat. His face was long with dark eyes, more like my mother's side, his height like my father's. And, he was elegant. I forgot men had manicured hands, and soft skin on their faces. The smell of his cologne gripped me, a lemony aroma of sweet nights and river walks.

I missed my family. How protected and cared for I had been.

"What a fantastic ship with a first class dining room! Delicious food. I met wonderful people on board," Carlo said as he slipped his arm through mine. I loved hearing him speak Polish. His enthusiasm enveloped me. It had been so long since I had seen my own flesh and blood.

The months Carlo visited were my happiest. The children bunked together to make room for him. After all, a gentleman needed space, especially for his toilette. Nathan worked long hours, often gone all day on Sunday, and Carlo wanted to see the city. After the children left for school, we took Rachel to Aunt Goldie's. Much to Nathan's chagrin Goldie had married her garment worker and was now pregnant with their first child.

"A union member no less! He's probably a Communist," Nathan muttered to me.

Carlo and I toured New York. His English was better than mine. To a gentleman free of the obligations of earning a living, languages were a hobby. On his arm I strolled with pride past my neighbors.

We bought tickets for a new folk opera, *Porgy and Bess* by George and Ira Gershwin. Carlo loved it because it was about southern Negroes, people he had only read about in books. I was fascinated, too, because I had not seen a Negro until I moved to America. "Summertime" buzzed in my head for weeks.

We attended the opening night of "Waiting for Lefty" about a strike in the taxi industry starring Elia Kazan. A few weeks later we saw "Awake and Sing" written by Clifford Odets. It told the story of a working class Jewish family in the Bronx and starred John Garfield. Such a handsome actor. We spent hours talking about the characters and the social significance of the working class. For an aristocrat Carlo presented himself as very open-minded.

Sarah attached herself to her uncle. To her Carlo was a gentle spirit compared to Nathan. Carlo listened to her struggle through sentences and admired her pictures from school. We took her to the Museum of Modern Art to see the opening of Jack Levine's protest painting "Feast of Pure Reason." It caused a sensation because it depicted millionaire banker J. Pierpont Morgan in the underworld. Nathan, my capitalist, thought it a travesty.

Carlo took us to dinner at restaurants many nights so I wouldn't have to cook. I'm sure my culinary skills were not impressive. Nathan appreciated his generosity, but sneered behind his back, "Your brother's a playboy without a job."

Carlo brought me new piano books, the inside page autographed with an inscription, TO MY TALENTED AND LOVING SISTER. YOUR BROTHER, CARLO.

We visited Mrs. Dreichspun, whom I now called Leah, music in hand. Chopin, Poland's national treasure, made me swoon. I attempted to play his Ballades, written in the mid-1800s, on her piano. Carlo mentioned the interpretation of them was linked to the lyrical poetry of Adam Mickiewicz. My out-of-practice fingers plodded through the musical narratives, flinging memories of Polish patriots and rustic love tragedies into the cramped room. Leah hugged me when I finished. I wasn't the only one who missed Polyn.

The Jewish holidays of *Rosh Hashanah* and *Yom Kippur* came and went in the fall, a flurry of cooking, cleaning and guests. Carlo watched my preparations with amusement.

"Mama would be impressed, especially without servants," he said.

Carlo and I spent hours catching up on the relatives who lived in our building in Warsaw, the cousins I played with as a child. Malka was married and a mother, too! Carlo didn't like the claustrophobic and communal way we lived in Warsaw and thought he might branch out, move to Brussels, start a business.

Carlo told me, "Grandmother Eva died in your absence. She had been complaining of being tired and thirsty. One morning when Yadwiga brought her tray, she didn't wake up." He shook his head.

What else had I missed? A sadness rolled over me. I could not be a comfort to my parents.

Eventually, our time together came to an end.

"I have to go back. Everyone's busy in America. I'm used to a life of leisure. I don't understand the way people live and work all the time." Carlo took my hands. "There are show horses who parade in feathers and sequins at the circus and work horses who plow the fields. My dear sister, we are show horses." He shrugged his shoulders. "Make plans to come and visit our parents. Stay for six months. They're getting old and miss you. Mendel's children are big and they don't know their cousins. You must come soon with Isaac, Sarah, and Rachel. Mama hasn't kissed the baby yet."

The morning Carlo left we took a taxi to the dock. The Queen Mary, set to sail for Nice, filled the area. People milled around ready to board, valises, hatboxes, and assorted containers at their feet. Children ran among legs to avoid relatives and their smothering kisses. One blonde woman with servants held a red leather, oval travel case. I eyed it with nostalgia. My mother had one like it for her jewelry with two miniature drawers on the bottom and velvet-lined compartments.

Carlo took me in his arms. His hand slipped a wad of cash and a small black bag into my coat pocket. I fished out the small package. A large diamond the size of a button slipped through the drawstring. It shimmered in the sunlight, winking at me.

"Why didn't you give this to me sooner?" I asked.

"No one needs to know. It's from Papa. Hide it. In case," he said with a nod. Then he kissed my forehead, and left as the foghorn sounded, his vicuna coat over his arm.

In case. In case of what? I pushed the cash into my brassiere. I hadn't found an Indian yet in New York.

I was devastated for weeks. Nathan said Carlo's visit wasn't good for me. He came up with an idea to cheer me. He decided to send the children to camp in upstate New York. The school year would be over soon.

"They need fresh air and supervision in the summer. We'll take a trip to visit them," he told me.

Nathan wanted to take his new Buick on a test drive. Preparing the children for camp, buying sneakers and shorts, sewing labels— it pulled me out of my malaise.

With a quiet apartment Nathan came to me on my side of the bed more often, his damp body looking for release. I was resigned. What could I do? This was my life. My mother said men had urges that needed to be satisfied.

One evening between my cycle he rolled off me and said, "At least I know the ones born here are mine."

In the light I could see his few gray chest hairs.

"What are you talking?" I asked him, forgetting my grammar. I pulled myself up onto my elbows. "The two born on foreign soil aren't yours?" I suppressed the insult in my voice. I didn't want to start up with him. He never struck me, but his words could hurt, stinging like a wasp. A preposterous idea. "You think Isaac and Sarah were from someone else because we were apart?"

He turned away from me. "They both have brown eyes and Rachel's are blue."

No longer able to keep the irritation out of my voice, I said, "What? You have brown eyes. Of course some of the children will have brown eyes. What do you think?"

Was this the reason he treated the two older children differently? I was resolute. No more babies.

His chest moved up and down in the movement of sleep. He never answered me.

Chapter Six

Paulina

August, 1936

Pregnant again. This had to be the last. As soon as Max was born I pulled some of the money Carlo gave me from my pink satin hiding place and slipped the bills to the doctor to tie my tubes. Forbidden to do the illegal procedure without a husband's permission, the cash incentive would create an "emergency" a few months after the birth.

Our baby boy arrived early in 1937, after the re-election of our president, Franklin D. Roosevelt. Nathan marveled over both of them, even suggesting we name the baby Franklin.

"The best president so far. Another Abraham Lincoln," he told me.

It was also the year King Edward VIII abdicated and married a divorcée. No one could talk of anything else. He must have been crazy to give up the throne. The children thrilled over the opening of *Snow White and the Seven Dwarfs*, a full length movie cartoon.

Later that year we moved to a larger apartment with a view of Central Park, renting out all the units in the previous building. Nathan returned money my father loaned us when we purchased it. Nathan bought me a new bedroom suite, a mahogany dining room table with velvet-covered chairs and a large rug with roses for the living room. I ordered a full set of Rosenthal china. The children had their own rooms, including a nursery for the baby.

We were comfortable.

Once again, a baby and diapers demanded my time. Tired to despair, Nathan relented and hired a nurse to help me the first few months. A Polish woman who had recently emigrated, she knew of my family.

"Oh, she said, "You were from the Kupfersteins. They were the nicest, the richest family in Warsaw." When she left I missed the company and my language.

Next, he found a Negro woman, Bessie, to help me. He called her a *schvartze*, the Yiddish word for a dark person. She washed and ironed clothes every day, so much laundry with four children. She'd stand over the ironing board for hours with a water bottle, the metal cap punched with holes, spraying drops. The steam from the iron rose around her face, crinkling her eyes and springing hair from her bandanna. With my accent and her southern slur our communications often ended in confusion and laughter. One thing I did understand though is that her grandparents had been slaves.

One night Nathan pulled a booklet out of his briefcase and handed it to me. "It's time. You must become a citizen. I did it when I first came. Now it's your turn to embrace America."

"A citizen? How will I learn this?" I asked him thumbing through the pages. It meant I was going to be a permanent resident. I wouldn't live in Warsaw again.

"I'll help you. Memorize everything. The test is in two weeks."

My comprehension of English was still limited. How would I learn this so fast? I started to read the information in bed that night—Presidents, the Bill of Rights, the Continental Congress, laws.

I spent days trying to learn the facts. Nathan shook me awake in the middle of the night. "Who's the first signer of the Declaration of Independence? What was the Boston tea party?" I didn't know.

"Nathan, I can't do this," I told him rubbing my eyes.

The pressure began to build. Isaac tried to help me learn the Presidents, drilling me for hours.

The day arrived for the test. I went to the beauty parlor so my hair looked nice set in waves. I wore gloves, a black suit with beading on the lapels and carried a crocodile pocketbook. I checked my seamed stockings and high heels in the full-length mirror.

I was so nervous in the taxi on the way over I didn't speak. Everything jumbled in my head—Presidents, events, monuments, wars, Indians.

The cramped room filled with immigrants waiting in wooden chairs, fidgeting with the booklets. Heads turned as I entered, all men except for me. A few held cigarettes, the smoke twirling toward the ceiling. As each man approached the desk in the front set high on risers, the judge looked over his glasses and asked questions. The first man, a cut on his face from a fresh shave, wore a shabby coat and transferred his hat back and forth in his hands. I couldn't hear over the foot shuffles, coughs and whispers. He must not have answered the questions very well.

The judge said, "Go to school for six more months."

The next man approached the front of the room. He was better dressed but nervous, and pushed at his cuticles with his fingers. I only heard the last part.

"Go back to classes."

"Next." The room became very quiet. I knew nothing. Had I ever read the booklet?

The judge asked me, "Who was the first President of the United States?" I answered correctly. "What was he famous for?" I don't remember what I said, but that was right, too. I responded with more confidence to the next questions. He said, "You passed. Go into the next room to say The Pledge of Allegiance."

I wandered shell-shocked into the next room filled with people. Nathan and some of his friends stood with flowers against the wall. He smiled at me. I sat down in the back behind a family of six and a few couples.

"All rise," a large man from the front said. The small group of people stood when a woman in a blue uniform entered. We turned and faced the flag in the corner. I put my hand over my drumming heart and couldn't remember a word. I moved my lips and that must have been good enough. A cheer went up from the crowd. Some cried. Nathan ran from across the room and hugged me, the flowers in green paper crushing my chest. That's all. I was a citizen of the United States of America and very proud.

Chapter Seven

Paulina

January, 1938

In the morning, a difficult time, I dragged myself out of bed, a chenille bathrobe wrapped around my chilled body. The children readied for school as I made their lunches. I drank orange juice, the only thing that made me feel better. At the kitchen table I stared at the frosted windows, my mind skipping from the cobblestones of Bielanska Street to the gray buildings of New York.

On New Year's Day 1938, a frozen dawn of icicles and clanking radiators slammed up the walls of our building. Nathan left for the Polar Bear Club, a towel on the shoulder of his overcoat. How many times had he forgotten to dry himself for me? His virility at stake, he wanted to prove himself.

At Coney Island he and other men ran through the snow into the water in their bathing suits, a *mashuga* idea.

"It's a tradition from 1903," he said to me proudly as he left.

A reporter noticed Nathan among the younger men poised to race into the icy Atlantic, its waves crashing to shore. The next day on the front of *The New York Post* Nathan appeared, stretched out on the snowy sand in his one piece bathing costume holding up the newspaper. An instant celebrity in the neighborhood, he reveled in it, smiling, nodding and puffing out his chest, a proud pigeon to the ladies in the elevator. One afternoon a widow in a hat, her eyes peeking through a netted veil, gave Nathan an alluring glance. I moved closer to him. Maybe I didn't want him all the time, but I didn't want anyone else to have him either.

After the attention from the newspaper picture died down, my energy faded, too, sliding me into an abyss. I don't remember how it happened, but I passed out, my head catching on the corner of the end table in the living room. While the bump healed I covered it with makeup and wore a burgundy fedora of Nathan's. Then, I lost consciousness again, this time in the kitchen. Isaac found me after school and insisted I go to the doctor.

Nathan was too busy to bother with such nonsense.

"Fainting? You don't eat enough liver. With you it's always something. Polish aristocracy? Huh! Take a tonic," he told me.

Doctor Gross, a specialist who trained in Vienna, took my blood and said he'd get back to me. Did I have an incurable disease?

A few days later as I sat on the cold table in the sterile room, I worried about what was wrong with me. I prayed it wasn't serious. The doctor entered without a smile, his glasses on his nose and a chart in his hand. His white starched coat, DR. GROSS embroidered over the pocket, looked brand new.

"You have diabetes." I sat up straighter, my heart ready to rocket out of me. He paused when I began to cry and handed me a tissue. I didn't know what diabetes was, but it sounded ominous.

"Your blood sugar has to be regulated. The good news is there's a treatment for it. Some Canadian doctors have isolated the elusive hormone. You'll need insulin injections."

He explained I had to give myself shots every day. I got up and ran to the little sink on the side of the room to vomit. I was petrified of needles. Would I die? Who would watch the children?

Once, when I was nine years old, the summer a blanket of humidity over Warsaw, I disobeyed my mother and ran outside to our courtyard without shoes. Malka and I were playing a game, Yadwiga was beating carpets in one corner and my grandmother sat in a wicker chair with wheels, a crocheted quilt on her lap, near the entrance. We hid and ran until a rusty nail found its way into the bottom of my foot. I tried to pull it out, but it wouldn't budge. In an effort not to step on it and disguise my lopsided walk, I wrapped my foot with bandages I stole from the servants' medicine cabinet.

At night under my bedcovers I inspected the damage: red. The next night: red and oozing. Then: red, oozing and puffy. Finally, I couldn't hide it anymore. Not only did I have a hideous limp, I also had a fever. When my mother discovered what I had done, she was furious.

"Look at you! You're foot is infected! The doctor will have to amputate," she screamed at me. I began to cry.

My mother and father huddled near the bed. When the doctor arrived, his clothes smelled of disinfectant. I was terrified. He examined my foot with humming sounds, poking and pressing the infected area around the nail. His mustache covered his top lip and twirled into points, shiny with wax.

It twitched when he said, "I have to operate. It's the worst infection I've ever seen."

Operate? *OhmineGott.* My parents, afraid of hospitals, knew people went in and never came out. In short order our dining room became a surgical suite. The table was cleared, chairs removed, layers of blankets and sheets set down, lights brought in and a hush fell over the room as my father and Magda's strong arms lifted me up.

My father gave me sips of kosher wine from a silver chalice while the servants and my brothers gathered and stared. The doctor warned me it would hurt. My parents held my arms so I couldn't wiggle. I saw the long needle go into my foot and screamed. The room swirled in my dizzy state, sweeping me in and out of darkness. I fell back on the pillows, cushioning myself into the makeshift bed and dozed off. When I woke up in my own room on top of the goose down quilt, my foot, propped on a pillow, was bandaged in white gauze. I still couldn't walk. My brothers carried me everywhere for a week. My papa brought me midnight blue satin slippers trimmed with swan's down as an incentive to get me out of bed. Finally, I got better and vowed never to go without shoes again.

A part of me was still that child petrified of needles. Where was my papa? Yet, once I listened to what Doctor Gross said, I prepared to do what was necessary. I had to see my children grow up.

"Insulin will help you escape certain death. You will not only cheat it, you're going to live a long and healthy life," he told me with a pat on the back.

In the beginning it was a challenge to give myself the injections and to buy needles and insulin at the pharmacy. I started with my thigh, which became sore. I switched to the other one. I removed sweets from the house, a difficult task with children. Eventually, the routine blended into my life and I was grateful for modern medicine. Just as I thought it would get easier, another problem arose to defy us.

After Max's first birthday Nathan received a telegram from my father.

Come at once. [Stop.] Can no longer collect rents from building. [Stop.] Bank has called note. Stop.] Will fall into receivership soon. [Stop.] Cannot evict in this inflation-ridden city of political uncertainty.

The apartment building on Bielanska Street my father gave us as a wedding present brought in substantial income. My father oversaw the manager, made the deposits and sent us checks.

Nathan crumpled the yellow message and pounded his fist on the table. "I have to go. Tomorrow. People have to pay their rent. They can't get away with this. Paulina, pack my valise."

"Let me go with you, to see my family." I began to cry.

"Impossible. You're going to travel with children and a baby on a moment's notice? You're a sick woman. Go in a few months with Mrs. Dreichspun. In the summer." He leaned over and held my arm. "Maybe things will be better."

I lifted myself away from the table to pull a suitcase from the top shelf in our bedroom closet. No time to shop for gifts for anyone. I knew I couldn't be ready in a day. I felt a steel beam lower into my chest, sinking my heart to my knees. A flood of memories whisked by me—my mother's face, my father's last hug, the gypsies warning. I opened the valise, stained with Nathan's many passages, on the bed. A sob crawled from my throat, unfurling into a wail. I threw myself onto the covers and curled into a ball. My mama, my papa.

Early the next morning Nathan left for the docks in his black overcoat, a wool scarf tucked around his neck. He purchased a round-trip ticket with ease on the Britannic to Southampton for $245, an off-season bargain. Few people wanted to travel to Europe. He returned in three weeks, his face pale, eyes rimmed in red.

"Your father looks bad. Your mother couldn't talk. She just cried. You must go." He laid a wad of bills on the kitchen table. "The building is lost. No one can pay. I changed what little I could collect at the bank. *Varshe*, our beautiful Warsaw, is gone. People beg on the streets. There's no work. It's the end." He dropped his head into his arms at the table. I had never seen him like this. I gnawed my lip in fear.

Nathan, so strong that nothing stopped him, saw doom.

"What about my brothers?"

"Mendel and Itzak are the same, but Carlo has moved to Brussels."

"Brussels? What is he doing there?" I didn't think he spoke Flemish.

Nathan's expression changed. "Your parents are quite upset. He moved to be near a Gentile girlfriend." Nathan noticed my frown and continued. "He's moved into a small villa with her family. He wants to buy a business."

My hand went to my chest. Two children moved away and one sick. My poor parents. "I'm going to buy a ticket. I'll leave baby Max behind. Leah will come with me."

The next day I bought tickets for me, Mrs. Dreichspun, and the other children. I was going to Warsaw.

Chapter Eight

Paulina

March, 1938

As I made preparations for my trip, Germany invaded Austria. When the Nazis impounded Sigmund Freud's passport and money, it made headlines around the world. Most of the Jewish population in Austria lived in Vienna. The oppressors came and started persecuting people right away, setting up restrictions as to where they could go, what they could do. People were threatened, businesses confiscated. Hundreds were forced to scrub the streets. The humiliation was too much to bear. Within that first month five hundred Viennese Jews committed suicide.

Nathan, angered by this news, sent my parents a letter begging them to leave Poland at once. He made a strong argument as to why they weren't safe. We owned our apartment building in New York, not as grand as where my parents lived, but he offered them a place to stay. My father responded with:

Dearest Children,

Thank you for your concern and kind offer, but your mother and I and your brothers are fine. Besides, your mother would never leave Itzak and with his illness he would never be allowed into your country. His condition is the same, but his melancholy brings us all down some days.

We have great sympathy for our Austrian brethren, but this, too, shall pass. We have a long history in Polyn and have always survived. The Parliament has passed legislation that revokes citizenship for Poles abroad. That means that many cannot return home to claim their property. I'm sure something will be worked out. This Hitler fellow has a small following. We have great faith in our Creator and the common man. No harm will come to us.

Our lives are filled with the turmoil of daily living. The scarcity of fresh fruit and lack of meat means long lines, but it is business as usual. The economy is suffering. I have curtailed my trips to Vienna and will buy goods in Belgium and other ports. Perhaps Carlo and I can set up trade routes.

We have trouble with our business partner, Godik, in Berlin. We have owned a movie theater together for years and now he will not pay us our share of profits. I want to go and collect but your mother is against the idea.

The influx of refugees with no place to go clogs the streets. Even Yadwiga, our loyal servant, is frightened and has returned to her family in the outskirts of Gdansk. Ludmilla left weeks ago. Only Magda stays to cook for us and it is difficult to find fresh food.

Our love to you and your family,
Papa

I tucked the letter into my lingerie drawer. Powder from pink sachet packets my mother sent from a Paris sojourn sprinkled across the front of the envelope.

Sadness filled my heart, an unending well of regrets that wouldn't go away. I didn't know how to help. I felt I had abandoned my parents. Would my children do the same to me? I had no control of anything, even the children.

With minds of their own, they wanted to experience the freedom of America, especially Isaac, a bright boy interested in college like others in his class. He and Nathan fought about it. And, in all fairness, Isaac wouldn't leave the subject alone. Nathan would come home, exhausted, a newspaper filled with the threat of war under his arm, and Isaac would be ready to nudge him before he could sit in his chair.

"College? I told you. A waste of money for a sixteen-year-old-boy. I only finished *kheyder*." Nathan saw Isaac's puzzled expression. "Elementary school for Russian Jewish boys. I had to support my parents. Work in the business like the rest of the family. Be glad you'll have a job."

Volatile together, Isaac and Nathan would argue until it deteriorated into pushing. I begged Nathan not to be physical in front of the younger children. Rachel and Max were petrified when the shouting started and Sarah ran out the door. Isaac was over six feet tall now, too big to push around.

First, they stopped speaking. Then, they began to avoid each other. Finally, Isaac escaped to Goldie's apartment, sleeping there instead of at home. He'd return to check on me after school or on Saturdays, change clothes and eat leftovers. He'd sneak into the apartment, wolf down food like a hungry, driven animal, then hurry out before Nathan showed up.

Isaac told me, "Mama, I hate him, his stubbornness. He doesn't want me to go to college because he didn't. People succeed in America with education." He leaned forward to grab my knees. "It's my only chance. I could be anything. *He* only wants me to work in a factory."

Nathan didn't ask about Isaac and I didn't bring up his name. I knew he was safe.

"Mama, don't worry about me. I'm fine," he'd say, hugging me. Then he'd kiss my cheek and disappear.

Soon, Isaac got a job working the night shift in a cap factory after school. Determined to save for classes I slipped him a few dollars when I could. He wanted to build skyscrapers, buildings to salute America, become an engineer or an architect. My father taught me it was better to be in business for yourself, not to be an employee. Were Isaac's grand schemes a good idea? I didn't know, but maybe he'd be like his grandfather and own the company. A boy so hotheaded and driven like his father would be a success. I had faith his spirit would guide him.

In a way, it was better not to have the conflict under our roof. The younger ones would sidle up to Nathan after dinner when he read the paper and smoked. He'd make a space for them in his chair and they'd cuddle next to him, Max with his thumb in his mouth and Rachel with a book. They were easier to manage.

Sarah, on the other hand, became elusive. She missed Isaac, her companion. She floated in and out, saying little, set with her own agenda. A beauty with long auburn hair, she wore it swept up to emphasize her neck. She had my petite figure, one with an ample bosom and long legs. She seemed unaware that she was attractive. With high school almost over she, too, wanted to continue her schooling.

Sarah approached Nathan after dinner one evening as he leaned forward to tune in the news through the static on the radio. Cigarette smoke swirled up from the ashtray beside him, his fingers playing with the dials. I could hear her stuttered plea from the kitchen and then Nathan's response.

"College? For a girl? A waste of money. Make a living. Get married. How long do I have to feed you?" I came to stand in the doorway drying a dish. He dismissed her with a wave of his hand.

Disappointment dissolved her face. She came to me in tears without a rebuttal to him. She pulled me back into the kitchen. I put down the dish to hold her.

"Mama, why is he so mean? I have friends who are going to attend Brooklyn or City College. I'm smart. I could be a teacher or more. I don't want to be a shop girl."

I smoothed hair off her forehead. I didn't know what to say to her. I didn't know any girls who went to college, but things were different in America. Would Nathan come home with someone for her to marry like my father? She'd run away. I comforted her as best I could and encouraged her to take out more books from the library.

She, too, avoided Nathan, slipping in and out of her room, saying she was going to the movies with friends or studying. She was a good girl. I didn't worry.

Perhaps I should have paid more attention, but Rachel and Max kept me busy. Besides, my trip was soon. Nathan was discouraging me from traveling, but he knew I was determined this time. My family needed me, so many clothes and gifts to get ready. The last thing I wanted my mother to see was me looking shabby. I bought a few things that needed alterations, looked for shoes, and purchased another fox collar unaware disaster lurked in my own building.

Leon, a nineteen-year-old, lived in the basement apartment with his elderly immigrant parents who got by on a small pension. At their age he was an afterthought, a change of life baby. I knew Sarah visited but said nothing. She was happy with this friendship, buzzing as she took the back stairs to avoid Nathan in the elevator.

A quiet boy with a skinny build and a downy mustache that reached his full pink lips, he'd greet me near the mailboxes, eyes cast down, Adam's apple like a pogo stick in his neck. I wanted to buy him a shirt with a collar that fit.

Anyway, his hobby fascinated Sarah. With a small camera he took pictures and developed them in a closet. I didn't understand how a picture came out after dipping paper in chemicals but she hung around him for hours. I warned her that her father would not like her spending time with someone of the opposite sex in the dark. Nor would he like her socializing with our tenants, especially Romanian refugees.

"Oh Mama, we're not doing anything. I'm learning photography. At first my images were blurry. Leon's teaching me how to get a sharp contrast." She saw a frown cross my face and touched my hand. "Don't worry. Papa won't find out."

Of course Nathan went to look for her one Friday afternoon when it was time to light the candles and Max, my little tattletale, blurted out where she was. Nathan pounded on the basement door, pushed it open when there was no response, and stomped through their living room. He found the two of them in the hall closet, Leon's parents asleep in the bedroom. Another scene that the neighbors heard. A *shonda*. Why did everyone have to know our business? Know our embarrassment?

Nathan dragged Sarah upstairs by her arm amid her protests of, "You can't do this to me. I want to live my own life. We weren't doing anything. I'm learning photography."

"Photography, schmography. A young woman cannot spend time alone with a young man in the dark. What are you? A *courva*?" he yelled, his footsteps heavy in the hallway. I winced when he used the Yiddish word for a woman of ill repute.

"I forbid you to see him. He has no job. What kind of *mishegos* is making pictures? For what? From this he'll make a living? People will talk that you're in his apartment. His parents are working class people without a business. Get a job and contribute to the household or you can live like your brother."

Sarah began to cry, her words and bravery slinking away like mine in a confrontation with Nathan. She ran to her room, slammed the door and didn't appear until the next morning after her father left for work.

She approached me as I sat at the kitchen table, surveying the morning mess. "Mama, I can't stay here anymore. I'm going to live with Aunt Goldie in Brooklyn until I finish school in a few weeks." With sour bitterness she added, "He can't tell me what to do."

"Sarah, don't run away. You're too young to be on your own. Besides, we're going to leave for Poland." I stopped to think. "Do you love this young man?" I asked, fearful her emotions might spin away from her.

"I don't know what love is. Leon's sweet, but I'm more interested in what he does with his camera. I see so many possibilities." Her face turned hard. "Papa cannot rule my life. I'll be eighteen soon and legal to make my own decisions. Boys my age enlist to fight for their country."

I covered my face with my hands and began to cry with the thought of losing my daughter, too. She, of my four children, was the brightest, the most sensitive, the most help. I looked up and watched her pace the small space.

"Sarah, I've never spoken to you about boys and girls. It's awkward for me. My mother told me nothing. In Polyn the servants teach these things." I hesitated. "Is there anything I should know?"

Sarah put her arms around me. "Mama, I'm innocent. There's nothing to know. Leon's a friend. Don't worry." She kissed my forehead, a reminder of how little affection we expressed to one another.

I put my arms around her waist and cried. I couldn't stop. I cried for my youth, my lost children, my loveless marriage, my family so far away. I cried like a giant ship pushing away from the dock, cutting through the ocean, its powerful bow setting a new course.

I planned to leave as soon as school was out with Rachel and Max. I held out hope Sarah would come, too, to see her grandparents. Isaac was living another life.

At night, when I draped myself into a chair, Nathan argued with me, a never-ending test of wills.

"Don't you see what's going on in Europe? It's too dangerous to go. Half of the Jews in Austria are scrambling to leave and you want to go in the other direction? You'll be trapped," he told me, puffing his cigarette.

"I have to see my family. Maybe I can convince them to come. We can smuggle Itzak someplace else. There has to be a way." I tried not to raise my voice because it would incite him, but it deteriorated quickly. My frustration leaked into my words.

"You want to be a *mashugana*, go ahead, but you're not going to take my children back to that sewer pit they're calling Europe. War's gathering like storm clouds and you're going to traipse through it. What's the matter with you? These Nazis are pigs. You'll be arrested doing something foolish and I won't be able to get you out."

"I won't be arrested. I'll smuggle in money and buy off people."

"What? With two small children?"

"You've never wanted me to leave because you think I'll stay. Or find someone better." My chin jutted in defiance.

He shouted in my face, "You'll never find someone better than Nathan Korsakov. I provide for you and the children. Where would you be without me? Living in Warsaw in your parents' building? For how long?"

He stymied me. What could I say? My head hurt.

"Don't you read the papers?" he continued. "They burned the main synagogue in Munich to the ground. Who knows what they'll do next?"

"How can I abandon them? How will I live?"

"I have no more patience for you," he told me.

It always ended with him slamming a door and saying, "Go, go by yourself. You'll never see your children again. You don't know what you have here in this America."

After our arguments, I'd delay getting my tickets, insecure with my ability to make a decision. I'd tell myself to wait another week, to see what would happen. I know I drove Leah crazy because I couldn't move ahead.

On one of our neighborhood walks she said, "Paulina, I can't go with you. I'm afraid, too. I don't think you should go either. Something bad is happening, Jews disappearing in the night. My neighbor, Mrs. Shapiro, hasn't heard from her family in weeks. Promise me you won't go." She pulled her cardigan close around her shoulders.

"But, Leah, that's why I have to go. What if something happens to my family? I could never forgive myself. Their pleas haunt me now." We stopped under an awning in front of a shoe repair shop. She held my arms.

"You must think about your family here, now. Wait. See what happens."

At the end of June Sarah graduated with honors and we attended the ceremony as a family. Nathan gave her a gold wristwatch as a truce, but she left anyway. She moved in for good with Goldie, sleeping on the couch, and visited me on Saturdays when she knew he would be in *shul*. I didn't ask if she stopped to see Leon. His parents lowered their eyes when they saw me on the street.

One summer afternoon Sarah and I sat at the kitchen table. "Mama, I got a part time job at Gimbels and I'm taking classes at night like Isaac." There was a thrill in her voice I had not heard before. "Look, Leon taught me how to develop my own pictures." She moved our seltzer water aside and took black and white pictures out of a paper folio. I didn't know if they were good or bad, but they were replications of trees in Central Park, leaves scattered on grassy knolls, Orthodox Jews walking down Orchard

Street in their black hats, coats opening in the wind and vendors in the fish market, their mouths in strange shapes of anguish.

"This is what you want to do?" I asked, fingering the large photographs. She nodded, her eyes alive with excitement. The mosaic of blacks and whites and shades of gray formed grainy images that told a story.

"Mama, I need a camera. I borrowed Leon's for these. If I had my own I could use his darkroom and develop my photographs."

How did she get such an idea to run around taking pictures? I slipped my fingers into my brassiere and gave her the five dollars I was saving for a Coney Island trip with the younger children. Nathan thought nobody ever needed anything.

Sarah threw her arms around me. "Oh, Mama, thank you."

"Don't tell anyone," I said as I got up to start supper. I knew I had made her happy.

One September evening Nathan came home enraged. Not about Sarah though. Hitler, Mussolini, the leaders of France and Britain met in Munich and agreed to give Germany part of Czechoslovakia, the Sudetenland.

"How can they capitulate to this thug?" he asked loudly, dropping his briefcase. I never knew how to respond. The world events were so much larger than I could understand. I only worried about my family. I had hopes of leaving after the Jewish holidays, no matter what Nathan said. What did this mean?

Nathan's nightly arguments and news reports wore me down. I couldn't fight back anymore and wasn't sure I had the strength to take on the world. Two months later on the seventh of November, 1938 the Germans, in retaliation for one of their diplomats being shot at the Paris Embassy, launched *Kristallnacht*, the Night of Broken Glass. I sat down to read the description in the newspaper about one-hundred-and-ninety-one synagogues set on fire and seven thousand businesses destroyed in Germany and Austria. The newspaper shook in my hands. Thousands of homes and businesses were looted, the glass of proud shop owners littered the streets, and thirty thousand Jews were rounded up. All because a Jewish teenager trapped with his family in a refugee camp near Zbaszyn, a border town in Poland where Nathan once arranged for two of his brothers to meet him, became frustrated and bought a gun. I couldn't breathe.

I urged Nathan to send my parents a telegram.

Come immediately. Stop. Don't wait. Stop. You are in danger. Paulina

A letter arrived written in Yiddish two weeks later.

Dearest Paulina,

Don't worry. The troubles in Germany and Austria are not ours. Good fortune saw that the movie house we own in Berlin was not a target during the rampage of destroying businesses. Godik still owes us money but we have hope. We take more precautions on the street because of hoodlums encouraged by Hitler. It is not safe for your mother to do the shopping any longer, but that is a minor inconvenience. Magda keeps us well-fed.

We cannot come to you, my dear daughter. Itzak cannot be abandoned, although he begs your mother to leave him. Last week he stood on the balcony prepared to jump, but little Natasha threw her arms around his legs and cried for help. It is a sin to take one's own life. We all must wait for God's will.

When are you coming? A visit would cheer your mother and we all miss you.

All Our Love,

Papa

My mother added in Polish, her artistic handwriting dancing across the page.

My Dear Children,
It is freezing here. I wish the troubles and problems would melt away like spring frost. We have to be strong. I shiver with chicken skin when I think of you alone in a big city without us and so many children. Send pictures.
God is merciful and keeps every human in his Almighty protection. Pray God will let us survive and come back to a normal life.
Kisses and Hugs,
Your Mother

I had to go. My guilt swept me away. In December after months of preparation, numerous shopping trips, and meal arrangements for Nathan, I was ready to leave for Europe with the younger children during Christmas vacation.

I came home one evening to find Rachel languid on the sofa. Her head felt warm. She lifted her shirt to show me red spots she was scratching on her stomach. I called the doctor who examined her, his black bag open on the floor. He listened to her chest, looked in her throat, examined the spots. Measles. He left, nailing a sign that read QUARANTINED to our door. Nathan, who wasn't home yet, saw the sign and slept at his brother Morris' for a week. Isaac and Sarah avoided the apartment as well. I was trapped inside with Rachel and Max, who came down with them a week later. Red spots and runny noses. I never got them, but I sat for hours with the hum of the radio.

One evening a Father Coughlin came on the radio and said the Jews were responsible for communism and all of Germany's woes.

I turned him off. Wasn't this supposed to be the land of tolerance?

Another trip thwarted. When would I see my parents? I left when Sarah was a child and now she was a young woman. Nine years passed by like the wind. When would I go?

Chapter Nine

Paulina

September, 1939

On September 1, 1939 Germany invaded Poland. Great Britain and France mobilized their forces and declared war. Nathan, enraged, banged the walls with his fists, cursing.

"Those bastards. I saw this coming. I'm always right."

"I must go to my family. I have to leave," I told him, grabbing my coat, my movements jerky in the hysteria of the moment. I stuffed table money into my pocketbook, grabbed aspirin, looked for my insulin.

"Are you *mashuga*? You can't go now. Hitler is unpredictable. Who knows what he'll do." He grabbed my arms to stop me and whirled me toward him. His eyes, hungry over my face, gripped me.

"I have to buy a ticket. My mama and papa need me. I'm going to Warsaw." A sob crept from a deep hollow place inside me, a raw beast of terror. I beat my hands against Nathan's chest. "Let me go," I cried, my fists in rhythm.

"Paulina, you can't go. That's it." Nathan's firm hold on my wrists stopped me. I collapsed against his chest, tears staining the front of his starched shirt.

"Sha, sha," he said stroking my hair, trying to soothe me. I listened to the rapid pace of his heart. "Let's go to Western Union."

The lines were out the door. With emotional despair, we telegrammed my parents to come, to get out, to leave everything, also wiring five hundred dollars. We heard nothing for weeks and then, finally, they responded with a letter on blue onionskin paper.

7 October 1939
Dearest Paulina and Nathan,
We received the money and have applied for visas. Such chaos. I waited for hours. I think it is hopeless. Four hundred thousand Jews in Warsaw and we all want the same thing.

The Polish Army mobilized one million men, but we could not defend ourselves without tanks and antiaircraft guns. The Germans marched through the Polish Corridor that leaves us so vulnerable and were on the outskirts of Warsaw in a week. What can a horse cavalry do against an air force? The Luftwaffe bombed our bridges, roads and rail lines. So many civilians killed. A garrison held out to defend our city until the 28 of September, but it was useless. The Germans have captured 700,000 soldiers according to a shortwave radio report we heard from Russia, and, they, too, have invaded. Once again, our Polyn will be sliced up like pieces of cheese.

Our immediate neighbors have fled because we are without running water. Even the barbershop owner and the night watchman next door have disappeared. Thank Goodness our loyal Magda has stayed and brings water for cooking from a well in the square. I don't know how she makes soups with so few things. Vendors have little to sell. Bathing is a challenge. The city government has promised us water soon.

We are hardy and have the staying power to outlast these clowns. We will manage. Do not worry about us.
Love,
Papa

A few weeks later another letter arrived. I tore it open in the lobby in front of the letterbox, my hands shaking, frantic with anxiety.

28 October 1939
Dear Children,
Hitler and his Nazis have an immigration policy that allows us to leave, but we would lose everything. Many of our friends are heading eastward to the Soviet zone. We cannot leave your brother, Itzak, who is too ill to travel. He sleeps for hours slumped over wherever we have moved him. Last week we found him in a pool of blood, an attempt to slit his wrists. We cannot allow such a thing. It's as though he knows people are beaten in the streets and shops are closed. At our family meeting we all voted to stay. This will blow over.
Unfortunately, Mendel's children are no longer allowed to attend school. Natasha follows her mama everywhere begging her to read. We are required to wear a blue Star of David armband on our clothes for identification. Magda spent hours sewing them on our coats. I am humiliated by this but continue to keep appointments. Your mother refuses to leave the house.
Take care of yourselves and kiss the children for me.
Love,
Papa
P.S. Can you send canned goods? There are no vegetables.

I read and re-read the letter and the others that followed, a ball of string unwinding, rolling out toward a cliff. The Nazis established a second ghetto in Warsaw but my parents were not required to move. Carlo wrote from Belgium that he was hiding in a basement closet, pieces of my mother's jewelry sewn into his coat lining.

Every missive was bad news. I retrieved the mail and opened each letter with dread. The servants fled. My parents' closest friend was carried off in the night. Bank accounts were frozen. My father traded antiques for food, silver chalices for medicine.

Nathan became obsessed with war news. He'd sit in front of the radio with his newspaper ruminating over troop movements, political announcements and politician's speeches. He bought a large map of Europe and placed it on our dining room wall with pushpins to track Germany's conquests. He complained in his brusque manner to everyone who would listen that the United States needed to get involved. Fortunately, our family agreed with him. We waited silently as Holland, France and Belgium fell. What about my Carlo living like a hunted animal?

Nathan, even in his anger, kept at business. He received a contract to manufacture boots for combat, but it was difficult to get leather. Did he make deals on the black market? I don't know. Maybe it came from South America like he said.

Sarah and Isaac came home more often. They remembered their grandparents and knew I was ripped apart with anxiety. Once, Nathan walked in on us sitting at the kitchen table, our drinks diluted from sharing the same tea bag. He joined us, a respite from previous tensions.

"How are things?" he asked Isaac.

"Good, Pop. They're good."

"And school?"

"I take night classes. I like it." Isaac was still cautious. Were Nathan's pleasantries a trap?

Nathan turned to Sarah. "And what are you up to?"

"W-w-working and school, too," she said.

Nathan stood up and took a wad of cash from his pocket. He wet his finger and thumbed through money. The three of us caught our breath. He handed each of them fifty dollars, a first-time acknowledgement.

Isaac stood up, taller than his father. "Thanks, Pop," he said, a smile grazing across his face. Nathan patted his back.

Sarah sat, her gaze transfixed on her tea. I nudged her foot with mine under the table. She was always so proud. I'm sure she was thinking about whether she should take it. Finally, she looked up at him and said, "I want to thank you for this generous gift, but I also want you to know that money can't buy me or heal our difficult past."

For a moment Nathan's face looked cross, the usual hurtful words ready to explode, then he said, "Ach, you've always been a pain in the *tookus.*" A wave of his hand dismissed her. He stood up scraping his chair on the linoleum and left. Isaac smiled at me but Sarah remained sullen.

Months passed. We went to see *The Great Dictator* on a rare family outing, a film by Charlie Chaplin that parodied Hitler and satirized Mussolini. Chaplin played two roles, a Jewish barber and a dictator. Nathan loved it. We laughed together, then went for dinner at a deli. Isaac, too tall for the low table, hunched over to eat his chicken soup, a giant matzo ball floating in the middle. Sarah smiled at me. Rachel and Max were thrilled to be served, even by a grouchy Russian refugee in a wrinkled white shirt and crooked black tie. For a brief moment I forgot how dangerous and terrible the world had become.

At the end of 1940, with France defeated and London under Luftwaffe strikes every night for two months, Roosevelt campaigned for a third term promising mothers not send their boys to war. I still had hope my family would be close to me, safe in America. That is, until I received a short note from my mother written on both sides.

14 December 1940

Paulina Dearest,

Polyn is no longer granting exit visas to Jews. We are trapped. Everyone is ordered into the ghetto and has six weeks to move. Once in, no one comes out. It is rumored half a million of us are inside the space of a few blocks. Many are dying of disease and starvation.

Your father with his many business contacts has managed to keep us in our house. You would not recognize it. Gone are the rugs, the art, most of the furniture, our expensive clothes, the crystal chandeliers. Everything traded for coal to heat a few rooms. We even burned chairs ourselves. We live in the kitchen now that we are alone. I sit by the fire in my fur coat to keep warm. We traded what's left of our valuables for food for your brothers and Mendel's children. Poor children. They only know they cannot go outside.

Carlo is in Brussels where all Jews are required to register along with their property. Since he is there in hiding, he has not declared himself. He is very clever and has many friends among the intelligentsia.

My dearest daughter, I love you. Kiss the children. This madness will be over soon and yes, we will finally come to you.

Your Mother

In 1941 Yugoslavia and Greece surrendered to Germany. Nathan moved pushpins in anger. Drops of blood from his thumb stained the floor, a reminder of lives lost. Letters kept coming. My parents avoided the Warsaw ghetto by paying off more people but food was scarce. Fifty to seventy people starved each day in an area surrounded by walls, barbed wire and soldiers with snarling dogs.

My parents asked me to send packages, which I did, but most never arrived. Confiscated.

In the summer of 1941 three million German troops invaded Russia. Hitler marched farther into Russia than Napoleon. The siege of Leningrad began in the fall. Nathan denounced everyone: Nazis, Communists, Bolsheviks. The pushpins covered most of Europe.

Nathan attended *shul* every day to say prayers of thanksgiving that his family was here. I was bereft mine wasn't. In coded language my father wrote they paid more people to escape the Nazi net. Letters arrived on scraps of paper, the emblem of an eagle whose feet held a swastika on the envelope, a symbol that sent icy fingers up my spine.

Our neighbors are gone. We are hiding, living like rats in a cellar. This letter has been smuggled out to be mailed. I cannot say who is helping us. The smell of fear pervades the lives of everyone. We will weather this storm as our people have many times before. Pray for us.

I joined Nathan at temple, secluded in the upstairs part for women. I prayed for my parents and more. What about our salvation? On the walk back to our apartment one morning we learned from shouting newsboys that the United States declared war. The seventh of December, 1941 the Japanese bombed Pearl Harbor. Shocked at first, we felt relief. Nathan was vocal in his excitement.

"Finally, we can go after these *momsers*," he repeated over and over. His fists would clench and unclench, his jaw set so hard it would twitch.

Conscription stepped up and I saw the effects in our neighborhood. Young men, their heads newly shorn, came in stiff uniforms and spit-shined boots to say goodbye. They looked so young, so nervous.

One afternoon Leon was at the door, his Army hat in hand.

"Is Sarah home? I've come to tell her I've enlisted."

I watched his Adam's apple jump in his throat, the fuzzy down of his lip gone. I explained she stayed with relatives and worked. Who would look after his parents?

"I'm leaving in the morning for Fort Benning and then I'll be shipped overseas." His brown eyes looked down. "I'm sorry if I caused you any upset. I was teaching Sarah photography. She has a talent, you know." With that he left. I felt sad for his parents. He was a good boy and now they were alone. I boiled a chicken and sent a few servings of *cholent* downstairs.

Sarah took his departure in stride. "He wasn't a true love," she told me. "Just a good friend. I hope he'll be safe."

In the summer of 1942 the Polish Socialist Jewish Bund leaked a report that was later verified and picked up by the BBC. As I crouched in front of our RCA, I heard the detailed account of deportations and killings throughout Poland. I became hysterical. Nathan could not calm me.

"The Germans have killed seven hundred thousand Jews," I screamed. Was my family among them?

Shortly thereafter, no more letters from Poland arrived, but Carlo continued to write from Belgium.

15 August 1942

My Dearest Sister,

I never thought I would be in this position. My money has run low and I need to pay my benefactors for room and board. Would you and Nathan wire money to me as soon as possible? I came for a visit and have moved in with Katerina's family. Gracious people. I am in hiding.

I have not heard from Mama and Papa in weeks. Things are bad in Poland. Until recently in Belgium we still strolled the streets, sat in the cafes, listened to concerts, but now I am without resources having sold jewelry I brought with me. Katerina, most generous and patient, knows I can no longer leave. She shares space with another couple and her parents. It is difficult for me to stay inside all day. For the first time in my life I am afraid.

My love to you, Nathan and the children. I await your response. Send the money to Katerina Lemur at the Riviera Hotel.

Love,
Carlo

Where would I get money to send? I approached Nathan with trepidation, knowing he thought my brother was a ne'er-do-well. Yet, he was sympathetic to Carlo's plight and gave me five hundred dollars to wire. I waited in line again until dusk.

The following week I checked with the clerk, a man too old to be drafted. His thin gray hair left too much shiny forehead. He glanced at me through his green eyeshade, his hands busy with papers.

"The money has not been picked up," he told me.

I checked back for weeks and it was not retrieved. Gone. Where was everyone?

Chapter Ten

Paulina

January, 1943

With no word from my family I could only hope they were safe and hidden from the Nazi scourge. My attention focused on our family, feeding them with war rations, coupons kept in leatherette envelopes that piled up in kitchen drawers.

Keeping Nathan happy was another chore, not an easy task. He followed every news morsel like a tracking dog, moving his pushpins around the map, giving me detailed accounts of battles.

"General Eisenhower has taken French North Africa. He's crushed those Nazi pigs in Tunisia." Or, "The Russians are being slaughtered in Stalingrad but they'll prevail even though they're anti-Semitic *momsers*, too."

In the Spring of 1943 Nathan and his brothers attended a rally at Madison Square Garden with 75,000 other people to "Stop Hitler Now". The American Jewish Congress presented a rescue plan to President Roosevelt. He came home riled up, chain-smoked cigarettes and fell asleep in his chair.

Sarah and Isaac moved home. All talk of college was forgotten. Isaac pestered Nathan to enlist. He went to the draft board and filled out papers. When he went for his physical, he failed the eye test. Devastated, he expressed his disappointment late one evening.

"They'll take me for a desk job after I get my glasses. I wanted to fight, to kill Nazis. Look how strong I am," he said showing us his arm muscles. A small bump the size of an apple appeared inside his upper arm.

"Never mind. Now you're going to push papers," Nathan said, dismissing him with a wave of his hand. "You could be learning the business."

Nathan didn't hear Isaac say as he left the living room, "I'll never work for you."

Our complex lives and intense relationships reached a limbo of live and let live. We sailed along until a tragedy rocked our building.

Leon, Sarah's friend was killed in the invasion of Normandy, June 6, 1944. It took weeks until we learned the news. His mother collapsed when the Army telegram came to say he was missing. Later, officers came with his dog tags.

We grieved with Leon's inconsolable parents, his mother, a limp dishrag, who fixed her eyes on the barred basement windows for the familiar legs to come home. Nathan, although he disapproved of Leon's friendship with Sarah, took the boy's father to pray at the temple. The rabbi cut his lapel to symbolize mourning. We sat *shiva*, a week where the family gathered on low stools and friends brought food for the bereaved. Nathan sat for a whole day. The tradition made sense to me. With the loss of a child you couldn't function anyway. World War II had touched our building. I made a noodle *kugel* with raisins to bring downstairs.

A few months later Leon's parents stopped Sarah and offered her his camera and equipment. We had no place to put the trays and chemicals, but Sarah begged me to turn the hall closet into a darkroom. I had reservations because of the odors, but finally, I agreed. A tribute to Leon.

Between her job and helping me wait on lines for food, Sarah took black and white portraits of our family. She pestered me while I worked in the kitchen, a babushka covering my hair. I pulled off my apron and sat in a chair, then jumped up to get lipstick. I made her take another one when I returned from the beauty parlor, my hair in waves. She enticed Rachel and Max to sit for her on our burgundy velvet sofa like two angels. The minute she was finished, a fight started.

Isaac refused to have his portrait taken at first because of his new glasses. He pulled them off, handsome in his Army uniform, broad shoulders pulled back.

She never took Nathan's.

Sarah tinted the pictures, our lips rose-pink and our cheeks blushed peach. When she tired of posing us, she took her camera to the streets and shot people waiting in lines, an older, heavyset woman with three net shopping bags, dirty-faced children, someone's shabby shoes with tape holding the soles to the uppers. She said it was art as she showed them to me late one night. I didn't know what to think. They depressed me. I saw the filthy littered streets, lined faces impatient with war and my own sad eyes, filled with trepidation.

Nathan's parents became ill with influenza and passed away within a few weeks of each other. He was caught up with grieving and sitting *shiva* at his sister's house. He allowed the rabbi to rend the lapel of his old suit, went unshaven, and draped all the mirrors in our house with black. One funeral blended into the other. They had been in America but not part of it, never learning the language or understanding the customs. They blessed the son who brought them all to safety.

One evening when Nathan got around to noticing what Sarah was doing, he went wild. "A young woman does not run around taking pictures. What for? It's dangerous. Get married and let your husband support you," he said to her.

She left the room without a word.

Nathan got undressed and sat in his undershirt reading the paper.

Sarah was strong-willed, not an attractive trait to most men. School was on hold. She worked the night shift at a factory to support the war effort, slept all morning and scoured the city with her camera in the afternoon. Her photos told a story. She took more portraits of me, but I was still critical of the lines around my eyes, the wings under my neck. Where had my youth gone? I vowed to get rid of my long hair worn in a snood and made an appointment for a wash and set the following week. I needed a lift.

Without my knowledge Sarah took her portfolio to a newspaper. With so many young men gone, they hired her to shoot human interest photos and cover accidents for one of the Yiddish papers, even though her knowledge of the language was limited. I helped her with some translation. Most of the headlines were in English. Leon's camera went with her everywhere in a beat-up brown leather bag. She quit her night job and forged into a new world. In secret I was proud of her.

One morning Sarah packed up the darkroom equipment from the hall closet and moved it to the paper. She took to wearing pants and a blouse, a scarf tied to hold back her auburn hair.

The first time Nathan saw her, he yelled, "I won't have my daughter become a man."

I thought she looked like that new actress, Katharine Hepburn.

Eventually their conflicts drove Sarah to spend most nights at the home of another female reporter. A Gentile one. Nathan had plenty to say, but was too busy to do much. I bought the paper at the corner and looked for her name in small print next to the photos. She was making something of herself in America.

Every day I searched for word from my family, but there was nothing. I convinced myself they must be well hidden and couldn't get word to me. We contacted the Red Cross and the HIAS, the Hebrew Immigration Aid Society. A postcard arrived that no Kupfersteins could be located. Eventually, I gave up looking for letters from Carlo, too. What a world we were living in, one where people disappeared into thin air, vapor swallowed by clouds.

Isaac received notice to report for duty after training in Georgia as a supply officer. Not what he had in mind, but better than being seen on the street and having neighbors think he was 4-F. Before he left, the United States took an unprecedented action.

After our President died, Harry Truman took over in April of 1945. The war raged in Asia. In May German troops surrendered. There were atrocities on the radio every day. I couldn't listen. I turned it off. In the summer of 1945 Truman ordered an atomic bomb to be dropped on Hiroshima killing 70,000 people. The next day they sent another one to Nagasaki. The Japanese continued to fight. Finally, in mid-August Hirohito stopped the war. One nightmare ended and another began. But, before that there was a surprise.

On the December morning of my forty-fifth birthday after the children left for school, Nathan presented me with a blue velvet box while I sat propped up in bed reading a magazine. I looked puzzled, I'm sure, as I pulled my flowered housecoat tighter around me.

"It's to celebrate the end of the war," he told me.

I opened it not knowing what to expect. I gasped when I saw pearls, the most exquisite two strands I had ever seen. Each one was perfect, nestled between small knots, held together with a diamond clasp in the shape of a leaf. The box fell onto the bed. The luster of nature's gift reflected light from every angle as I shifted them around in my hands. Nathan leaned forward and kissed me with tenderness on the lips. I couldn't speak. He had never given me an extravagant gift.

He shifted his feet in embarrassment. "Maybe I haven't been demonstrative or communicative, but I want you to know, I love you." He said the last part quickly, as though the thought had never been uttered before. His spare words reverberated from my heart to my head and back again. He loved me. I suppose my expectations were small, but I felt appreciated. I dripped the pearls into the velvet box and clutched it to me. I was a lady, a lady with pearls.

I don't know where he got them, maybe as payment for something. Or maybe he bought them, but they were the most beautiful gift I had ever received. We went to dinner and I proudly wore them over my bosom, the diamonds close to my heart instead of at the nape of my neck. I wished I could show them to my mama.

It had been a long four years. Men started to come home, their shirtsleeves pinned up or with crutches. So many with eye patches or fingers missing. Thank Goodness Isaac was never shipped overseas. Now I could begin to look for my family in the rubble that was left of Europe.

I came home one afternoon from the kosher butcher, the roast beef and chickens wrapped in brown paper, tied with string. Sarah waited for me outside. She took my packages and escorted me into the elevator.

"Mama, I have bad news. I wanted to tell you before you saw it on the newsreels. General Eisenhower has liberated death camps in Poland. They've killed all the Jews."

At first I couldn't understand what she was saying. Death camps? *Vos es dis?* Where was my family? Why? I heard the phrase repeated many times in the next weeks and months. They rolled over and over in my head like the trains that took them all away.

"And, Mama, the paper is sending me overseas to cover the story. To bring back photographic evidence. I'm leaving in a week.

They want me to go to the displaced person's camps to take pictures of survivors."

I didn't register all she was telling me. "But where is my family?" I grasped at the wall.

"I don't know. I'll look for them. I'll be traveling with a reporter." She might have thought I would be concerned about her traveling with a man, but I could think of nothing else except my mama and papa. "Don't worry. I'll write to you."

Sarah readied herself for her trip without much assistance from me. She had to travel light. After she left, I went to the movies with Leah. The images Sarah warned me about flashed across the screen: bodies stacked like potato chips, each soul abandoned. I dropped my bag of popcorn and fled from the theater. I never saw the Barbara Stanwyck film. My life stalled in a never-ending nightmare.

I searched Red Cross lists, sent telegrams that were returned, and watched with horror as surviving Jews tried to return to their homes in Poland and were killed by their neighbors who had confiscated their homes and belongings. The pain was too much to bear. I stopped reading the paper. Nathan showed me an article that ghetto documents were excavated on Nowolipki Street in Warsaw, a history of what went on during the Nazi occupation. I made phone calls. The Kupfersteins were not on the list.

A letter arrived from Sarah in Germany.

September 14, 1946

Mama, I have searched for our family. The Nazis shipped people all over. They kept methodical lists of whom they killed and what they took from them but the Russians confiscated most of the material. We have no access to them. I can't find grandpa and grandma but I will never stop looking.

My job is to record what happened here. It has changed my

life forever. I have lost faith in God and the sanity of man. The Nuremburg Trials have begun and I am not being sent there to photograph the criminals. I don't know how I'd look at Hermann Goering, the murdering bastard.

I bought a fine Hasselblad camera in a pawn shop here. I tested it on menorahs, prayer books, and yellow stars ripped from clothes jumbled together in a case. A couple bought a few of the photographs for souvenirs. All I could think about was whom they might have belonged to and where they ended up.

I love you, Mama. Kisses to my brothers and sister and yes, even Papa.

Love,
Sarah

I continued my routine of cooking, shopping, taking care of my family, but I couldn't sleep. The horrific visions of what might have been my family's fate wrapped itself around my head, a band of steel that squeezed itself into a headache. What was my daughter doing traipsing around Europe in their chaos?

Another letter arrived from Sarah.

October 10, 1946
Dear Mama,

Perhaps I should have waited to tell you this bad news until I got home, but I cannot wait. I tracked down a neighbor from Bielanska Street in the DP camp who works on the Yiddish paper. The place is filled with wretched souls who have no way to rebuild their lives. Everyone wants to go to Palestine and the British won't let them in. Many weigh less than 75 pounds and can't digest their food.

Moishe Feigelbaum, the barber whose shop was next door, who says he knew you as a girl, told me what happened to grandma and grandpa. I remember holding their sweet hands so many years ago. Please promise me you will sit down while reading this. I am so sorry to write terrible news but I can't bear the agony of having you in limbo.

Mama, everyone's dead. They were murdered in Auschwitz. They stayed out until near the end, hiding in sewers until the Nazis trapped them. Moishe saw them in the camp handing in their clothes.

Oh Mama, I am so sorry. I love you. At least we are no longer waiting. I'll be home soon.

Love,

Sarah

I collapsed on top of the kitchen table, sobbing. Nathan and the children found me in the same spot hours later, my reservoir of tears drained. My voice escaped with my grief. I could only croak. Rachel tucked me into my bed. I didn't speak for days.

We went to temple to say *kaddish*, the prayer for the dead. I mouthed the words. Nathan broke down, sobbing for my father who had been his mentor and my mother who had treated him like a son. Rachel and Max were sympathetic but never knew the family I mourned for with blinding grief. They tiptoed around me and spoke in hushed voices.

A few days later my friend Leah received word no one in her family survived either. We cried together.

Book Two

Sarah
September, 1946

Chapter One

Sarah

September 1, 1946

On my inaugural flight to Germany filled with reporters, advisors and medical personnel, I jiggled upon take off, teeth chattering, a macabre novelty toy in endless movement. Strapped into a pull-down seat with my rucksack and duffle bag tucked underneath, the plane vibrated like a wet dog shaking off droplets of water through the night.

The only other females, three nurses in fatigues, sat side-by-side across from me, their starched white caps tucked into netted cubicles above them. A blonde with apple-red lips smiled at me. She mouthed the words, "Are you afraid to fly?"

I shook my head. Conversation meant shouting over the clatter. The former troop carrier rattled like a hollow gourd, the plane's khaki insides marred by scratched messages of love and fear. Besides the engine noise loose straps slapped the curved sides in a syncopated rhythm interrupted by an occasional snore from trusting men who slept, slack mouths and loose lips opened.

I gripped the sides of my seat, leaned my head back and allowed my mind to fill with thoughts of Mama and her loss. How would she go on? Exhausted anticipation blotted out a solution.

Cold air seeped down the back of my neck. I wrapped an Army

blanket around me. After a re-fueling stop in England I fell asleep against Saul, the middle-aged reporter assigned with me to write about displaced persons. I didn't know what I would find but I knew the camps sheltered 250,000 human beings who had lost every person and possession dear to them.

What a relief to reach our destination after hours of racket. I stumbled into the gray morning light with a fuzzy mouth and unkempt hair. Saul guided me toward an Army transport truck and pulled me up over the tailgate into the back. They dropped us at our first destination, enclosed in barbed wire.

Saul filled me in on the history as we walked toward the Camp Commandants compound, a low cinder block building surrounded by grass and a white picket fence. "This is a former concentration camp near the towns of Bergen and Belsen, originally established in forty-three for prisoners-of-war." He reached inside his wool jacket and pulled a cigarette from his shirt pocket and offered me one. I refused. "It became more than that," he said his voice filled with sarcasm.

Appalled at the condition of people in rags, some still wearing their striped uniforms, or worse yet, Nazi ones, I slowed down to stare. Which obscene reminder did they hate more?

"How many people were left here at the end of the war?" I asked. Saul moved ahead at a brisk pace, his brown lace-up shoes kicking up dust. A hollow woman approached, hand out. I stopped to search my bag. Saul grabbed my arm to hurry me along. She caught the apple I threw her.

"Sixty thousand abandoned without food or water. The cowards ran when the British liberated camp in April of forty-five. Sarah, this is only the beginning. It's going to get much worse. No gas chambers here but 35,000 died from starvation, disease and overwork. This one and Dachau are the only concentration camps they used for displaced persons. The others were German

Army barracks." He turned me toward him, his sad eyes in a permanent downward droop, his face unshaven. "Toughen up. We've a job to do."

My fingers circled my throat in an attempt to keep air moving through. Is this the kind of place in which my grandmother perished? My grandfather? The sweet man who sat me on his lap? It had been almost a year since the war ended. Americans, Jews, and some Europeans were outraged at the chaotic conditions for the people left behind. I forced my mind to focus on the importance of telling the story to the world.

The Camp Commandant's building looked like home, sweet home. "How come he gets grass?" I asked.

Saul lifted the latch on the gate to enter. He snuffed. "Grass is nothing. The commandants lived like kings in hell. The asshole at Theresienstadt made the inmates build a swimming pool for him and his family. Can you imagine walking past that every day while you were starving?"

The Commandant, an Allie appointee, shook our hands when we introduced ourselves, then sat down. A middle-aged man with horn-rimmed glasses didn't look at us. He shuffled papers on his desk, lifting corners, moving piles, searching for something. A stack of folders fell to the worn carpet. He ignored them.

"Damn. Can't find anything in this mess. Stupid reports. Ya' think they'd give a shit about moving these people outta here and all they want from me is paperwork."

He must have realized he'd used curse words in front of a female. He looked above the rim of his glasses. "Sorry, ma'am. Bit overwhelmed."

It didn't stop his hunt for the elusive report. The faint aroma of a pipe hung in the room. I noticed a rack and humidor behind him on the credenza.

Saul spoke up. "We're here from *The Yiddish Press* and we

need your permission to interview and photograph the detainees."

No response. I glanced at Saul and could see he was doing a slow burn. His foot tapped on the carpet. The man sighed in exasperation. A manila envelope sailed over the side of his desk.

"What? Photographs? Yeah, sure. Anything's fine. Just don't make the office look bad. I've got enough problems with the Zionists exciting them about Palestine, the British turning back the ships and people escaping to get there illegally. Where the hell do they think they're going?"

He waved us away, the glasses pushed to the top of his head. His indifference sickened me.

Saul directed me toward a low clapboard building. "We sleep on different sides. They didn't want to put us in with the detainees. Your stuff is in there waiting for you. I'll meet you for dinner in the mess hall. Don't expect much."

I pushed through the screen door to the rows of iron beds, my rucksack sitting on the bed of one near the door. Gray. It was all gray.

The dining hall shocked me. I stood at the entrance and watched tables and tables of children and adolescents eating in almost silence. Orphans. All orphans. Many were un-groomed and needed a haircut or a bath. I thought of the care my little brother and sister got at night. Some held toys and stuffed bears. After I sat down I asked Saul, "What's with the toys?"

"The Allied forces requisitioned them from the town people when they liberated the camp. They couldn't believe what they saw—stick figures in the late stages of starvation, most bald from lack of nutrition, horrible conditions. The Negro soldiers were the most upset. The survivors were too weak to walk so they carried many in their arms. They thought their people suffered under prejudice and injustice in the U.S." He made a *harrumph* sound and began to eat. "This was a real awakening for some. Many broke down and sobbed."

At our meager meal of soup and a skinned potato, a male detainee, his hair missing in patches, sat down with us. He shared that he had been there for three years, a witness to the British hanging of Josef Kramer, the "Beast of Belsen."

My mind flashed to the Commandant's chair, his desk neat and orderly, precision at every corner, and I envisioned a German officer carrying out his job of destruction. At *Yom Kippur* we always repeat the words: who shall live and who shall die. Did he feel like God with that much power?

The man noticed me pushing the potato around with my spoon. "If you don't eat that someone else will. We only got sugar cubes in the beginning until our stomachs could handle more. Now we're hungry all the time." I cut the gray potato with my spoon and ate it.

Afterwards Saul and I sat outside and shared cold beers that he had commandeered from the kitchen with a bribe of cigarettes. He muttered, "That bastard. Responsible for so much of this human misery."

I said little.

Later I fell into the hard cot with a frayed gray blanket and turned to face the wall. How could I do my job in such a terrible place? I cried myself to sleep.

Over the next weeks Saul, his fingers stained yellow with nicotine, wrote notes in his own shorthand in a small spiral notebook. He didn't care about anything but being witness to what he called the most horrible crimes of the century. He wore the same sweat-stained shirt for days. Once I made him give it to me so I could rinse it in the bathroom sink. Without soap the collar wouldn't come clean. His gait rolled from side to side because of his stocky shape and his oozing belly gave him a heavy gait. He grew hair in places I tried to ignore, tufts popping from his ears.

Yet, I loved his commitment. We developed a routine. Saul asked questions in jumbled Yiddish of the Poles, Romanians, Germans, Austrians and Hungarians, leftover bodies with wispy souls. Sometimes we were lucky enough to get an interpreter or they spoke a little English. He'd start taking notes, then give me a fuzzy raised eyebrow or the jerk of a thumb to get it visually. In the beginning I cried when stick-figure thin people told their stories. I shot Kodak XX film of vacant faces, thin hands, bony feet, requisitioned boots. Soon, I became numb.

Eventually, I took the cigarettes Saul offered. After an initial nausea his Pall Malls calmed me. I turned away when people dug into the dirt with their fingers for the butts.

Aid for the camps dribbled in slowly. The inmates, some of whom had been there for years, could tell no difference between incarceration and liberation. There still wasn't enough to eat. Their 2000 calories a day consisted of black, wet bread, too unappealing for me to eat, and black coffee. I lost pounds the first weeks. At night on my cot, my stomach growling, I thought about a Nedick's hot dog, Mama's *cholent*, and a Hershey bar with almonds. A cream soda. I'd kill for a cream soda.

Nor was there enough to wear. In sharp contrast the German population didn't sacrifice clothes. Not only did they keep their own, they were the beneficiaries of finery collected as people entered the camps with their fate buried in naïveté. Families had dressed in their Sabbath-best waited in lines, many women in furs, the men in starched shirts with cuff links and pocket watches, and children, the precious children, in wool coats and angora hats.

When we hitched a ride to town for a decent meal, we could see the Germans were still the best-dressed in Europe, huddled into mink coats and seal skin boots, undisturbed by the crowded conditions a few miles away. Did they think about where it all came from? I wanted to rip their clothes off them and take them back to the people in striped pajamas and uniforms.

Saul interviewed an Army chaplain, a Rabbi Goldberg who told us, "I personally attended twenty-three thousand burials at Bergen-Belsen alone in the first weeks after liberation. At least this camp is all Jewish now. In the beginning the Jews and the Nazi collaborators were thrown in together. Terrible confrontations."

How could people be so insensitive? The three of us sat on a makeshift bench at the edge of the camp looking through the barbed wire, sipping a bottle of cheap red wine. The numbers staggered me. Saul passed me a cigarette. I smoked more, bumming from him with promises to replace his cartons when we returned.

I tuned out of their conversation about Palestine to rifle though my portfolio. I focused on the portrait I took of the rabbi in his uniform at twilight the day before, tallit prayer shawl draped over his shoulders, skullcap pushed to his crown, his mouth twisted into tormented resolution.

I heard the rabbi tell Saul, "We survived almost three thousand years without a country and managed to preserve our identity among alien cultures. It's time. We need a homeland."

Repetitive stories of missing loved ones, pain and torture, the need for medical supplies, a good pair of shoes, an unending hunger and the desire to go to Palestine echoed through every interview. Most of the interviews ended with the questions, "Why did I survive and everyone else died? What is it I'm supposed to do? What's God's plan for me?"

I couldn't understand why they still believed in God.

Our mission was to let the people at home know the suffering wasn't over. We traveled to more DP camps, many of them former German Army barracks. When there wasn't room for us in the dormitories, Saul and I slept in makeshift beds on other workers' sofas, behind counters in stores in a nearby town and one time in a barn. Sometimes I felt relief that I wasn't sleeping in a Nazi's bed. What about the detainees? Did the irony grip them they were sleeping in their oppressors' beds?

We didn't shower often either. I let my grooming go, not wanting to attract male attention from military personnel, some of whom hadn't seen a female in a long time. Not that I was such a beauty, but my thick auburn hair pulled back and a slash of Vaseline on my lips meant I was a woman.

"Hey, babe, take some photos of me," soldiers would call out if I passed by, camera on my shoulder. Once as we headed toward a mess hall, I heard, "Only reason a broad travels over here is to get laid."

I moved closer to Saul. He may have been short and funny-looking, but he was my protector.

In the evening we smoked and drank warm beer through the night with whoever was left over at the end of the day: relief workers, other journalists or some lost, trapped being we had befriended. But, as soon as the dawn lit the sky, we were ready to record what American eyes and the rest of the world had not seen.

With almost sixty displaced persons' camps throughout Germany, Italy and Austria, the human wreckage was widespread. We visited the ones in Germany and Austria, skipping Italy, Saul taking notes and me, snapping pictures. The sound of a German accent made the hair rise on my neck, but I knew I was recording history.

Over a period of three months we moved often. Not all the camps were as barren as Bergen-Belsen. Some had activities, music, art projects for the detainees, but most of the people just waited for a sliver of hope: a relative found alive, a sponsor in America, property returned to them, a trip to Palestine so no one could persecute them anymore. A few showed me their most precious possession, a wrinkled photo of a loved one that they had hidden in an armpit, under a floor board, buried beneath a tree.

Once in a while another photographer arrived for me to commiserate with about the difficulties of processing. I developed my film in Associated Press offices when I could, but a few times we were so far from civilization that I mixed my chemicals in a rations cup with water from a stream. A moonless night became my darkroom. Grainy images of a young woman balding from malnutrition, hunched forward on a stool talking to Saul haunted my paper. Her large head, hollow eyes and thin lips, hung above a dress with big holes for her pencil-thin arms. Beatrice. I took rolls of her with my Kodak Retina.

Europe's spoils were divided into zones by the British, Russians, and Americans. Instructed to stay in our area, I learned about the conflict the British faced. People impatient with being stateless felt they couldn't rebuild on the same soil that punished them. Trapped survivors with no place to go. I couldn't conceive of not belonging some place. Many wanted to go to Palestine, a place they wanted to call their homeland, and the British wouldn't let them. Two ships, the *Eliyahu Golomb* and the *Dov Hos*, with about a thousand displaced persons weren't allowed to depart from Italy. The refugees went on a hunger strike. Finally, they left for Haifa on *The Mediterranean*. Upon arrival they were transferred to detention camps. Would it never end for these wretched souls?

A relentless campaign started for people to immigrate to Palestine, the only place that wanted the remnants of a culture. Hand lettered signs appeared around the camps: SPEAK IN YIDDISH, THINK IN HEBREW. SUPPORT ZIONISM. WE NEED A STATE. Passions ran high and people argued for hours about the possibilities of a Jewish state. Saul translated for me while we listened to one rabid Zionist tell a dilapidated group they were going to be farmers, but first they had to dig wells.

One man, who looked seventy but was probably only fifty said,

"I was a doctor in Vienna. I know nothing of farming. What else can I do?"

"Livestock. You'll take care of goats and cows."

"A shepherd?" He held up his hands and looked at them. "With these you want me to milk cows?"

I turned away from the absurd conversation. At first I thought I would go to Poland to look for my family, but I knew it was futile after speaking to Red Cross volunteers. When the Soviets liberated Warsaw in January of 1945, only two hundred Jews survived. How could anyone be left? Over eighty percent of Warsaw was destroyed with only one hotel standing. I wouldn't have known where to begin.

Besides, travel was risky. Aaron, a Zionist relief worker with dark, curly hair returned from recruiting men for the Haganah, a Palestine self-defense team, training in Germany. *Never again* was the motto that guided them.

As Saul and I sat across from Aaron at a cafeteria table, he told us, "I accompanied one old man afraid to go to the Jewish cemetery even in daylight. Poor guy. He wanted to leave a stone for his dead mother. Ghouls rob graves looking for gold. They're using Nazi methods to pull teeth. He told me he usually waited until there was a funeral so he wouldn't be there alone." Aaron shook his head. We were silent. What had man degenerated to?

Reports also came back that Jews were murdered when they returned to claim their property. One lady found the mayor of the town living in her house, and he refused to leave. Worse, custody of almost half the Jewish children sheltered during the war remained with their Christian parents even when their real parents survived. Many wouldn't give them back to relatives. The French newspaper reported the church said parents left them because they wanted them baptized. My anger, a nasty ball that hung in my chest, wove a web across my forehead, a permanent frown of frustration.

While Saul telegraphed a story on conditions in the camps or wrote about yet another walking tragedy, I spent hours perusing bulletin boards reading lists of survivors and notes from people who were desperate to find loved ones, especially children they left behind:

Vera Rubenstein from Krakow, Poland looking for Israel Rubenstein, her four-year-old son. Last seen at Theresienstadt train station.

Aaron Klemowitz, Prague, Czechoslovakia, searching for his wife, Bella, last seen in front of the opera house wearing a brown coat.

I listened and read so many terrible stories I ached. I couldn't cry anymore. My tears, the pool we're given at birth, dried up. What no longer gushed forth turned to empty resolve. The world was a terrible place.

Only Moishe completed my journey.

At a camp in Austria, Moishe Feigelbaum, a lively man with missing teeth, showed up to tell his story. Saul interviewed him as they sat on crude wooden stools under a tree. They took longer than usual. Moishe, better dressed than most of the inhabitants, wore a shirt with rolled-up sleeves and black pants. No belt, just a piece of rope around his skinny frame, and shined shoes, the laces missing, a premium commodity. With small, dark numbers tattooed on his arm he motioned with his hands when he spoke. Deep creases in his face, lines of loose skin, played around his mouth.

After working all morning I sat on the ground under a nearby tree, my back pushed up against the trunk smoking another bummed Pall Mall. French cigarettes were scarce, expensive and awful. I leaned back and closed my eyes. The sun danced in and out of clouds. Oh, how I missed a beach. Coney Island with kids and noise and rides and the ocean, the blue-green water with white whipped waves and a Nathan's hot dog. Saul would call me if he thought the man's story worthy of a picture.

"Sarah, get over here. This guy's from Warsaw and says he knows your family."

"What?" My eyes opened. I'd spoken to many Polish people and no one knew anyone from my family. Once, a woman said she knew their name and told me they were a prominent family from the rich section, but she didn't know what happened to them. She wanted a tip afterward, which I gave her. I scrambled to my feet and approached, wary that this might be another false lead.

The man spoke in Yiddish and Saul translated for me. "He says you look like your mother." Saul waited until he spoke again. He sat with his knees apart, intent on the man's face. "Says he hasn't seen her since she was a young woman. You don't have her eyes." Moishe's skeletal fingers clutched his chest, gripping the loose material of his shirt.

"You speak English?" I asked.

His hand gave a seesaw motion and he grinned his toothless smile. "I am learning. Your friend will teach me," he said nodding at Saul, a pause between each word.

"You know my mother? Paulina Kupferstein?"

"*OhmineGott*. Yes, yes," he said nodding vigorously.

"How?" I asked.

"Family lived next door. I am barber. My shop on Bielanska Street. She would pass to go to her courtyard. One of the most beautiful women." He tapped his eyes. "Such violet eyes."

A hard ball rocketed into my chest and moved into my throat. I blinked in disbelief. My chest moved up and down, a panting dog waiting for a bone. I couldn't talk. Of course I remembered the barbershop next door. I passed it many times with my mother and grandmother, my small hand in theirs, when we went to visit or shop.

"Do you know what happened to my grandparents? My uncles? Their families?" I spoke in a loud voice, as though he would understand me better if I raised the volume.

Moishe grabbed my arms, drawing me closer to his face. "Listen, I tell this man my story. A miracle I survive. No one. Just me. Wife. Children. Parents. Gone. Many times I am almost dead. Can you imagine I give haircuts, shaves to Nazi criminals?" He stopped to lick his lips and take a breath. "You think I don't know torture you feel? Come. Sit down. I tell you what I know."

Saul said, "I'll be back in a little." He got up and gave me his rickety stool, lit a cigarette and handed it to me. I crossed my legs and cupped my chin in my hand.

Moishe swallowed. "I did not know your family in a social way. Your grandfather, his sons, come for shave once in a while before Sabbath." He shrugged his shoulders. "Servants help with their grooming. One son, something not right with him. Slept in chair and then older brother come to get him. Your grandmother leave to buy meat from kosher butcher a few streets down. Your mother, *GottenHimmel*, pass by many times. I never spoke to her. But I dream about her. Like an angel with smooth skin. And those eyes."

"What happened to them? Do you know?"

He closed his eyes for a minute and nodded. "Yes, yes, I know. The Nazis careful, collecting people by streets. No one knows what will happen. People with money, your family not so fast. They after the little guys like me first. Working people. Your grandfather, a gentleman. Maybe they think he has money hidden." He shrugged again and looked away.

I clutched his arms in anticipation, my fingers touching the numbers. A chill coursed through my body. I felt frantic. "What happened to them? You must tell me."

"I don't know much. I take clothes from people at Auschwitz before they find I cut hair. Your grandfather stood in line, met my eyes. We could not speak."

I began to sob, heavy waves of grief, but without tears.

"*Oy*, I am sorry. Maybe I shouldn't say. I know them from Bielanska Street, such a wonderful place. One time I am not so busy and stand in the doorway on a spring day. The whole family come by. Dressed up very nice. We exchange a few words. They going to have pictures taken. Your grandmother in a fur coat and diamond earrings, your mother in a fox jacket, like an angel."

I took his hands in mine. "Please, I am the one who is sorry. Thank you. Now I know." I pulled his wrinkled fingers to my mouth and kissed them.

"May I take your picture?"

"Yes. You show it to your mother. She see what she missed." He smiled at his joke, patted down his hair with his hands and sat tall on the stool, his mouth closed to hide his missing teeth.

With shaking hands I recorded the last person to see my family alive. Afterward I was afraid to hug his frail body. I hurried back to the other tree to get my knapsack and reached for most of my money. Saul would cover me until we got home if I ran out. I handed him fifty dollars. He stared at it.

"I cannot take this." The survivors, rewarded by American soldiers, knew the value of a dollar.

"No, you must. You will need it. What are your plans?"

"I go to Palestine."

I could say no more, grabbed my things and ran to my cot to blot out silent screams.

That night I wrote to my mother. We were alive and they were all gone. No pleasant way to couch it I told her the truth, what little I knew.

Perhaps that's when I lost my faith. What God would allow this to happen? Most of humanity was worthless. I put my belief in the images that emerged from my camera, stark black and white replicas of emaciated men and women who thought they could rebuild their lives if they could only find their mother or their child or their friend or go to America or Palestine. What would happen to my life? I didn't want to waste it. Photography had to be a part of it. I only believed what I could see, and I couldn't see God anywhere around me.

The Yiddish Press decided not to send us to Nuremberg since the trials were over. Other news agencies covered it. Just as well. I don't know how I could have sat in the same room with Goering or Hess or any of them. After six months we headed back to New York.

Chapter Two

Sarah

February, 1947

After we returned Saul left the paper and moved to the Midwest with his family in an effort to erase all we had seen, an escape to a slower pace.

I walked in the door of our apartment in the afternoon, angry at a complacent world and anxious to take a long, hot bath. Mama, glad to see me, exhibited a melancholy that kept her from being effusive.

She hugged me. "Sarah, you look so tired. Long trip, huh? I need a rest myself."

"I want to talk you about what I saw, about Moishe, the barber," I told her.

"Shaa," she said, putting her hand up. "Not now. I can't." She left the room, her eyes filling with tears.

I stood there, out of place, awkward, wondering if I belonged anywhere. My beat-up knapsack at my feet held what had been my reality for the last months. How could I make the transition to warm clothes, enough food and luxurious surroundings?

I stayed in the apartment for a few weeks but the noise of the younger children and my father's intractable ways annoyed me. He didn't understand the need for reflection unless it was prayer at temple. I needed time to decide what I would do next, but he wasn't willing to give me that luxury.

He'd come home at the end of the day, a cigarette dangling from his mouth, smoke twirling around his head, drop his case at the door, pull off his scarf and coat and yell, "Paulina! I'm hungry."

My mother's eyes, surrounded by fresh lines and dark circles, lacked the makeup she usually wore. Creases folded around her mouth allowing her prettiness to fade like Sabbath flowers on a Sunday afternoon. She'd groan and lift herself from the sofa, the effort a blinding illness. Sometimes the damp rag she had over her eyes would fall to the floor. She'd shuffle into the kitchen, light the gas and start heating his supper, leftovers from meals eaten earlier in shifts by the children first and then the two of us, an endless evening of pots and dishes. The kitchen was never closed. I began to resent her lack of backbone. Why couldn't she stand up to him a little?

She took the letters from her parents, Carlo and the others, blue and white onionskin frail to the touch and tied a lavender ribbon around them. Then she put them in a shoe box, storing them on the top shelf of her closet, far away from the temptation to read them again.

My mother asked me not to bring up the war. "I can't talk about it. Best to leave it alone."

The stories from neighbors and the news never stopped, but she wouldn't speak about it. Frankly, I'd had enough, too. If my father with his hardened shell tuned in a program on the radio that dealt with the war, she left the room.

I don't blame her for wanting to bury unpleasantness. Why pick at scars? They'd never heal. So for her sake I didn't talk about the family we lost or what I had seen. But my own internal snapshots rotated across my mind, a slide show of horrors that played and deprived me of sleep and any hope that I could believe in a Higher Being. I searched through the catalogue of faces for the ones that might belong to me.

"Mama, you can't go on like this," I said. One night we shared a dairy meal of pierogies, borscht, and pickled herring, dipping pumpernickel pieces into the sour cream and onion dressing. "Your family disappeared like vapor. All the weeping in the world won't bring them back. Tell Father you need to go to the Catskills to get away. Go with Leah. The fresh mountain air upstate will do you good. You deserve it. Get away from here for a while."

"How can I leave? The children are in school." She had tied a scarf around her hair like a washerwoman.

"Summer is a few months away. Take a place up there and do what other wives do. Leave your husband in the city."

She brightened a bit. "You think your father would pay for such a thing?" She tore a piece of bread and dipped it in the sour cream.

"Mama, don't ask him. Just make reservations and tell him you're going. Get out of this stifling apartment. Fix yourself up." I motioned toward her scarf and she touched it with her hand. I went over to the window and looked out through the melting snow, rivulets of my rare tears drowning the brick landscape. Why did I feel so alone?

I wiped my eyes and came back to where she was sitting. She stared up at me, her clear blue eyes wavering in the light. I pushed a strand of hair behind her ear. "I'll help you. We'll look in the paper tomorrow. Nature is healing."

At first my father opposed my mother leaving for the summer. Anything new took time to digest. Then he liked the idea of taking the train up and getting out of the muggy city, too. My mother and Leah spent weeks in preparation: clothes, more clothes, hats, bathing suits with matching robes, sandals, shorts.

"Should I wear shorts?" my mother asked me, turning her body around to look at the back of her legs in the cloudy mirror behind the bedroom door. "I'm no Betty Grable." She lifted herself onto her toes and swept her hair off her neck with her arms.

"You're still very beautiful," I told her.

She smiled at me with wistful eyes. For a woman close to fifty she was stunning.

She bought board games, checkers and Monopoly for Rachel and Max. They were excited about the prospect of being away from the city, a humid oven in the summer. Rachel, the quiet one, liked to listen to music and Max, my annoying little brother who took everything apart with his insistent fingers, even my father's small alarm clock, marked off the days on the kitchen calendar until they were ready to leave on a Sunday morning.

I saw everyone off at Grand Central Station, including my father who was going to make sure he was getting his money's worth for the fancy accommodations. Was anyone else thinking about trains in Europe that left with people who never returned? The scene, a confusion of food baskets, suitcases, hatboxes and the latest movie magazines for Mama and Leah, reminded me of the chaos in the streets when the war ended. So many parades and endless pieces of paper floating down from buildings, decorated vets marching proud.

"If I don't like it and the food's no good, we're coming back. At these prices they'd better have decent pastrami," my father told me as he boarded the train, a blanket under his arm.

I had the apartment to myself for a few days, an unusual treat of solitude. No radio, no shouting, no loud children, no telephone. My mind rested. I spread enlargements of my favorite photographs around the room to study them.

When my father returned from ensconcing the family at their hotel, we lasted a week. He thought I was going to take my mother's place.

"You can't cook a meal for me? Look how hard I work. Clean up. It's a *schmutz* with all these papers and pictures."

I didn't say anything. My stutter returned as the tension escalated. I refused to let him cower me into doing what he wanted. One evening after work he came in with a scowl, his unshaven jowls a dark warning. He started ordering me around.

"You can't boss me the way you do Mama. I'm a grown woman not a child."

His booming voice shook the walls. "In my house you tell me what to do? Get out!" He pointed his finger toward the door. "Get a job and see how hard it is to work. I'm tired of you ingrates. Contribute to your upkeep."

"I want to be a photographer, develop my skills. I know I can be good."

"Again with the photography? What kind of a woman wants to take pictures instead of settling down?"

He made a move toward me and I didn't feel that brave. His explosive temper scared me. I grabbed my camera bag. Thank goodness my wallet was in it. Running out the door I heard him yelling, "Go. Go to your men, you *courva*," as the door slammed.

I sat in the stairwell and cried. I vowed never to go back if he was there. I hated him. I hated him for the way he made me feel. I hated him for what a tyrant he was. I hated him for the misery he caused.

I pulled myself up with a grip on the railing, wiped my nose with the back of my hand and went out to the street. At least I didn't need a coat in the warm summer air.

I walked over to Leah's. Mr. Dreichspun answered the door in a striped bathrobe and a pair of my father's slippers. "Come in. Sarah, what's the matter? Your eyes are red. Have a glass of tea. Tell me."

He sympathized. Nathan, as I had taken to calling him because he felt so little like a father, wasn't easy to work for either. We made a pact not to let anyone know I had been there. I slept on the sofa. In the morning he loaned me a little money for the train.

I surprised Mama when I showed up in the Catskills. The duplex with a screened porch was better than I expected. I hid out for a few days with everyone smuggling me food from the sumptuous meals, but eventually the manager caught on and said my mother would have to pay extra. The waiters, usually law students, executed a head count at supper.

Max, newly tan, was thrilled to be out of the city. He bragged to me, "American Plan means all meals are included, unlike European plan which means you pay separate. We're on American Plan. We get to eat as much as we want."

My mother joined me on the double swing out front; the stars clear in the country sky. A breeze rustled leaves and a cricket sang its one song. Our feet found a rhythm and rocked us back and forth. She sighed.

"Sarah, I love you, sweetheart, but you cannot stay here. Your father will be angry and he'll be back this weekend. Go home. Make peace with him." She hugged me and slipped a few dollars into my pocket, money she had squirreled away from my father and his budgets. She got up to go inside and I rocked by myself for a long time.

She knew my father would be furious to see me added to his bill. The next day I kissed the little ones goodbye before they rushed off to swimming and horseback riding. I left on a train for the city with a sad resolve. I wasn't going to be a dishrag to any man.

On my return I stayed at the YWHA. I sneaked back into the apartment in the middle of a Saturday and collected my things. I didn't want to see Nathan. As I gathered my clothes, a few books and my pillow, the ceiling creaked with a heavy-footed person upstairs. I jumped. It made me hurry.

Unfortunately, the next week the newspaper let me go. They told me budget cuts were the reason. I searched the papers and saw the ad for my job. I called to inquire and when they heard a female voice, the position was filled. I loved photography, but with all the GI's home, they weren't hiring women. I went to Gimbels in heels and hose, my slacks folded on the top shelf of my tiny locker at the YWHA.

Department store salary meant meager pay, long days and rude clientele, but I persevered. In a few months I moved out to a rooming house only a few bus stops from work. A shabby place, but quiet and clean. No company was better than bad company.

I continued to search for photography jobs at newspapers or magazines. I couldn't get an interview even though I knew my portfolio was better than the men who worked there.

Finally, the manager of a small magazine, *New York City Life*, called me back. I stood in the hall outside my room, the black receiver cradled in my neck.

"Sarah? Irv Moskowitz here. You the broad who came in with the black and white pictures of people?" My heart leaped. "I've got a lead for ya'. A Mrs. Bertram Shapiro wants someone to shoot her daughter's wedding. Everyone I know is booked. Can you shoot a bride?"

My heart fell. "Yes, I can do that, but I don't want to. I do photojournalism."

"Listen, sweetie, either you take it or not. I don't care. She's my wife's friend. Might take you in a new direction. She likes you, ya' might get referrals."

I could practically hear him pop the cigar plug out of his mouth. "Okay, what's the number?" I grabbed for a pencil at the end of a string tied to the phone wire.

He gave it to me. ". . . and don't forget to give her a good price." With that he slammed down the phone.

Mrs. Bertram Shapiro and her daughter, Shelby, never said a civil word to each other or me the entire time they planned the wedding. The mother was a *balabusta*, which even if you didn't know Yiddish is close enough to ball buster to figure out. She managed every detail as though she was launching the Macy's Day parade. Either she shouted orders to poor Mr. Shapiro who groaned with worry about the cost or she pointed to the hapless groom whose name I never learned. The family treated him and his parents as though they were *trefe* at a kosher banquet.

Mrs. Shapiro launched the beginning of my whirl on the wedding circuit: chubby brides squashed into dresses, nervous grooms in too tight jackets, hysterical mothers yelling about the relatives, worried fathers shelling out bucks for sumptuous meals, guests complaining they were seated too close to the bathroom, the ice sculptures melting before the envelopes filled with checks and cash were passed to the groom, and me, trying to take their pictures and make sure everyone looked good. Or that Aunt Sadie didn't appear in too many shots.

I moved to a better rooming house in the Village below Houston Street and started back to school in the fall. I begged, borrowed and scraped together money for tuition and books. My mother, back from the Catskills with a renewed spirit, wasn't happy I was living on my own, but she didn't relish having more conflict in the house either. She helped me out where she could, but I began to see her as so self-preserving, so lacking in fortitude. Why couldn't she stand up to my father and say what she wanted? Take my side? Nathan, who thought college for a woman was a waste, harped to my mother that I needed to find a husband. Ironically, because I wasn't interested in sharing my life with anyone, a man appeared.

My rooming house in a brownstone for single women sat next door to another house for men. A blond man watched me as I left for school or work. A pensive sort with a cigarette and work boots, he'd lean across the railing, then flick his cigarette into the street. Finally, one Saturday afternoon as I headed out before dusk to a wedding, dressed in a long black dress with my bag over my shoulder, he stopped me.

"I want to introduce myself. I'm Wilhelm Studer." He put out his hand. I looked at it.

I stopped because I didn't want to be impolite, but I knew he was Gentile from his looks and his name. He had the bluest eyes I had ever seen, an example of the Aryan race that Hitler wanted to promote. I felt guilty looking at him, thinking what it would be like to shoot his sculpted face with its planes and squared lines.

When I didn't introduce myself, he spoke again.

"Are you a photographer?" I nodded.

"It was my hobby before the war. Can I see some of your work?"

I didn't recognize his accent as one from Eastern Europe.

"I don't have time. I'm on my way to a job. Maybe some other day," I told him and hurried off.

After that he waited outside, perched on the banister, giving me a nod as I came and went. I had no idea what he did and caution wouldn't allow me to start anything. On a Sunday afternoon, as I hung laundry to dry on a clothesline across the tiny backyard, Wilhelm's head popped over the fence.

"Sarah, I'm not going to bite. Let me see your photographs. I have my portfolio, too. I work at a factory in Staten Island. No time for creative pursuits."

I kept pinching the clothes with pins. How did he know my name? I peeked at him from behind a sheet. Those eyes so clear, so purposeful.

"Okay, I'll meet you on my front porch in a half an hour." It couldn't hurt to talk to another photographer. Besides, every once in a while I was booked for two events at the same time. Maybe he could share the load.

Wilhelm, who asked me to call him Will because it sounded

more American, shared his photographs of Amsterdam landscapes, canals crowded with commerce, flower markets brimming with tulips and streets clogged with bicycles. Life before the war. He smoked dropping the ashes over the side of the porch. He offered me a cigarette, lighting it from his. Our fingers brushed as I took it.

I showed him my portfolio. He asked questions about lighting and equipment, impressed with my Hasselblad. I felt myself drawn into the conversation. He ran back to his room to bring me his camera, a Leica IIIC with a big lens.

"I smuggled it out of Europe," he said, stroking the side.

"It's a treasure," I told him.

As I lay in my bed that night I realized how solitary I had been since the DP camps. Isolated from Mama who was trying to rebuild a world without any of her relatives, I didn't have much to say to my siblings after our childhood turmoil and my father was a monster. Nor did I have much in common with the shop girls at work and their silly chatter about young men they kept company with or which hat would go on sale. A passion burned in me to make life more than what it had been so far.

Will took to waiting for me outside, watching as I returned from work, my hands laden with my camera bag or books. Often I wore a cloche that covered half my face so I could hurry by with a wave. I couldn't get involved. I only had an hour or two before my night classes anyway. He seemed pleasant enough but his good looks distracted me. His jaw line created angles in the shadows of the porch as he smoked under the eaves.

One evening after class, when the winter chill made all New Yorkers turn up their collars and shrink into their coats, Will called my name. I looked up to the porch. Moths flipped around the yellow light, a halo around his head. He offered a cup.

"What is it," I yelled from the sidewalk.

"Coffee. Hot coffee. How 'bout a cup?"

I hesitated. My stomach growled. I shrugged my shoulders. Five minutes. "Okay." I sat down heavily on an old upholstered chair someone meant to throw away. He pulled a wicker stool in front of me and handed me the cup. I took off my gloves so it could warm my chilled fingers.

"I hardly see you anymore. What have you been doing?" he asked.

He was trying to be friendly, but I didn't know how to be friends with anyone. His butter-colored hair, the cleft in his chin, made him too handsome for that.

"I'd like to take some pictures uptown next Sunday," he said. "See how the other half lives. I was hoping you would come with me. Show me around." He gave me a relaxed smile then leaned back a bit to drag on his cigarette.

At first I thought no, the danger hairs on my neck at attention. Then I realized he was an immigrant alone in this country. Perhaps his family had dispersed because of the war. What would be the harm? I could use a fun day of photography myself.

"Okay, we'll go Sunday." I handed him back the cup, grabbed my pocketbook and packages and ran down his steps and up mine.

Had I made a mistake? It wasn't a date I kept telling myself. Still, I'd better keep him out of my parent's neighborhood.

We left early on Sunday morning stopping for breakfast at a corner shop. He ordered ham and eggs for both of us. I had never eaten ham before and watched as he sliced and gobbled it down. He noticed me pushing the slab of meat around my plate.

"Don't eat pork?" he asked, his mouth chewing it. I shook my head.

"Time to try it," he said. He leaned over and cut off a small piece. "Open." He held it in front of me.

What would happen? The God who turned his back on my people would strike me down? I opened my mouth, chewed the salty morsel and then swallowed.

"Good, huh?" he said, sawing at his own piece and drowning it in egg yolk.

I picked up my fork and knife and finished the ham.

"Are you a Jew?" he asked me as we left.

"Yes," I said, bristling. "Why do you ask?" Was he going to make an issue of it?

"I saw you didn't want to eat the ham. I suspected it because you've been so standoffish. Am I like the pork? Forbidden?"

Our pace quickened. "Look, I don't want to get involved with you. I want to take some pictures today that don't involve white gowns and bleary-eyed brides. Let's just enjoy the photography, okay?"

Will remained silent for the next half hour, until we became distracted with lighting, apertures, tripods and buying more film. One of us watched the equipment while the other took a roll. The morning's soft light rewarded us with dappled sunshine. On the way back we spoke little.

In front of our buildings he asked, "How are you going to develop yours?"

"I have a darkroom upstairs."

After an awkward silence he held a few rolls toward me in his palm. "Could I use it?"

"Men aren't allowed into our rooms."

He looked down, disappointment on his face. "I'll do it next week." He slipped the film into his pocket.

I regretted not offering to help. I knew he didn't make much money. He had paid for breakfast and the subway.

I ran up the steps without a goodbye.

Eventually, weeks passed and his film was not developed. I devised a plan to smuggle him into my room so he could use the closet I had turned into a darkroom. I waited until the house was quiet, slipped downstairs with my bathrobe and a shower cap. We giggled as I made him put them on in the foyer. We ran upstairs, breathless, as we shut the door to my room. He looked around at my sparse furnishings. I felt uncomfortable that my clothes were hanging from hooks and set in boxes on the floor. I pointed toward my closet. It had taken me hours to prepare the water, trays and Amidol, a developer I mixed by hand. It stained my fingers, but the familiar septic smell comforted me.

"In there?" he whispered, pulling off the cap and robe.

When he came out after a few hours I had fallen asleep on the bed. He touched my arm and I looked up, his intent expression a mirror of determination. I moved over so he could sit down.

"How'd they turn out?" I asked my voice filled with sleep.

"Come, look," he said dragging me into the closet. His images hung from a line with wooden clothespins: a woman in a full-length mink coat with her poodle, another of twins dressed for Sunday school with caps pulled low over their eyes and a flower vendor in a dirty apron selling chrysanthemums to an elderly woman in black. He was an excellent photographer.

I felt his warm breath on my neck as his arms slipped around my waist.

"No. I can't. I mustn't."

His face played in my hair. "Sarah," he whispered, his voice husky.

He turned me around to face him. In the darkness I saw only the outline of him, but I felt his lips on mine, then his tongue, searching, searching for something in me. I tried to push him away but I lacked conviction. The solitary core of me needed to be squeezed to feel secure. My mind echoed: nice Jewish girls don't do this. He held me close, his mouth on mine, a warmth spreading through my lower body. When he stopped to breathe his fingers found my face and outlined my lips, the tip of his forefinger playing between them. My accelerated breath scared me.

"No, not here, not now. You must go. If my landlady catches you, I'll be thrown out in the street." I pulled his wrist toward the door of the claustrophobic closet.

The air was cooler in my studio, bathing my face. I swallowed it as though I had been pushed under a drowning sea. What was I doing? I grabbed his coat, pushed it at him, opened the door to check the hall and hurried him away. He tried to protest but knew we couldn't make any noise.

The front door squeaked. I locked mine and leaned against it. I could breathe even though my heart fluttered like a trapped sparrow.

I moved toward my bed under the small window, fell face down into the quilt and thought about that kiss. I had been kissed before by boys at school, a hurried, brush-the-lips, had even been fondled a few times, but never this.

Will unlocked something in me I couldn't put back. Warm ripples rocked my hips. I turned over and pushed the pillow under me, pulling my skirt above my waist.

I had never touched myself before; two fingers found their way into my panties past the curly hair. A warm flush crept through my belly as my breath magnified, the thought of his mouth, full and parted over perfect white teeth. I smelled his fragrance, a blend of salty sea and fresh lemon, as he leaned over me, the fine blond hair I felt on the back of his hands as he reached for my face.

Without warning I convulsed in a sob, sweat erupting in an animal smell, at once pungent and delicious. A place I had never been. My chest heaved, an emotional wrench that pulled me to a stop. I put my hand on my heart to stop the pounding. Had someone heard me?

In the morning I awoke still dressed.

Chapter Three

Sarah

February, 1948

I knew it was wrong to become involved with Will. For a few weeks I did my best to avoid him. He'd wait for me as I hurried by his brownstone, a shift of my hand saying later. It didn't mean I wasn't thinking about him.

I looked forward to climbing between my well-worn sheets where my dream-mind took me back to the saved kiss. My body amazed me. I didn't know it could perform that way. In the sanctity of my room my fantasies became more elaborate. I imagined conversations, how Will would look disrobed, and what his member might feel like inside me. The only ones I had ever seen were my brothers'. Sometimes in my fervor I rubbed myself twice, the wetness flowing out of me, dampening my bedclothes. I always started with the kiss.

My life, a solitary one by choice, suited me. I liked the distance between me and my tumultuous family. The chitchat of the girls I met at work annoyed me. My refuge was always Mama, but she had her own life to contend with, grief and guilt absorbing her lost family. Why did any of us survive?

Finally, Will waited by my stoop as I returned one evening after a Saturday night wedding, my bag heavy with cameras and extra food from the bride's mother.

"Sarah, I have to talk to you." He grabbed my arm to turn me toward him. "Sit," he said, loosening his grip. I resigned myself to the bottom step, feet on the ground looking up at him. "I want to spend time with you. I'm alone in this country. We share interests. I don't understand why we can't share company."

"I can't see you. You are not of my faith. This will never work. Please, forget about me," I said with rehearsed pride. The air was cold and clouds of breath ballooned out as I spoke. I made an effort to pull myself up dragging the camera bag onto my shoulder.

When we were eye to eye, he said, "I want to be friends. I enjoyed the day we took photos. Let's be like brother and sister. I'll even try to find you a nice Jewish boy." He tapped his cigarette pack until one moved out, offering it to me with a smile.

I hesitated, then took it. He lit the cigarette for me, shaking the match out in the frosty air. I blew a smoke ring toward him. We both felt the electricity of our attraction, but I thought I could be strong, could avoid involvement.

In the ensuing weeks we shot pictures at the Bowery, the Statue of Liberty, the U.N. with its stark architecture and flags flying. I kept the subject on photography. He'd been to school and knew so much about composition, lighting, form. He showed me how to experiment with color, setting his tripod at the right angle to backlight the leaves on evergreens in Prospect Park.

One Sunday when we were caught in a downpour without umbrellas, we ran home, my camera bag clutched to my chest. We could only make it as far as his porch. Out of breath and shaking off water, I saw him staring at me, his wet hair matted into a low crown on his forehead. My drenched white blouse stuck to me, outlining my slip. In turn, my nipples, hard against the fabric, were two small bumps, a red light for my arousal. The warmth of embarrassment flooded my neck and face.

"It's okay. Everyone has nipples. Even me," he said.

Mortified, I looked away. The rain stepped up its intense beating, a musical tympani of rhythms.

"I'll just make a run for it and get my things later," I told him from the top step.

"No, don't go. Let's talk. And I want to show you my photos from the last time. At least dry off. You'll get sick." He reached for my hand.

What happened to my judgment in that moment? My principles? My strength?

Without warning I no longer wanted to be a good girl. What was I waiting for? Marriage? A virgin with no purpose?

"Come upstairs for a bit. No one's in the house today. They all go to church." He opened the screen door. "Come, I won't touch you." He held up his hand. "I promise. I have a hotplate. I'll make you tea."

I hadn't been alone in a man's room, other than the makeshift places I stayed when I worked with Saul. Empty except for his bed, a chair and dresser, the starkness felt clean. A rag rug covered the floor area near his bed. He'd hung unframed photos on the walls, wonderful photos, stuck with tape to the swirled plaster. Some we'd taken together, moving cars and New York skyscrapers, cops at intersections, their white gloves an artistry of abstract shapes. Still others were from Holland, pictures of the tulip market at Aalsmeer, a dizzying knot of bicycles on an Amsterdam street, widows in black at an outdoor market. Each told a story. I wandered around looking at them. He handed me a towel. I wrapped it around my hair, remembered my blouse and tried to pull it away from me.

"I would really like to do a black and white study of you," he said.

"Me? No, you have great subjects here."

"I don't think you've ever been photographed properly."

"Maybe one day." I became uncomfortable. I may have been

naïve but I wasn't dumb.

He picked up his camera and shot my profile, not my best angle with its Roman nose and chin tipped forward. "I like the turban style of the towel. You look like Nefertiti," he told me.

"No, please. I must go." I hugged myself rubbing my arms for warmth.

"You haven't had your tea." He placed his camera on the dresser. He rushed over to a corner of the floor where a hotplate was plugged into an outlet. The boiling pot gurgled as he poured the water into a cup without a saucer. He handed me a tea bag I dipped in and out. "Sit for a minute. I won't bite you."

I perched on the only chair, an unpainted wooden one near the window looking out at the street flooded with debris. A small leak in the ceiling near the corner of his bed left a wet, shiny trail down the wall. The windows, cloudy with steam, felt cold to my touch.

He pulled the towel off my hair and began shooting pictures, his hands moving fast to advance the film. I gazed out the window, a reverie of warmth flooding me, then I looked at him with a small smile. I felt relaxed, calm. Then a shiver rocked my body.

He put down the camera. "You're cold. Take off the wet blouse." I began to protest. He took the tea from me. "Take it off." His voice dropped. "I want to see you."

He came closer and unbuttoned my top button, then the next, then the next, each pearl bringing me to the reality that I wouldn't stop him. I might have tried, but I didn't. I wanted him.

My damp blouse dropped to the floor, a wet rag crumpled like my resolve.

"I want to shoot you. It's art to see a woman this way."

I volunteered the skirt, pulling my panties off from under my slip, turned around to unhook my bra, sliding it through the armholes. It, too, fell to the floor. A bolt of lightning, then thunder clapped, illuminating the room for a few seconds. A burst, a flash and then silence.

"Here, lie on the bed," he said plumping his pillow, smoothing the case. "I've never seen anyone look more beautiful. The light is wonderful."

I stretched out in my blush pink slip, free of the confines of my clothes. The silk clung to me, the ivory ornamental netting provocative over my breasts. I put my arms behind my head, waiting. Without lights the room melted into a hazy gray, the sound of the storm, a familiar cadence. A lacy rain stained the windows.

Will sat next to me, the camera on the floor near his feet. With a quick movement, he pulled his shirt over his head. His body reminded me of flawless alabaster. With hesitation I reached up to stroke his chest devoid of hair.

I caught my breath as his slow fingers explored what I had only recently discovered. First, his hands ran down the silk of my slip, past my breasts down to my thighs. Static crackled through his fingertips. The second time he brushed my erect nipples and slid a strap off my shoulder, exposing me. He leaned forward to kiss me, my back arching toward him, a small moan escaping from my lips.

His hands lifted my hips pulling the lingerie to my waist. When his fingers found my moist curls, I began to let go.

"Such wetness," he said.

The strokes of his fingers alerted every nerve in my body, a heightened awareness exposing itself in degrees. I closed my eyes to complete my escape. His pants and belt buckle hit the floor. He rolled on top of me, and with a few adjustments, entered me with a force that made me gasp, taking me in that foggy light on his small, cramped bed, warming my chilled body with unexplored passion. My hips responded in kind, rocking with his thrusts, until a wrenching noise pulled him over the top where time played in slow motion. My first experience. I thrilled with the newness that I was complete.

He nestled into me, his mouth covering my neck and shoulders with kisses. His fingers traced my hairline ending on my ears. I felt myself dropping into the abyss of arousal again.

Will got up, put on his pants and picked up his camera. I rolled to face him, lips slightly parted, unashamed of my nakedness, comfortable with our lovemaking. Could I ask him for more? He took another roll without either of us speaking a word. A gust of wind shook the windowpane.

Later, when I viewed the grainy photos he took of me that day of my de-flowering, I saw sensuality on my countenance, an expression of fulfillment. I remember his, the high color of his cheeks, the perfection of his skin.

Soon we had a routine with me sneaking into his room a few times a week, my naughty secret. He brought me to a place I knew only as ecstasy. However, I knew I could get pregnant and that would be a disaster. We used condoms after the first time. My body refused to be without him, my addiction.

One Saturday afternoon after Will and I spent the morning together in bed, I returned to find my landlady had left a message on my door. Mama called. Big news! Isaac was engaged! Come home for Sabbath dinner.

I couldn't imagine my brother being mature enough to marry anyone. I went home the next week to see my family and meet Isaac's bride-to-be. Mama made a feast, Papa was on his best behavior and Rachel and Max were glad to see me. Mama had set the table with her best tablecloth, crystal, silver and Rosenthal china with a gold and blue band. The Sabbath candles burned low next to an arrangement of fresh red roses and ivy.

Isabella, Isaac's fiancée, a small dark-haired girl with a slight lisp, didn't seem to notice Isaac's nervous energy. She watched him, the dark tendrils around her face shifting with her eyes. Small diamond studs graced her ear lobes, an engagement present from my parents. Obviously, they wanted to impress her family, people born here who spoke without accents.

"What will you do now that the Army is releasing you and you're going to be a married man?" I asked my brother.

He fidgeted, playing with the utensils. "I'm going to work for Papa."

Papa? Those two couldn't get along for five minutes. I tried not to look surprised.

"Doing what?" I asked. I took a sip of wine. My father jumped in. "What difference does it make what he'll do? He'll have a job. Maybe someday he'll learn enough to be the boss." My father sat back, puffing on his cigarette, an ash falling into a cut crystal ashtray Mama slipped beneath his hand.

I didn't respond. I knew what was coming. "What's the matter with you running around taking pictures? Find a nice husband and settle down with babies. Who do you think will take care of you in your old age?"

My father began to cough and reached for his glass of water. I pushed my chair back. Mama, uncomfortable, started clearing dishes.

"What? You don't respond to your father? What are you making of yourself? Twenty-four and an old maid? Stop this nonsense and do something useful. Look, even your brother is settling down with a nice girl and a job."

The others at the table looked down or away. Max played with his food. I got up and carried my plate through the dining room swinging door and into the kitchen. Mama stood at the sink washing dishes with Lux.

"Mama, it's going to get unpleasant and I don't want to ruin the occasion for Isabella and Isaac." I grabbed my coat from the kitchen chair and put it on. I heard my father cough again. "I have to go. Tell the others I had an emergency or something. I love you,

Mama. I'll call you soon."

I kissed her cheek, her expression sad, then exited through the kitchen door that led to a hallway. I hurried back to my bohemian world, one with an illicit lover and photographic passions.

It could have gone on like that forever. For the first time I experienced joy, the hardships of my home life and the horrors of the DP camps swept away. Maybe because I wasn't alone anymore. Will and I became a couple in our Village neighborhood, strolling for coffee in the summer, ferreting out art shows, wandering Bleecker Street with its galleries, book shops, and photography exhibits. We made friends with a musician who owned a beat-up guitar and sang songs on the stoop a few doors away.

One afternoon on a corner near Washington Square we set up our photographs of New York sites against the brick wall. We had matted them with black paper and sold quite a few. The money bought us dinner at a cozy spot in Little Italy with lanterns and red and white checkered tablecloths, the smell of an afternoon rain cleaning the streets. He held my hands across the table.

"Marry me, Sarah."

"Oh, Will. I don't know. Give me more time." I stalled.

He ordered another glass of Chianti, finished it, and paid the check. We left the restaurant without speaking and sat in silence on the subway home.

Will had asked me to marry him before, after making love when the air reeked of sex and I melted into his body, my legs wrapped around his.

"We could be together in the morning, all night. I don't want to sneak between our two places," he said as his fingers teased my nipples.

Once, during the day, we coupled in the balcony of a seedy movie theater in the Bronx that only showed reruns. I climaxed while Fred McMurray gave his speech in *Double Indemnity*, a film

I first saw in 1944 during the war.

Although I experienced lust I knew it couldn't last. First, Will was a follower of Martin Luther. I didn't believe in God anymore, but I abhorred what Hitler had done. God, who abandoned the Jews. I owed something to my people. Secondly, my father would disown me. Not that I cared, but I felt for Mama. And, third, Will had so little ambition. He headed for Bush Terminal every morning to take the ferry to Staten Island to work in a factory banging steel into parts. A few beers, a couple of dollars in his pocket and he was happy. Something more burned in me. I loved him but not for a lifetime. It caused me great guilt. What kind of a woman has sex and doesn't want to marry the man forever?

Chapter Four

Sarah

April, 1948

Perhaps I'm not saying too much about Will because I don't want to remember what a fool I was, how I ignored the flags of danger, how I did what was easy. He didn't talk much, but I assumed his reticence was his Gentileness. My family communicated with such intensity, voices rising, hands flying, sometimes in different languages, passionate and opinionated about every subject. Will and I spoke about photography, people he knew from work, but little else. I got used to silences. We whispered after sex in the soiled air. He fell asleep after a few beers. A simple existence after the complexity in my home.

Although I was never regular, when I missed my period for the second month in a row, I knew something was amiss.

"I think I might be pregnant," I told him as we sat on my porch with our cigarette camaraderie. He looked up at me from his position at the top of the steps. I rocked back and forth in a brown wicker chair.

"How do you know?" His eyes narrowed as the smoke snaked around his head.

"I've missed. I have to go to a doctor."

"I'll go with you next week."

"No. I'll go myself." I stopped the movement of the chair, got up and went inside where he couldn't follow me.

How could this happen? He used condoms every time. Or did he? Was I really paying that much attention to what happened under the covers? Was this my punishment for breaking the Commandments? Even though I didn't believe, was it a vengeful God who took away my pleasure?

Under a false name I visited a doctor not in my neighborhood. A short man with a bald pate covered by a few strands of hair, he called me into his office after an uncomfortable exam. His small pig eyes glared at me. I perspired in anticipation, my hands clammy with sweat. His fat fingers drummed my chart.

"Mrs. Smith, I'll have definite results for you next week, but my opinion is that you are pregnant." My heart beat so fast I thought I'd explode. A large, wounded crow, frantic for freedom, wings bent, fluttered in my stomach.

Without tears of joy and my unchanged expression, the doctor added, "I see no marriage band. You have options. One is adoption. The other, which I do not advocate, is termination. It is illegal but the nurse out front can give you a number of someone in Harlem who takes care of such matters."

"When?" I asked, my voice dead of emotion.

"As far as I can tell you're in your first trimester. Probably around Thanksgiving."

I grabbed my purse and fled into the street, the anonymity of the street crowds assuaging my guilt and fright. My cloth coat wasn't enough in the chilly April air. I hurried back to my room to think about my choices without interference from Will.

That night when we met on my porch, I thought out loud as he sipped a beer, watching me, his face serious. "I could get the number of the person in Harlem who will fix things, but I'm afraid. A botched job can leave me sterile or worse yet, dead. I've heard about those kitchen table butchers. Or, I could go away when I start to show and give the baby up for adoption."

I began to cry, sinking like a ship's anchor headed toward a sandy bottom. "I don't know if I can do that. So many Jews murdered and I'm thinking about giving one away? I have to honor my grandparents and name a child after them."

Will didn't speak while my tears deteriorated into sobs. He leaned his head back to finish the beer. I turned around as screen door squeaked. One of the other residents came out. A moth battered itself against the yellow porch light and he reached for my hands, his blue eyes enlarged with the news. "I'll marry you. We'll keep the baby."

Will leaned forward to give me a hug.

His tenderness moved me. "But how will we live? We have no money, no apartment."

"I can get overtime. We'll manage."

"Will, you're not Jewish."

"So what? You told me if the mother is, so is the child. The baby will be. Isn't that what's important to you? Marry me."

"I don't know what's important anymore. How could I have been so stupid?" I wiped my nose with the back of my hand.

"Go upstairs. We'll go to City Hall to get the application. I'll take off early to look for a place. Give your landlady notice. We're moving." He held out his hands to pull me up, wiping my cheeks with his sleeve. "I'm heading to the tavern at the corner to celebrate. I'm going to be a Papa with the girl of my dreams." He kissed me on the forehead. "Get a good night's sleep," he called skipping down the steps.

I leaned my head back against the post. "Sadie, Sadie, Married Lady" with a *shaygetz*. Oh, my poor mama.

The following Friday, when we could both take time off, I waited for Will in front of City Hall. What if he didn't show? A signal from the angry God that I should give the baby away? A few minutes late, carrying a carnation corsage, the tips dipped in blue, festive ribbons held on with green tape. His hands shook as he pinned it on my shoulder. We linked arms and strolled up the steps. I couldn't talk in the elevator. What was there to say? I'm trapped? I'm not sure I'm in love. Lust placed you in my life?

In our best clothes, Will in a blue serge suit and me, in a rose-colored dress and corsage, a small felt hat with a veil on my head and a cheap pair of shoes on my feet, we went into the courthouse. The wedding took five minutes in front of a Justice of the Peace. Will slipped a thin gold band on the fourth finger of my left hand.

After dinner we spent the first Friday night at The Amsterdam Hotel, a brief honeymoon of one evening. Our lovemaking, sweet with fulfillment, lasted through the night. His previous hunger turned to adoration of what the early pregnancy did to my breasts, full and supple, the cleavage an inviting territory, my copper penny nipples stretched into wide nickels.

The next day we studied the newspaper ads for apartments, scouring the streets to look for a place to live. It took a few rejections until we figured out the G.I.'s were getting all the good flats. We needed to offer money under the table for a place without cockroaches, and neither of us had much cash. By the afternoon, with swollen ankles and a few blisters, I decided to call Mama.

Will stood outside the claustrophobic phone booth while I dialed in my stocking feet, my high heels fallen to the side.

"Sarah, dalink, you sound terrible. What's the matter?"

"Mama, I have to talk to you. It's very important, but I don't want to come if Papa's home."

"Come now. He's busy with the Slonim Society after *shul*. What? You're crying? My brave Sarah? Come over, tell me."

We took the subway to the stop a few blocks from my parent's high-rise building. Will, impressed, looked up, then sunk his hands in his pockets. He waited across the street in a doorway, watching me walk through the glass doors etched with gold numbers into the lobby.

I opened the unlatched door to a quiet apartment. The smell of *flanken*, a stew of beef short ribs, carrots and potatoes in a thick gravy, greeted me. It mingled with the smell of cigarettes and Mama's perfume. I headed toward the back of the apartment calling out, "Hello."

Mama, in her bedroom at her vanity, was pulling down her lower lid to apply a kohl pencil around her eyes. Pond's cold cream, an ornate silver brush, comb and hand mirror on top of a *Modern Screen* magazine, lipsticks, cotton balls in a glass jar, crystal perfume bottles from Bohemia, their atomizers decorated with tassels, an empty box of Barricini candy filled with broken jewelry, screw-on earring backs, needle and thread, and a jar of Vaseline, pomade, hair nets as fine as spider webs, bobby and hair pins scattered throughout the debris covered the top of her make-up table. She got up to greet me. I started to cry when she hugged me.

"*Shayna meydele*, I've never seen you like this." She took my hand and led me toward her bed, her eyes worried.

The words stuck in my dry throat. I knew how disappointed she would be in me. I opened my mouth, but the truth remained trapped. My stammer came back.

"Ma-Mama, I'm in trouble."

"Trouble?" Her expression changed to scared. "Female trouble?" I nodded.

"*OhmineGott*." Her hand slammed against her chest. Her voice rose. "Who did this thing to you?" She got up to pace. "Sarah, answer me."

I tried, but I couldn't stop crying. She brought me a glass of water and I began to speak. I started with my loneliness, spoke about Will, then told her my reality.

"I got married yesterday. Mama, Will's a good person."

"Married? Without me? Without a dress?" She collapsed on her upholstered vanity stool to face me. "Who is this boy? What kind of a family does he come from?"

When I didn't answer right away, she knew.

"He's not a Jewish boy?" her thin eyebrows rose to the top of her forehead, lost in the wrinkles. I couldn't speak.

"*Vey iz mir.* Your father will kill you. Go, quick, before he comes home." She became agitated, wringing her hands and pacing again.

"No, he's not Jewish, but he doesn't care too much for religion. I'm not sure I do anymore either. We're looking for a place to live and we need cash for the landlord." My voice pleaded. "I don't like to ask you, but we need money. We saw one place that has possibilities with some paint."

She got up with a heaviness that made her move like she was swimming in oil and went to her closet. She reached toward the top and caught the string of a flowered hatbox as it fell toward the floor. She brought it back to the bed. Hidden inside the crown of a ruby felt hat was an envelope she had stuffed with bills.

"How much do you need?" she asked me fanning out the money. "It's yours." My hand trembled as I took five hundred dollars, enough to get us in and pay the first month's rent and a deposit. I felt terrible and relieved at the same time. Maybe I could pull this off.

She nestled the hat back into its place with her knuckles. "When is the baby due?" she asked, her voice small and sad.

"You'll be a grandmother around Thanksgiving."

That made her smile a little.

"I'd better go. I don't want to see Papa."

Her face became long.

"Mama, bless you. Thank you. Please. You tell him. I know he'll never want to see me again. I'm sorry to leave it for you." My head dropped, my eyes wet. "I'm so sorry." We stood and I hugged her for a long time, my face in the soft skin of her neck, smelling L'Heure Bleue, a perfume from Paris that she'd worn since I was a child.

I took the stairs so I wouldn't have to see anyone. When I ran to Will across the street, I looked back and I saw Mama standing in the window staring at us. I raised my hand in a wave. She touched the window.

I never bothered to call the doctor's office for results. I was pregnant and needed a doctor in my neighborhood. Mrs. Will Studer. I stroked my belly, still flat, and smiled.

I also quit school. Luckily, I never felt too ill to go to work. The girls were surprised when I showed up with a marriage band. I had never been too friendly so after the initial questions, they left me alone.

Will and I moved our meager furnishings into a fourth floor walk-up on a Saturday night after I finished an eight hour day on my feet. The slimy landlord in his undershirt announced himself as we dragged the last mattress up the stairs. With dirty fingernails, a corpulent belly and a goulash fork in his hand, he gave us a lecture about paying the rent on time.

When he left we showered and made love, even before we pushed the twin beds together. Will, aroused by touching me, lost control, the sweat of the humid air dampening his hair. I touched his chest, so smooth and firm, not believing anyone so beautiful could be mine. Still inside me, he held himself above me, afraid to crush me, his eyes searching my face.

"I love you. We're going to make this work," he said.

"I know," I replied. He didn't hear me he was so involved in his completion.

When the early light crept through our undraped windows, I

looked over at Will, his profile so perfect in the morning. Maybe having my own family was a better path for me.

The hardest part of the pregnancy slammed into the stifling summer heat. My legs swelled. I gave up on heels and wore Red Cross shoes like the nurses. Doctor Farber insisted I buy support hose, ugly thick stockings that rolled above the knee. I was too fat for a garter belt. I didn't have a big wardrobe selection either. Three different maternity tops in blue, white, and pink, all with capped sleeves, like a child's smock, and a few skirts with elastic panels in the front for my expanding stomach.

I wouldn't allow Mama to come to the apartment. I didn't want her to see how shabby things were, although we made an effort to paint and upholster pieces we found at the Gramercy Park flea market. We found a crib in a secondhand store and painted it white.

Mama met Will at the restaurant in the Metropolitan Museum for Sunday afternoon tea. They made awkward small talk about family and the baby. I knew both were trying. Isaac's wedding was in a few weeks and I wouldn't attend.

"Sarah, your father yelled and then cried when I told him about you. He says God punished him. Then he blamed me, that I wasn't a good mother." She looked down as though she believed him.

"Mama, this had nothing to do with you," I said reaching for her hand. Will looked away, embarrassed by our emotion, excusing himself to the men's room.

"Look, for now it's better to stay out of his way. He's not well. After the baby, maybe he'll soften up." She always had hope.

"What's wrong with him?" I asked. Not that I cared, but I felt obligated.

"I don't know. He coughs, he's tired. He won't go to a doctor. A *bulvant*. You know your father. *It's nothing. Leave me alone. I'm strong like a bull*, and then he shoos me away with his hand."

Mama changed the subject. "What should I tell people at the wedding?"

"Tell them the truth," I said, my resolve strong. I wasn't the first girl to start a little early. People always adjusted the birthdays of their children or pushed back anniversaries.

"Ay, but, Sarah, such a *shondeh* for the family. The neighbors, the friends, all the whispers. And with a *shaygetz*." She reached in her purse for a hankie and blotted the corners of her eyes.

"It's done. I can't change anything. Mama, he's a swell guy. And he loves me."

She smiled weakly, glancing away. I knew what she was thinking. Thank goodness her parents weren't here to know about this.

Will returned and escorted us toward the front. He offered to pay, but Mama wouldn't let him. We faced each other outside on the steps of the museum near the massive stone lions. Mama held my face in her hands and kissed my cheeks. I looked down at my puffy fingers and her manicured nails. She hugged me.

"You'll be missed at the wedding. It's going to be some affair. Isabella's parents are having it at the Waldorf Astoria. Four hundred people. I'll ring you after they leave for the Catskills." She headed toward the subway in her high heels and seamed stockings, a straw hat with a black and white polka dot band shielding her face from the scattered sun.

Chapter Five

Sarah

November, 1948

Thanksgiving Day rolled by without a turkey dinner. The day before, my last day at work, I could barely move around anymore. My belly, a lurching sack of potatoes, shifted as I waddled around, my hand in my lower back. Will stayed overtime at the plant to make extra money. Exhausted, we fell asleep without cooking anything.

The weekend passed and still no baby. But, a few days later, in the early morning hours of December 2, 1948, on my mother's and father's birthdays, I awoke with a terrible backache. When Will heard my moans he got up and brought me an extra pillow. I shifted to find a comfortable spot.

"Maybe it's labor," Will said, worried that we might not recognize it. He stood at the end of the bed, his striped pajama bottoms slung low on his hips.

Spasms waved across my lower back then shot down my legs. "This is not labor. I've seen women in the movies. They scream and yell. I'm just uncomfortable. Get me a glass of water. Please."

An elbow or maybe a knee pushed my belly into a strange shape. "Maybe you're ready to come out, huh?" I asked my stomach, stroking the elliptical mound.

Will turned on the light next to the bed, casting a yellow glow over the black and white matted photos hung around the room. The empty bassinette loomed large in the corner. I sat up, the pillows propped behind me, my neck and head bent back toward the wall and dozed off.

Will asked, "Honey, should I go to work or should I take you to the hospital? It's almost seven."

"No, I'm okay. Go. I'll call the doctor if anything gets worse. Labor takes a long time. I'll call your manager to get you off the floor if there's any big news. See? I have the number in my pocket." I reached down to show him the piece of paper folded into my housedress, the kind with snaps down the front. I had been wearing his shirts, but even those were too small now. The last few days I felt like I was pregnant from my neck to my knees.

Will left, his lunchbox filled with a liverwurst sandwich he made himself wrapped in wax paper, an apple and a thermos of coffee.

I stayed in bed until ten o'clock. The excruciating back pain, no longer bearable, prompted me to call Doctor Farber's office. I got his nurse, anxious to tell someone about my symptoms, my agony. This was the worst backache I ever had.

"Doctor is with a delivery now," she told me in nasal Brooklynese.

She wasn't much, but she was my only salvation. "What should I do?"

"Are you wet?"

"What?"

"Never mind. Come to the hospital with your bag. Do you have transportation?" She sounded as though I was an annoyance.

"I'll take a taxi," I said slamming down the phone. A sense of urgency and excitement propelled me forward. I was having a baby!

I felt so mature, so grown up, so much an adult hurrying out to the street, a coat over my shoulders, my bag in hand, taking myself to the hospital. I thought about calling Will, but there wasn't much to tell yet.

The cab dropped me at the emergency room. I rolled myself out of the back of the cab like a slick watermelon trying to grip the doorjamb. Orderlies came out to greet me with a wheelchair. I waved them aside even as they argued with me. I was doing this on my own.

With my hand on my hip, my pocketbook over my shoulder and my navy canvas overnight satchel with the tan leather handles that had been packed for two months, I made my entrance.

Two nurses got me into a gown in a semi-private room with a drape between the beds. I handed the one with the yellow hair Will's number at work.

"Thanks, hon, but no point calling now. You got a long way to go. Right, Shirl?" she said, cracking her gum. Shirl nodded, her bleached yellow curls moving with her head.

Labor got worse than I imagined. I yelled, screamed, cursed, sweated, invoked every horrible thing I could conjure up and still the pains came, insistent waterfalls of powerful stinging rain. When my thrashing subsided, I panted in relief until the next wave pushed its way to shore. Shirl wiped my damp forehead with a washcloth. Doctor Farber arrived and checked me, but treated me with mild disdain, as though I had ruined his day by delaying the process, his third delivery of the day.

I had no dignity left. Everyone came to peer under the sheet to see if I was dilating. Heads would bob up between my legs and ask me questions or make comments.

"How ya' doin'?" or "Breathe deeply. Whoosh, whoosh."

Dr. Farber addressed the nurses. "I'm going for a late lunch. Call me if anything changes. It's not a breach, just a slow one."

He patted my hand. "You'll be a mother soon, kid. Shirl, get an epidural ready. I've got theater tickets with the Missus tonight."

Chapter Six

Sarah

December, 1948

I held my daughter in my arms, overcome with emotion. That special moment, when I saw what I'd created, is unique to every mother, but this was my baby. She scrunched her red face as she yawned, tiny hands and feet at the end of scrawny limbs pawing the air. After I counted her fingers and toes, I stroked the thin light hairs on her soft head, the veins mapping across her translucent scalp.

"Someone anxious to see you, hon," Shirl said, cracking her gum. She smiled, exposing teeth yellowed from cigarettes.

Will came into the room with a burst of daisies in his hand, his expression hesitant. He stood next to the bed and leaned over to kiss my forehead.

"Look, look what we made," I said as I unwrapped our daughter. "She's perfect."

Will didn't speak, his throat swallowing without a sound. He shook his head back and forth.

"Say something. Are you all right?"

He placed the flowers at the end of the bed, the imprint of his fingers creasing the wax paper, pulling the flannel blanket down around our daughter's face to get a better look.

"She's beautiful. She's very beautiful. And so are you." His voice sounded hoarse, as though he had not spoken in a while. He leaned over to kiss me again. After our lips met, he didn't pull back. He stayed close to my face searching every pore for answers to this wonderment. For me, with my lack of faith, the new life became my belief system. Miriam wiped out my memories of the DP camps and evaporated family.

"You're a papa. How does it feel?"

Will straightened. He found a chair to pull close to the bed. He rested his elbows on his knees. For a while he said nothing. The hospital hummed in the background as we remained in our own private world.

"I can't believe it. They called me off the floor to come to the phone so I knew. The nurse said you had a few more hours. I needed to finish my shift. I went home to shower, change. Sorry I wasn't here earlier."

Will wore a starched sky-blue shirt that made his eyes the brightest thing in the sepia room. In his haste he had forgotten a few wisps of hair that stood up at his crown. Nothing took away from the fact that he was still the best looking man I had ever seen. How long would it be before we could make love again?

"It's okay. Oh look, she's making sucking noises. The nurse will be here soon to show me how to breastfeed. I ache so my milk must be coming in."

"When can you come home?" he asked.

"Doctor says three or four more days. Tomorrow I can dangle my feet and the next day they let me out of bed."

"I'll get the apartment ready. I still need to buy diapers and pins." Will came over to my side. "What are we calling her?"

"Miriam. After my grandmother."

Will kissed the baby's forehead and then mine. He smiled at us.

"My girls. I'll call your mother in the morning, after your father's gone." He glanced at the clock over the door. "Mike and the guys from work are waiting to buy me a few beers and smoke cigars at the tavern near our place. I'll be back tomorrow night."

As Will left he turned in the doorway to let the nurse in her crisp white uniform slide by. He mouthed the words, I love you.

"Don't forget to tell my mama Miriam's arrived."

Shirl pulled the drape to encircle my bed. She leaned over and began to undo the bedclothes. "Okay, hon, this here's a breast pump. Now position the baby like this," she said waking my bundle of joy. Miriam began to fuss, her small gulping noises reminding us her needs came first.

Will slipped away.

Mama came to visit a few days after I came home from the hospital. After the two a.m. feeding, I camped on the living room sofa, a relic with faded poppies from a second-hand store. Miriam nestled on my chest so Will could sleep a few more hours. He worried about dozing at the plant, afraid he'd lose a finger if he wasn't more alert.

Even though my mother arrived late morning, I hadn't showered, washed my hair, straightened up the flat or eaten breakfast. Miriam, however, was bathed and changed. The latest batch of clean, boiled diapers hung in the bathroom, dripping onto the tile floor. The earlier batch hung out the window, trapped under the sill and probably frozen.

Mama, ecstatic over her first grandchild, arrived dragging a carriage, the inside filled with baby clothes, blankets, and a plush teddy bear. My mother wore a lavender wool dress with a matching duster coat, galoshes over her shoes, a black raincoat and umbrella, and a patterned scarf covering her hair.

"The bear's from Mrs. Dreichspun. She'll come with me next time. Your father doesn't know I'm here. A baby is the best birthday present." My mama smiled at me, hanging her raincoat and umbrella on the bedroom doorknob. She sat down at our two-person kitchen table to remove her galoshes.

"Did you tell him I had a baby?" I moved Miriam over my shoulder and rubbed her back to get the burp.

"I told him." She didn't look at me.

"What did he say?"

"I don't want to repeat it." Mama stood up and smoothed her dress. She stretched her arms out.

I handed her Miriam, the first time anyone else had held her other than Will or me. Miriam's limbs curled inward, eyes fluttering, as she folded herself into Mama's bosom. My mother paced to get her to sleep, settling next to me on the sofa.

"Sarah, she's beautiful. She has your lips but looks like your husband." She touched the blond down on her head.

An awkward silence hung in the air. I thanked her for the gifts, especially the carriage, which I knew we needed. Maybe what my father uttered was better left unsaid. What was important was that Mama came.

"Mama, will you visit again soon?" Suddenly, I felt I needed a mommy more than Miriam.

"I'll try. I don't want to antagonize your father. When you married this young man he declared you dead so the child doesn't exist." She turned away. "It's difficult for me. I'll do my best to help, but he's not a generous man. He'd be furious if he knew I was here."

"Why can't you stand up to him? I'm your daughter." I felt my face flushing with anger at his Old World righteousness.

"You don't understand. I have nothing. I'm dependent on him. I have to survive. Maybe, before the war, when my family was alive, I had other choices, but now--" Her voice faded. She handed me Miriam rearranging the blanket. I put her in her bassinette.

After another hour of chitchat about Isaac and his bride, she fluffed the back of her hair and fiddled with her scarf. "I have to go."

She dressed herself in her raingear and stood at the door. I hugged her despite my anger, the thought dancing through my head that I would be stronger for my daughter.

"Sarah, wash your hair while the baby's napping. Fix yourself up a little. A man doesn't like to come home to a house *frau*." With that she handed me a folded twenty-dollar bill. "For the baby."

Chapter Seven

Sarah

May, 1949

Six months passed as I wandered zombie-like through my days, my limbs in slow motion. Finally, when Miriam slept though the night, we developed a routine of breakfast, bath and walk. I delighted in her smiles and sounds. The spring days, a welcome relief after a cold, wet winter, found me strolling through Washington Square with Miriam sitting up and pointing to hydrangeas and robins. My life became so basic that bright green grass made me happy. I took my camera with me and Miriam learned to ham it up, the most photographed infant in New York.

Mama visited once a week. Sometimes she stayed a few hours while I ran out to do errands without the burden of a carriage to manipulate though doorways and drag down four flights of steps. Other times she stopped by to check on us, her net shopping bag filled with *babka* and *rugelach* in white boxes tied with string from Entemann's Bakery.

We didn't always pass inspection. Once, we were out of laundry soap, bread, and Pablum. Another time, the rent was late. Often, the place was a mess.

"Mama, we're just not making it with what Will brings home. I can't stretch a dollar any farther with a baby. I don't dare miss her pediatrician visits."

"Have you thought about going back to work?" Mama folded her hands on her lap.

The idea made me nervous. "Who will watch Miriam?"

"I'll come once a week, but I don't want your father to know." She looked at me, her violet eyes blinking.

"Mama, look how this man forces you to be deceptive."

She stiffened. "Sarah, I have to do what makes my life easy. I am not going to tell him I'm coming here."

"What will you tell him?" The irritation in my voice, the raspiness of a hoarse opera singer, filled the room.

"That I'm with Leah or shopping. Why should I cause myself aggravation?"

I sighed in frustration. My mother never stood up to my father. She skipped over the issue and continued.

"What about your neighbor downstairs, Mrs. Malley, for the other days? Doesn't she watch her grandson? Nice Irish lady. They always do a good job with children because they have so many." My mother reached for me, but I wasn't willing to be hugged. Yes, I got myself into this, but it didn't make it any easier to accept. I didn't want to leave my baby with a sloppy, Irish lady with an abnormally cheerful attitude.

My mother shifted around wringing her hands, adjusting her hat. "I don't have much money to give you. Your father isn't well and the business has to support Isaac and Isabella and Max. Ach, more problems. Isaac with his big ideas for expansion with another outlet in Jersey. Oh, and he bought theater tickets for a musical. Called it a business expense. More arguments. Your father says Isaac just wants to spend money instead of making it. No one works as hard as him." My mother looked away, her mouth turned down, the sarcasm in her tone a new note of discord to my ears.

"Is dad sick?"

My mother shrugged her shoulders, perplexed with her family's motivations. "Who knows? He coughs, he wheezes. You know him. *A doctor? What for? It's nothing.* Some days he comes home early, weary with upsets. He's pushing sixty, not a kid anymore."

My mother shook her head, her body sinking into itself. For the first time I saw deep lines in her face, her fleeting beauty a testimonial to a difficult marriage. She gathered her pocketbook, shopping bag, umbrella and stood up.

"I'll help you. Don't worry, Mamala." She hugged me.

I didn't want to think about my father who rejected me. What kind of a man wouldn't want to see his grandchild?

"Rachel, I'm surprised to see you," knowing my tone sounded cool. I opened the door wider to invite my sister into our cramped space choked with baby equipment. We embraced with distance between us.

It was my last weekend off. Macy's hired me to work Tuesdays through Saturdays in ladies undergarments, which meant Will could watch Miriam on Saturdays, Mama took one day and I only needed Mrs. Malley three times a week. I introduced Will, sprawled on the sofa reading the paper, an awkward moment. He got up to shake my sister's hand, his gangly height towering over her.

"Look, you two want to talk. I'll take a walk, have a beer. Nice to meet you."

Will grabbed his brown jacket from the hook behind the door, took a few rolls of undeveloped film for his pocket, patted himself to make sure he had cigarettes and left.

Rachel turned to me after he left. "He's very good-looking."

"I hardly notice anymore," I said as I bent to pick up the dropped newspaper and empty an ashtray.

It had been over a year since my sister and I had seen each other. I knew she worked at a hospital during the day and took classes at night, creating her own world without conflict.

Rachel's face had matured, her figure filling out, her hair grown longer, twisted behind her ears. I thought, an attractive young woman with pretty features who ignores her assets.

"Will seems nice. I'm sorry I haven't come sooner, but . . ." She didn't finish when she saw Miriam's head pop up in her crib pushed against the wall. She went over to lift her out, Miriam crying at a stranger's touch. I took the baby away to comfort her. Miriam, with suspicious eyes, hid her face every time Rachel looked at her. Even though she had celebrated her first birthday, she wasn't ready to embrace someone new.

"How are things at home?" I asked bouncing Miriam on my hip.

"That's why I came. I mean, I came to see you and meet Will and Miriam, but I really came to tell you what's going on."

"What do you mean? Mama okay? She was just here last week."

"Mama's fine. It's Father." Rachel spoke in measured tones. Her bland personality rarely reached high levels of expression.

"What's wrong?"

"He's ill." She glanced around the room–Will's shirt draped over the back of a chair, baby toys on the floor, unwashed pots on the stove burners. I wished I'd cleaned up, the shabbiness of our surroundings glaring in the late afternoon light.

I busied myself clearing the table with one hand. "Can I make you a cup of coffee?"

"No. Thanks."

Rachel sat down on the sofa, the poppies covered with a beige blanket. She crossed her legs. Brown nursing shoes and brown stockings peeped out from her long skirt. She had not inherited my mother's fashion sense. She patted the seat next to her.

"Come. Sit down."

I placed Miriam near her toys on the floor and I went to sit next to my sister.

"What is it?" My heart sank in my chest. Was I going to get pulled back into a family crisis?

Rachel cleared her throat, then stared at me with her large blue eyes. "Papa's dying of cancer."

I felt the bomb of information settle into my stomach. A small gasp of shock came out of my mouth.

"How do you know?"

"He's been hacking and coughing for a year, but you know how stubborn he is. He'd never go for a check-up. I saw blood in his sputum in the sink a few times. I finally convinced him to come to the hospital and get a chest x-ray. The radiologist told me it's already begun to spread."

"What does this mean?" I was concerned about Mama. How would she manage?

"The prognosis isn't good. He probably doesn't have that long. It's at advanced stages." Rachel looked glum, which made me realize how little I knew her. The ten-year difference in our ages seemed larger now than when I was a young woman and she remained stuck in childhood. I felt resentment for all the battles I fought so she could be the favored daughter.

"Does Mama know?"

"Mama knows he's sick, but she doesn't understand the extent of it. She and the Dreichspuns whisper about the big *C*, but they don't realize the consequences."

"What can I do?" I felt strings pulling me back into my parent's stifling living room as though I was a wooden puppet, my painted mouth false with rage.

"Come. Make peace." She pushed at her cuticles with her thumbnail.

"Why should I when he hasn't made peace with me? He declared me dead when I married Will. Sorry, Rachel, it's too late for family harmony." My mouth felt dry.

"Look, I keep to myself. I'm saving money to move. Dad doesn't know it. He'll be shocked. To him the purpose of children is to have someone take care of you in your old age. That's why *Bubbe* had so many. He reminds us all the time of how he fulfilled his obligation to his parents."

"Doesn't he know he's driving us all away? We're not in the *shetl* anymore. This is America, land of the free. We all want to branch out," I said, steaming with indignation.

She stood up. "I came to tell you what's going on. Once he's gone, it's too late. You don't want to hate your father the rest of your life. Think about it. Mama's having the family over in a few Sundays."

"Don't count on me. Until Father welcomes me into his home with my husband and child I'm not coming."

I stopped for a moment so my mind could wrap around the news. So Papa was sick and Rachel was setting up an exit. I remember mama telling me, "I'm not close to Rachel like you. She's quiet, studies into the night, a boarder who tiptoes around the house."

Rachel reached in her pocketbook for an envelope. The clasp made a popping sound. "It's for Miriam." She handed it to me and I peeked inside. A twenty-five dollar gift certificate from Gimbels.

"Rachel, this is extravagant. You shouldn't have."

"I didn't know what to get her. I never got you a wedding present either. I know I'm lax in the sister department." Rachel's inability to express herself reminded me that we didn't talk much. She looked down and left. I watched her walk down the hall, her gait slow and measured. From the floor Miriam's small hands gripped the hem of my dress to pull herself upright, each handful of material a slow climb to independence.

Rachel called, "Hope to see you soon," her voice fading down the stairwell.

I thought about my invincible father dying as I stumbled through my routine of bath, diapers, food, walk. Did I want to make peace with my father or leave the situation estranged? Was Rachel trying to pull me back into the caretaker role so she could escape? I didn't feel ready to forgive his Old World ways for rejecting me with such finality. While I slept that night I awoke, gasping for air, my life trapped in a brown paper bag, the top twisted tight.

Chapter Eight

Sarah

October, 1949

One Monday after my working routine had been established for months, Mama arrived to stay with Miriam. Miriam, her face covered in oatmeal, watched from her high chair.

"Mamala, guess what?" Her face flushed with excitement, she rushed in, hand against her chest, purse swinging from her arm. I stood back to let her by me. "I can't believe it. Someone is alive! My cousin Malka wrote to me!"

Mama handed me a torn blue envelope, the cream paper dull with a watermark design. I turned it over in my hand as my mother went over to greet Miriam. "The postmark says, Buenos Aires. What's she doing in Argentina?"

My mother grabbed the envelope back when she saw my perplexed expression.

I remembered Malka visiting us in my grandparent's elegant living room before we moved to America. A few years younger than my mother, Malka, a short, stocky woman with gray sloe-eyes and long dark lashes that almost dusted the top of her cheekbones, she had an animated mouth, her lips smacking as she spoke at a rapid pace.

"Let me read it to you. She wrote in Yiddish so I'll translate."

She cleared her throat for the task and put on glasses that hung on a pearl chain around her neck. We pulled out chairs at the table.

"My dearest Cousin Paulina,
I hope this letter finds you in good health. I apologize for the length of time it has taken me to find you. Two previous letters were returned. Even with the help of the Red Cross it has been difficult."

My mother pulled off her glasses. "How could they not forward them to me after we moved from Brighton Beach?"

"Mama, read the letter."

"I don't want to share the horrible details of what we went through during the war. Early on, when Poland was partitioned, I was one of 250,000 Jews sent to Russia, separated from my husband, Elias. He survived with the partisans for a while, was caught, and perished in the camps. Fortunately, my daughter, Ruth, stayed with me. She was fifteen and very resourceful. I would not have had food if not for her daily efforts. Conditions were hard in the bitter cold of Siberia. The only difference between the Russians and the Germans is that the Russians didn't gas us. When the war ended we were transferred to a DP camp at Bergen-Belsen."

"Mama, I was there! I could have helped her!"

"Shaa. Let me finish." My mother waved her hand for me to be quiet.

"In the beginning I thought I would go to Palestine to start again. It was the only hope in the DP camp, especially when I learned Elias was gone. As months passed, I met Avram, a

man who had the energy to help us. Ruth and I were in better shape than others who survived so the three of us organized a school for the children, an arduous task without books or paper. Eventually, Avram Pons and I married in a small ceremony by a rabbi and a violinist but without flowers. Ruth cried for her real daddy, but Avram has made us a family again. He, too, lost everyone including his wife and two children. What kind of monsters murder the innocent? We clung to each other like ship-wrecked souls afloat in a devil's sea. Avram's brother, a doctor, left Hungary in '38 and settled in Argentina, the only country to issue him a visa. It took him a long time to get a medical license. That's who sponsored us.

It was a big adjustment for us—a strange country, another new language, no friends. With his brother's assistance we bought a small doll factory. We manufacture different types, including ones in native costumes for tourists to buy in the markets. It seems to be a success. I have to believe in a world where little girls will be safe and want dollies to tuck in beside them at night. It is the only way I can wipe out the past.

Ruth married another immigrant's son. I am a grandma with a grandson who speaks Spanish! Eduardo is the light of my life. I hope and pray Ruth does not let her mind dwell too much on the bad years we had.

I am happy, dear cousin. What about you? Nathan? My thoughts and solace for your losses. I look forward to hearing from you and news of your children. Sarah must be a grown woman now. I remember the copper light shining on her beautiful auburn hair as she played in the courtyard on Bielanska Street. You were so smart to follow Nathan to America. Our girlhood was so sweet.

Perhaps one day you will visit me. Buenos Aires is the Paris of South America.

Love,
Malka"

My mother clutched the letter to her chest. "I can't believe someone is alive from my blood." My mother pronounced the last word as *blut*, her Polish accent accentuated by her memories.

I hugged her. "Mama, I remember her. Gray eyes?"

"Yes, gray eyes like a winter sky. She was my favorite cousin. We had the same music teacher. Later, when I was married and had you and Isaac and still lived in Papa's home, she visited me. We'd stroll to the cafés and concerts near the king's summer palace. She encouraged me to follow your father to this country when I had so many doubts."

My mother's reverie broke. She put the letter into the torn envelope and placed it in her purse. "Your father is not well. You must come to see him and apologize."

"Apologize? For what?" I stepped back.

"You have not behaved with the respect a daughter is supposed to show her father." My mother's lips set in a firm line.

"Mama, I may not have married in the faith, but he's the one who is angry with me. I don't have to apologize." I moved to the other side of the room to boil water for tea. Running the water in our stained sink, I banged the kettle onto the crusty burners. I opened the paint-chipped cabinets for cups and saucers, making as much noise as possible.

"Sarah, he's dying. Bring Miriam. She will soften him up. Make peace before he leaves this world."

"He doesn't know the meaning of the word." I toyed with the leaves of an ivy plant on our windowsill, poking the dry soil with my finger.

"Do it for me. Let me have some solace."

I was stubborn, but my mother's plea and our collective

survivors' guilt clutched the center of my being. My thumbnail poked a hole in an ivy leaf. "I'll think about it."

The teakettle began to whine. I reached for it. "Right now I have to return a call. I may have a wedding photography job for next weekend."

I waited a month before I ventured to my parent's apartment. Will thought I was foolish to go. He had no family so why did I need mine? After a heated discussion Will planned to come with me. As I placed a hat on Miriam's head and tied a pink ribbon under her chubby chin, I felt the deluge of my father's stinging words from the past. I almost changed my mind. What compelled me forward was that Miriam, who was more than a year old, should meet her only grandfather, even if I didn't like him much.

My mother had prepared Sunday brunch for the family, a delicious spread of Danish, bagels, cream cheese, lox, onions, pickles, white fish, pickled herring in sour cream, chopped liver and *tsimiss*, a combination of shredded carrots and sweet prunes. It sat untouched on platters until everyone's arrival. The smell of fresh Chock Full of Nuts coffee made me breathe in and hold it for a moment.

My mother, wearing an apron, nodded at us, her hands filled with utensils. She said little and pointed toward Isaac's old room that had been turned into a sick room. Will looked uncomfortable in his suit, his hair slicked into a side part. I carried Miriam in a pink dress with smocking, her starched skirt covering my arm, a cotton shield.

Will followed me down the hall. As I entered my father's sickroom, I realized I had rarely ever seen him in bed. He was always dressed, leaving for work, pacing in agitation, or sitting up and reading the newspaper. Repose was new. With his eyes closed he looked so small and frail. Where was the towering, intimidating figure that caused me to flee?

The sick aroma in the room assaulted my nostrils. Cancer, with its peculiar smell, permeated the walls, the drapes, the sheets, and him, a reminder of how little time remained.

I walked close to him, the nightstand next to his bed covered with an array of gauze bandages, scissors, brown bottles of cough tonic, Bayer aspirin, green jars of Vaseline, a pitcher of water, eyeglasses, a dozen small bottles of prescription pills, a pack of Pall Malls, the red cellophane strip on top of a cluttered ashtray.

"Dad?"

It took a few seconds for his heavy-lidded eyes to flutter open.

"Dad, this is Miriam." I waved her little hand for her.

At first his eyes didn't focus in recognition. Then the feisty temper returned. A finger emerged from under the covers to point at Will.

"What is he doing here? You brought this *shaygetz* into my house? Out, I want you all out." His hand slashed the air and his voice became stronger at the passion of his words.

I refused to let him intimidate me. My boldness took me a step closer. "I came to introduce you to my husband and my child. They are innocents. Be angry with me, but don't deprive your grandchild of a family. Will, this is my father."

Will stepped into the room from the doorway and held out his hand. My father didn't reach for it.

"You defied me and God and married this, this . . ." He stopped himself from saying a derogatory epithet, the first sign of restraint I had ever seen in him. He turned his face sideways on the pillow so he wouldn't have to look at us.

I licked my dry lips. "It's time to put differences aside. You won't be here forever." I didn't want to beg and cajole, but I wanted this to work for Mama's sake.

Will touched my shoulder. "I'm going. I don't need to stay and listen to this."

"Wait. Don't leave yet," I answered him in an angry whisper.

"I'll be at the diner with the boys." Will loosened his tie as he left the room. I didn't know whether to follow him or to stay and fight. A few moments later I heard the front door close.

My frustration turned to tears. "Why do you ruin everything? I love him. He's a good person. Look at this beautiful baby. Don't you want to know her?"

Miriam started to whimper at my upset and I did my best to shush her with a bouncing motion, wiping a lone tear with my finger.

With a shift of his head on the pillow my father looked at us, his unshaven face sprinkled with gray, his cheeks slack with weight loss. The stillness of the room intensified.

My father tapped the bed for us to sit down. I accepted the invitation.

"Why did you marry a *goy*? This *nogoodnik* who looks like a Nazi?" asked my father waving his arm, his voice weak.

I stood up. I should have known it was a trap. "I'm not going to apologize for my decision or my child." My eyes welled up with tears. "Will is Dutch not German."

"What difference does it make? You turned your back on your ancestors." He motioned toward Miriam. "For this, your mother's family was murdered?"

As I readied to leave my father began a coughing fit unlike anything I had ever heard. Thrashing on the bed he motioned for the water. In that split second I could have walked away, but I didn't. He raised himself on one elbow, grasping the glass and gulping the liquid, drops wetting the top of his gown and the sheets. He flopped back into the pillows.

"Does she talk?" my father asked in a raspy voice.

"A few words. Not much we can understand yet."

He reached a finger, stained from nicotine, to touch her baby-soft arm. "How 'bout walk?"

"No, she doesn't do that either."

Silence drowned the room. Instead of the private conversation that I craved, my father ignored me. The tension escalated with his difficult breathing. Miriam pulled out of my arms to crawl closer to him. My father made noises with his mouth that delighted her, then hid half his face behind the sheet. She pulled it down to discover him, clapping her hands with joy. Had my father ever played with me this way?

I reached for a cigarette from his pack. "You still smoking?"

"Why not? What's the difference? You think these doctors know everything? Ach. It's bullshit all their advice and medications. You get sick? The body can heal itself," he told me, pounding his chest with his fist.

The Nathan I knew still resided there. I lit the cigarette for myself and blew the smoke over his head. Miriam sat on the bed playing patty-cake with him.

The doorbell rang. I heard muffled greetings and laughter of people arriving and my mother's shushes.

"Do you want me to help you into your robe so you can come into the living room? Mother made brunch."

"Okay."

I took a long drag on my cigarette and balanced it in the ashtray. I picked up Miriam and placed her on the rug near my feet. My father flung back the covers and with great effort, sat on the edge of the bed. His knees and legs were bony, almost devoid of hair. Miriam pulled herself up to the edge of the bed anxious to resume patty-cake. I brought my father his striped robe from behind the door.

He stared at it. I grabbed his elbow to propel him to his feet. His skin felt cool to my touch. The back of his gown peeked open to reveal a raw, red grid of burned flesh on his back. Cobalt radiation. Rachel had told me it was the only treatment. I shivered in revulsion at the open wounds.

My mother came in. "Everyone's here. They can't wait to see you and meet this *shayna maydele*," she said moving toward Miriam. "Nathan, what are you doing? Sit down."

She propelled him backward toward the bed, moving me out of the way. "First, before the robe, you need Vaseline on this," she said pulling down the top of the gown. His chest was devoid of hair, too.

"Sarah, hand me the gauze and scissors. The doctor says air is good." She cut a piece of gauze, dipped it into the Vaseline and spread it over the rare-meat flesh on his back.

My father winced in pain. "Go. Go be with the guests," Mama told me. "We'll be out in a minute."

I picked up Miriam and went into the living room to greet Isaac, Isabella, Max and his girlfriend, Selma, Rachel, the Dreichspuns, Joe Blatter, a boarder from years ago, and Mr. Altchuler, a widowed neighbor.

Miriam, of course, was the star of the show as we sat balancing plates on our knees in the living room. She crawled from person to person, enticing them to give her a taste of cream cheese or the cheese filling from their Danish. My father, although weak, became lively, dominating the conversation with talk of the slipper business, even showing off the latest style of burgundy leather mules on his feet.

Isaac and Max made eye contact as if to say, "The business will be ours to run soon."

I stayed until everyone left, knowing Will wasn't waiting for me at home. My father insisted on lining up the dining room chairs in a row along the rim of the living room, coughing and shuffling to do the chore. He refused my help.

"Help your mother in the kitchen. Leave Miriam with me."

I lit a cigarette and sat in the kitchen watching my mother who also refused to let me assist her. With rubber gloves she manipulated the large platters into the soapy water. I offered to dry, but she insisted they should drip.

"What happened to Will?" she asked me.

"Dad insulted him and he left," I said taking a drag.

My mother sighed, leaned forward and rested her elbows on the sink.

We made small talk after that.

I stubbed out my cigarette. After twenty minutes of quiet from the living room I peeked out to see my father enticing Miriam to walk between the chairs, spacing them a little farther apart each time. She reached toward each one with delight, her polished white shoes bright blossom specks on the rug.

By the time we left, Miriam learned how to stumble into her first steps. My father and I had forged a silent truce.

Chapter Nine

Sarah

March, 1951

After work I rushed home to prepare for a small wedding on the Upper East Side. I needed to change clothes, gather photography equipment and kiss my daughter. My coat pockets bulged with film from the forty-seventh street camera store. I opened the door to find Will asleep on the sofa, newspapers strewn on the floor near his feet, his uncombed hair a yellow haystack. Miriam wailed in her crib with the bedroom door shut. I rushed in to take her out, her face red with anger, nose runny, hair limp with sweat.

"Poor baby," I repeated as I bounced her against me to calm her down, wiping her face with my hand. I took her back into the living room.

Will began to stir with the commotion. I tapped his ankle with my foot.

"Didn't you hear her crying?" I asked in a throaty whisper, controlling my anger.

"What? Huh?" He stretched his arms out with a groaning sound. "Guess I fell asleep."

"Have you been drinking? How could you not hear a baby screaming in the next room?" My voice was shrill.

"I had a few beers with the guys." He elbowed his way out of the depression of the sofa to his feet. The air in the room was fetid with stale cigarettes, rancid beer, and sour formula.

"I have a wedding to shoot tonight so I have to leave soon. Are you going to watch the baby or not? Otherwise, I'll take her downstairs. She needs dinner, a bottle, bath." My tone dropped a few decibels.

"Yeah, I'll take care of her." He reached out his arms. "Come to your daddy, little girl."

In response to his slurry words, Miriam hid her face in my neck.

"I've got to shower and be out of here in thirty minutes. How 'bout you get the food ready? I'll take her in the bedroom with me."

I calmed Miriam down by playing with her on the bed for a few minutes, marveling at her large blue eyes and perfectly shaped head covered with blond fuzzy curls. Mama and Will's genes. How could a child look so much like her father? What part of her would be like me? I played "This Little Piggy" with her pink feet, the tickling distracting her from the upset. I loved her anticipated chortle when she knew I was getting to the last tiny toe.

I picked her up and hugged her. I would never let anything bad happen to this child. I sat her back on the bed and she watched me undress, curious about every article of clothing I flung aside. I grabbed my chenille robe from the hook behind the door and walked her into the other room.

Will picked her up and placed her in the wicker seat of a high chair, a treasure from a second-hand store on Castro Street. I watched as he tied a bib around her neck.

I couldn't wait to get into the shower, my only hope for washing away anger that was swelling to a crescendo. As the warm water flowed down my body, the rat-a-tat-tat on my shower cap reminded me of the nagging ache swimming in my worried head, a shark's fin in dark waters. By the time I left, Will and Miriam were friends again sitting on the sofa with a Golden Book.

My frustration grew as months passed, especially since my hours at Macy's were so long. I delighted in Miriam's stages of development, but I was only with her for a short time in the evenings. My aching feet developed corns and my cheeks hurt from smiling at condescending customers, ladies of leisure with pin-curl hairstyles and shiny pumps. They clicked open patent leather pocketbooks and pulled folded bills from change purses, mad money from husbands who made a decent wage.

So many times I saw great places or people to photograph, but there was never time to pursue it. I thought about black-and-white studies of faces or rooms, but over the months my creativity waned, scraping muscle from bone, peeling away in layers. My desire to express myself couldn't compete with daily survival. What brought Will and I together faded like my unfulfilled dreams, dissipating like morning fog on the Hudson.

I searched the want ads for something else, anything else. I interviewed for a few positions in offices, but I didn't know shorthand. My mediocre typing on mandatory tests left a supercilious sneer on the faces of the office managers. Confident stenographers with a sway in their hips and matched seams won the best jobs.

Finally, I spotted an ad for a photography assistant. I called Arturo Patchelli, an older man from his telephone voice, who owned a studio in Little Italy.

"You comma tomorrow. Be early. And don't wear perfuma."

I took the Six subway to Canal and Lafayette Streets. With newspaper in hand I found Mott. Number thirty-four was an office building with a brick façade and a shop on the first floor.

A glass door with its peeling gold letters greeted me, PATCHELLI'S PHOTOGRAPHY SINCE 1935. Bells hanging from a red rope of threads tinkled as I entered. On pale blue walls pictures of graduates in caps and gowns, brides in ornate white lace dresses and chubby babies in christening outfits, beamed expectant hope. Beat-up metal folding chairs against one wall looked like the aftermath of a choir practice. An old wooden desk in the center of the room needed straightening. On top of it sat an open appointment book on a shredded ink blotter, a black telephone with numbers taped to the bottom, bits of paper with notes, a message pad, packages of pictures and a few errant rolls of film in an ashtray. I tapped the bell at the edge of the desk, then looked up at a large picture of the Madonna in repose gracing the wall, her calm features satisfied.

Mr. Patchelli's arm swept aside the black drape on the back wall. A man in his sixties with silver wavy hair, bushy eyebrows and heavy cologne, he entered the room. The formality of his navy three-piece suit seemed odd without a tie. My mother would have thought him debonair, a Cesar Romero type. His fragrance tickled my nose and I tried not to sneeze. He offered me a chair next to his desk, ignoring my outstretched hand.

After initial questions of my name, address and work history, he began his negotiation.

"You can make appointments, deal with anxious brides, nervous mothers, eh?"

I nodded.

"What about graduations? I take all the photos for Saint Teresa's. You gotta make sure the kids don't gotta hair in the eyes, keep the negatives straight, sell the moms and grandmas the packages. I don't make much on individuals and wallet size. Packages with 5x7's, 8x10's is the ticket." He pulled out a dusty, gold rococo frame from behind his filthy desk. "I sell 'em frames, too. You can do that?" He wet his fingers with spit and rubbed a place on the frame.

"Yes, I can do all that. As long as there's not too much typing I can help you run an efficient studio."

"Okay! You hired." He slammed his hands on the desk and he rose to show me out.

"Wait, Mr. Patchelli. What's my salary? When do I start?"

"Twenty-five dollars a week and you start tomorra. You no like it, that's all I offer." He turned to face the mirror on the wall next to the door where hundreds of young people had smoothed their hair and dampened their lips. He wet his fingers again and touched his temples.

"Twenty-five dollars a week isn't enough." I picked up my purse. "I have a baby, bills to pay."

"Okay, okay. You getta percentage of the packages."

I stood tall behind him. Our eyes met in the mirror as he examined his jaw line, pulling imaginary specks from his jacket.

"Ten percent. That's it. See you." He shooed me away.

I smiled. I would've asked for five.

"Mr. Patchelli, I can't start so fast. I have to give notice at my other job. Give me a week."

"Okay. Go already." With that he disappeared into the back.

I smiled all the way to the subway, down the stairs, and into my seat, until a man began to leer at me. My grin disappeared so I could adopt a New York stare.

For a while my life improved. I liked riding the Six to the studio. Maybe I wasn't taking pictures, but I was around film and photos and people. And, I could sit down during slow times. I even got a lunch break, which I convinced Mr. Patchelli I didn't need. It enabled me to leave a half hour earlier. Some nights I stayed late so I'd have the next morning off, a chance for breakfast with my doll. I appreciated the flexibility. It wasn't challenging booking appointments, dusting powder off Italian girls with downy lips, or listening to Mr. Patchelli talk about his invalid wife and her sisters with their big behinds, but I respected the lulls in the day. It gave my mind time to wrap around more pressing matters, squeezing it as I did through warrens of discomfort.

I worried when I left Will with Miriam. He stopped drinking for periods of time, but then it'd lure him back. The blinking of a neon sign and his buddies were a lot of competition for a sparse home and a cranky wife. We fought a lot, hardly making love anymore. I'd look at his handsome face and think, how could I have been lured by a cleft chin? His camera, pushed to the back of the closet, never came out of its leather case anymore. I knew my choices were few. Where does a woman with a baby go? Not home to her parents, not mine anyway.

My father deteriorated in stages. I went every few weeks with Miriam to visit Mama and sit with him. We never had the conversations we needed to have to say what needed to be said. It was as though my marriage or Will's religion or anything of importance didn't exist. He never asked me to bring Will over again. That hurt me, but I didn't press the issue. What was the point of upsetting him when he was dying? I was there because Mama asked me to be, as a cutout figure without a past and hardly any present. The future looked too complex to explore.

Rachel and my mother took care of my father. He needed visits to the hospital for treatments, bathing, fresh linens. His great bulk shrunk to the size of an empty, small boy's suit. He weighed so little Rachel could lift him herself and take him into the bathroom. Without health insurance his care was all done at home. He wanted to live, to see his precious Miriam go to school, graduate, perhaps marry. It wasn't going to happen.

My father doted on Miriam, whom he nicknamed Mimi. She began to call herself that, too, adoring his attention. He sent my mother out to buy her a doll that was almost her size. She loved her surrogate sister, dressing it in clothes she had outgrown, combing her blonde hair until a bald spot appeared on the back of her rubber head.

Isabella, Isaac's wife was pregnant so another baby would arrive soon. I doubted it would be the same interaction he had with his first, his precious Mimi. I watched him play patty-cake with her and teach her Russian songs, lost opportunities from my childhood that were manifesting themselves now.

One Sunday my mother and I sat at the kitchen table with our glasses of tea. She wore cold cream and a flowered housedress, a bandeau wrapped around her hair. After a discussion about Mr. Patchelli and my talent for selling packages of first communion pictures, she fretted over how much my father's care cost.

"What will I do? How will I live? The boys are running the business and send an allowance, but I'm afraid it won't be enough. What if I have to move?" She glanced around at the familiar space.

I touched her arm. "Mama, it'll be okay. Isaac and Max are smart. They'll keep it a good business and take care of you. Besides, Papa saved money."

"What money? It's not so much. The hospital, doctors. They thought he would go quickly, but the man is such a *bulvant*, like an ox who works the fields. He's been sick for almost five years." She paused as she looked into her glass.

When she spoke again her voice was filled with sorrow.

"Money's been eaten away like moths feasting on a cashmere sweater."

I pushed back my chair and hugged her, my cheek slippery against the cold cream. She looked grim, her shoulders slumped forward. I wasn't used to seeing her without hope, my Mama who had gone through so much.

I wanted to ask my mother how she felt about my father. I sensed her privacy and the mixed feelings she harbored for the man who made her life safe and miserable at the same time. She knew none of us would be alive if it wasn't for his stubborn persistence. Making it in America had always been the goal, whatever the cost.

I, on other hand, felt an outward peace toward my father because he no longer threatened me. Inside, I quartered resentments for the unhappiness he caused all of us, but what was the point of creating more conflict for my mother?

I patted her knee. "Don't worry. We'll figure something out."

I gathered Mimi, as we called her too, and her giant doll. She sat on a fluffy rug next to my father's bed talking and pouring pretend tea into a plastic set of cups and saucers. He slept, mouth open, an arm hanging off the bed. His other hand lay across his chest and I saw the scarred imprint of the Timex he had been so proud of until the man stabbed him on the street so many years ago.

Mimi and I moved around the room in hushed tones. When it was time to leave, I touched his stubbly face with my hand. Cool to the touch, I pulled away. I leaned over and put my ear to his chest. Nothing. My father had glided away to the sounds of his granddaughter's tea party.

Book Three

Mimi
September, 1952

Chapter One

Mimi

The year of mourning after my grandfather's death became a slow dirge of cleaning out closets, consolidating bank accounts, and shuffling papers. One year later at the unveiling of his headstone at the cemetery, the adults left a smooth rock on the new granite, proof of their attendance. I clutched my mother's hand. My relatives, save for Aunt Rachel who didn't show, all dressed in black. While the rabbi droned on in Hebrew, I glanced at the empty plot for my grandmother.

My dad didn't come because he and Grandpa didn't get along.

At my Grandma's apartment that September afternoon, a heated discussion ensued after everyone settled into her velvet chairs, my uncles in their starched white shirts, sleeves rolled up, neckties loosened, jackets swung across the backs of the dining room seats. A small spider inched along the upholstered cornice above the drapes. A window fan whirred with an incessant clank, a rubbing noise of irritation in the muggy heat. The adults called it an Indian summer.

After my Aunt Isabella told how she prepared the pickled herring—one-third of a cup of sugar to a cup of white vinegar overnight—my Uncle Isaac started clearing his throat.

"Mama, it's been a year. Rachel has moved to Syracuse. Have you thought maybe you don't need such a big place?"

I glanced at my grandma, her hands folded on her lap. She pursed her lips as though a sweet candy had turned sour in her mouth.

Aunt Isabella added, "Paulina dear, we need to cut expenses. More mouths to feed." She stroked her big belly. With her lisp, "mouth" came out "mouse." My little cousin, Ernie, with his perpetual drool and wide, dark eyes, clung to her leg.

"Where do you want I should go? I'm familiar with what's here." My grandmother scrambled her grammar when she was upset.

My aunts and uncles looked at each other. Isaac spoke.

"Mother, we're thinking it would be better for you to live near us. You could see the children more often. Maybe stay over." He stroked Ernie's head.

My grandmother narrowed her eyes. "What kind of place?"

"Okay, a little smaller, maybe not so fancy. Do you need a doorman? An elevator?" Uncle Isaac picked lint from his pant leg.

"You want me to live in a dump? What would I do out there away from my friends?" Her voice rose like a train spewing steam when it screeches to a halt. Grandma reached for a hankie in her bosom to blot sniffles. She had the most beautiful eyes I had ever seen, amethyst bonded with a sapphire.

My Uncle Max butted in, circles of sweat under his arms. "No one wants you to live in a dump. This is a big place for one person. Can't you consider something more practical? Isaac and I are afraid the business can't support so many families."

Max's fiancé, Greta, leaned in to hug his arm, crossing her legs to reveal silk stockings beneath a cotton eyelet skirt. Her dirty blonde hair fell in waves to her shoulders, painted red lips and nails adding a bit of color to the scene. When her hands moved, one finger with a big diamond, her gold bracelets jangled. She lifted her chin to blow smoke rings, then tap-tap-tapped the ashes into an ashtray, giving me a knowing smile, as if to say, "I'll be part of this soon."

Of course my mother got into the fray. She stood and set her plate on the dining room table. "You're asking Mama to move? Where's she supposed to go? A wasteland like Fox Hills in Staten Island? She'll wither without her friends."

Grandma added to the drama by bleating out big sobs into her hankie. "My husband's dead. My children don't want me." She covered her face with her hands.

I went over and sat on the floor next to her putting my head on her knee. She began to twist my curls around her finger. The rest of the people in the room glared at each other. Greta rolled her eyes.

As a quiet child I observed adults, their dress, speech and habits. I'd mimic their behaviors in front of the bathroom mirror as I perched my skinny legs on the sink, especially the way they smoked, taking a deep drag, puckering my mouth. My favorite was Greta because she'd throw her head back and shake her wavy hair as she exhaled. She also held out her pinky when she drank tea.

My Uncle Isaac raised his voice, shaking his hand with a fork in it. "I can't carry the whole burden of this family on my shoulders. How many slippers and pillows do we have to make to support everyone? Max and I are the only ones working."

"Wait a minute. You're not supporting me or my daughter," my mother said. She walked over to face him, hands on hips. "And, Rachel takes care of herself."

"So why can't *you* contribute to Mama's upkeep?" asked Uncle Isaac standing up. His pink scalp shone through damp strands of the thinning hair combed to the side in a low part. Even though he was acting mean I still liked him when he took the time to play with me, spinning me in endless circles.

My mother moved a step closer to his face. "You've got some nerve knowing my circumstances. Besides, why should Mama make changes because you can't manage a business? It was a profitable one until you got hold of it." My mother's hands dropped from her hips as she turned and marched toward the door, grabbing at her coat. "Mimi, let's go."

I didn't move.

"Who told you to get knocked-up by a no-*goodnik*?" Uncle Isaac hissed.

The room spun in silence. No one took a breath.

My mother's eyes widened and her brows climbed in shock. She turned to Uncle Isaac. She looked ready to strike him. "Have you no respect? What *chutzpa*. Who do you think you are, big shot? A *schbernik* who got handed a business on a silver platter."

"You're talking like that in front of the child?" my grandmother asked. Her hands covered my ears.

My grandmother began to weep, a trapped, wounded puppy in a box.

Through her tears my grandmother said, "Stop it. Arguing on the day of an unveiling. What kind of children did I have? A *shonda*. Lower your voices. What are we? People of no breeding?"

I hugged her legs harder. The room stayed quiet except for her snuffling and the squeaky fan. Uncle Isaac sat down and my mother leaned against the wall, arms crossed.

Grandma pulled a hankie from her bosom and brushed imaginary crumbs off her black skirt. "I'll solve your problem. I'm leaving on a trip."

"What? Where are you going?" asked my uncles in unison.

"I'm taking money your father left and I'm going to visit my cousin Malka in Buenos Aires. When I return, we'll decide what's what. Enough." She looked down at me with a self-satisfied smile and stroked my hair. "I'm going to bring you a lovely present."

My mother hung her raincoat, scarf and hat back on the stand in the foyer. "I think that's a wonderful idea, Mama. When are you planning to go?"

"I don't know."

I couldn't ask then, but I remembered the knocked-up part for years. It explained why she married my father.

Labor Day, 1953, my mother and I sat under a rented umbrella at Coney Island. My father, who never put on a swimsuit, drank beer all day. It was supposed to be a celebration because I was starting my first year of school the next day, but instead it felt sad. We rarely went on a family outing. If my mother worked on a Saturday for Mr. Patchelli, my father took me on the subway to my grandmother's and left me there for the day.

My dad would hold my hand on the street without saying much to me, as though he didn't know how to talk to a little girl. On the train he didn't read like the other men, just stared with a vacant look, the white part of his eyes shot with red. Sometimes he'd drink beer from a bottle wrapped in a brown paper bag. He told me not to tell my mother, which I never did.

On those Saturdays that I visited my grandma I helped her get ready for her trip. She wanted to leave in the winter because it was summer in Argentina. I couldn't understand how that worked, but I knew it had something to do with the equator.

My grandmother spent hours on her clothes. She'd mend them, switching buttons on dresses and jackets for more expensive tortoise shell or mother-of-pearl ones, storing the discards in a cigar box. She added a fox collar to a suit, the head of the animal with its beady eyes draped over her shoulder. She'd iron garments, the steam dampening her face, then fold the item into tissue paper, all the while telling me stories of when the dressmaker came to stay with her family on Bielanska Street. Sometimes she told me about how she played with Malka in the large courtyard of her father's building with its fountain and flowers.

My grandmother said, "Mimi, life is not made-to-order like my childhood dresses. My idyllic one is gone forever. In those days my cousins and I watched for the flowers to bloom in the spring—wisteria, roses, hollyhock—so we knew it wouldn't be long until we could be outside. My *bubbe* from my mother's side would sit in a wicker wheelchair in one corner of the courtyard. She was supposed to watch us, but she always dozed off. Yadwiga, one of the servants brought out rugs, put them on a stand, and would beat them to get out the dirt. Deliveries had to go to the kitchen entrance. Did I ever tell you about the time the gypsies read my palm and predicted my life?"

"Yes, Grandma." I plumped her pillows under my side as I stretched out on her bed.

"Anyway, everyone who came to visit passed by, friends for my mother and a steady stream of business people to meet with my father. He kept his desk in the front hall so the workmen didn't traipse on my mother's carpets, beautiful thick rugs my parents brought back from their travels. The men would stand there, caps in hand, waiting for him to pay them their week's wages before the Sabbath started. Sometimes I hid under the well of the desk, watching their eyes as they looked around at the paintings on the walls, the fine wallpaper and beautiful woodwork."

I loved her stories of a world so far away, my imagination dancing through brick buildings and forests. When I asked her how her family got to Warsaw, she said, "From the fifteenth century my family was in Poland, but in the late 1700s they moved to Praga, a fashionable suburb on the east bank of the Vistula River. At the time a few hundred other Jewish families lived there. By the late eighteen sixties over two hundred thousand Jews lived in Warsaw."

"Where were they before that?" I wanted to know.

"You sure you want to know all this, Mamala?" She sat next

to me for a rest and tipped my chin toward her. I nodded yes. "We left Spain and wandered eastward to rest. *Poh lin* in Hebrew means 'Here, stay overnight.' Poland linked the Ottoman Empire to Central Europe so merchants traveled with their goods on land instead of sea where they might encounter pirates or bad weather. Unfortunately, they always accused us of something—the Black Plague or murdering babies or witchcraft."

I had no clue about the Ottoman Empire or Europe but I stopped her, demanding she explain plague and witchcraft. I wanted to know who hated us and why.

"We don't believe in their Lord." She stopped. I wanted her to continue even though I couldn't comprehend all of it. She rarely talked about the past, where she had come from, what her melancholy was about. I wanted more.

"What happened after they got there? Grandma?"

It took a while before she began, her voice low.

"Originally, the Jews who came were called *renders*. They leased land from the nobles, managed estates for the rich and collected taxes. In return, the king made them court Jews. People hated them because they controlled the wine and liquor trade in the countryside, too. Ach, then there were wars and conquerors and Poland disappeared from the map for a while. A sad history."

"Did your family know the king?"

"At one time my family was part of the King's court. He gave us land. Many pieces of my mother's jewelry came from that time, passed down by the women to their daughters."

"Where is it? Did you get a crown?"

"Gone. That's enough. No more."

"But what happened to them?"

"Gone. Everyone, everything. Gone."

The story seemed incomplete even though it had jewels, kings, and monsters. "What happened to your family?" I asked again. She wouldn't continue.

"Enough." She waved me away.

"How did you learn all this?" I wanted to know.

"My father and mother had tutors for me. Papa thought history was important. He wanted me to know where I came from. And, now, you know, too." She reached for a small pile of letters tied with lavender ribbon on her nightstand.

My grandmother, her hair tucked into a terry cloth turban, moved through the past and present, a never-ending carousel that played the same tune over and over without a beginning or an end. She sat on the edge of the bed and read me her cousin Malka's letters.

Later, I helped wrap gifts for Malka, her husband, Avram, their children and grandson. The items lined the edges of her powder blue Samsonite suitcase, a new purchase from a luggage store downtown. The steel-cased outside made it so heavy I couldn't lift it even when empty. In it she placed lace handkerchiefs, wind-up toys, an alarm clock, Cobb's chocolates, stockings, slippers, ceramic salt and peppershakers, cards of mother-of-pearl buttons, and photo albums.

"Grandma, why are you taking so many presents? Is it a birthday?" I asked.

"Malka says there's inflation since the rebellion. She and Avram never liked Peron, their leader, or Eva, his wife, although the people loved her, especially after she died." She stopped to tsk, tsk. "Four thousand people killed in Buenos Aires. They threw Peron out. He's in Spain or Paraguay now, probably with Nazis who escaped." She made a clucking sound with her mouth and turned her back to me to search her closet. I loved that she talked to me as though I was an adult.

"Is it dangerous to go? What are Nazis?" I pronounced it with the *z* as an *s*.

She ignored my questions. "Mamala, I'm going to send you wonderful picture postcards. Listen to your mother. Don't make trouble." She came back to me and took my face in her hands and kissed me on each cheek.

"I'll be gone three months. My plane ride is to Los Angeles, then on to Buenos Aires. Twenty-three hours for my first time in the air."

Finally, my grandma's departure date arrived. My mother and I took a taxi to Idlewild Airport to see her off. Grandma wore a blue cotton dress, her hair styled in waves, white cotton gloves and a cosmetic case filled with her creams and paints. After she boarded the airplane, we watched it take off into the cloudless gray sky. My grandfather's death had freed her.

The first postcard with a picture of a wide boulevard and impressive buildings arrived a few weeks later.

January, 1956
Dear Children,
Having a wonderful time with Malka, Avram and Eduardo. We cannot stop talking about our childhood. We've even prepared some Polish food. She saved our recipe for cholent with small potatoes and onions. What a beautiful city! The Paris of South America. Went to waterfalls in the country. Better than Niagara! Miss you all.
Love,
Mother

The second and third ones were similar to the first, but finally, a letter came in a blue envelope. My mother read it to me.

"Dear Sarah,
Malka sends her love. She remembers you and Isaac playing

in the courtyard on Bielanska Street.

This trip has taken me to a place that I buried long ago. Being with my cousin who knew me so well as a child is both heartwarming and sad. It's difficult for me to talk of my parents and brothers, but speaking Polish every day has brought forth a flood of memories. Malka remembers our suite of rooms furnished with style and my brother, Itzak, dozing on a low couch in front of the bay window, my mother hovering over him. We talked about our grand Passover seders that always started on a full moon, the light through the tall windows blending with our candles. They went on for hours, my father in his elegance leading the service, the rest of us slouched in our chairs. Why did Carlo tantalize me with a visit to New York and then leave? Why was I left with no one in a strange country?

Yet, Malka's life is more difficult than mine. She has never learned Spanish and depends on her children for shopping and news. It's not free here like America with political views expressed openly. Nathan was right. The United States is the best place in the world. Here, the Catholic Church controls everything. Before Peron left he passed measures legalizing divorce and gave children borne out of wedlock, legitimacy. It caused a lot of conflict but made things more liberal.

Malka and Avram live well in a lovely hacienda in a predominately Jewish area so their grandchildren can attend the temple school. Avram goes to the doll factory every day and works with his sons, Eduardo, Manuel, whom they call Manny, and Solomon, whom they call Sonny.

I must tell you, though, I get chicken skin bumps when I hear German spoken in the shops or streets. Are they Nazis or refugees? I look into their faces as though their eyes will reveal the truth. Are they murderers? Or just children like me searching for their parents?

My love to you and precious Mimi. It will grieve me to say goodbye to Malka because I'll never see her again. The distances between us are too great. I love you. I'm looking forward to coming home to what's familiar.

Your Mother."

My mother read the letter in a flourish and handed me the postcards.

As I tore off the foreign stamps with the pretty designs, I asked her, "What are Nazis?"

"Never mind."

Chapter Two

Mimi

After my grandma left on her trip, my father didn't come home a few nights. I nuzzled in bed next to my mother.

"Where's Daddy?" I wanted to know.

"I don't want to talk about it." She pulled me closer to her and I could smell her mommy smell, a combination of perfume and cigarettes. She may not have wanted to tell me, but I knew. He drank and fell asleep at friends' houses, or worse yet, on a bus bench.

One Monday morning he showed up at six, pounding on the door because he had lost his key. I opened the door. He smelled of liquor, smoke and the street, a fetid odor that made me step back. Dark raccoon circles ringed his blue eyes, wet pools surrounded by mud. He wanted to shower and change for work. My mother, furious, stood in the bedroom door, her chenille robe wrapped tight around her. She harped on his being gone all night. Her face, tired and void, wasn't pretty.

She spit out the words, "You drunken bum. You barely make a living."

"Who could support a bitch like you with your demands?" He staggered a bit and reached toward the sofa for support.

"Demands? Food on the table, rent? Those are demands? Get out and don't come back. I won't have you speak to me that way in front of Mimi." Then she turned to me pointing her finger. "Go downstairs right now to Mrs. Malley." She guided me toward the door, her hand on my back.

"But I'm in my nightgown," I protested. She ignored me. The door shut like a slap.

I didn't go right away. I put my ear against the hard surface, my legs growing goose bumps in the chilly hallway. I wrapped my arms around myself to keep warm.

"I can support myself and Mimi, if you don't drink away our money."

"I'll do as I damn well please. I'm sick and tired of your Jew-bitch ways."

Glass broke. I heard a scuffle. I didn't know who was doing what to whom, but my tears carried me down three flights of stairs toward the warm arms of Mrs. Malley.

"What is it?" she asked me through the space between the chain and the door.

I shook my head back and forth. I couldn't tell her.

I heard the locks move. "Would you like some hot cocoa?" She wrapped a blanket around me after I crawled into her lap.

By the time my grandma returned from Argentina, my mother had filed for divorce. She said she didn't want Grandma to talk her out of it.

Divorce was unheard of in our family or in anyone else's either. I was a pariah at school. Kids whispered behind my back, the teachers gave me pathetic looks.

My mother said she left my father because he drank. He seemed sad to me the few times he came by to pick me up. We didn't do much, just walked around, sat in the park, bought candy. She complained he had no ambition, that he never grew up. I didn't know what that meant. My father would watch television, a beer in hand, our small black and white TV with rabbit ears flickering until the test pattern appeared. Then he'd drink another beer and stretch out.

Once, my mother showed me photos of them when they were younger as she packed them away in a box. She told me, "Don't marry because you're lonely or desperate. Find someone where there's a meeting of the minds."

"What's that? Weren't you in love?" I asked.

"For a time, yes, we were in love." She looked away. A pensive expression crossed her face. She hugged me. "Don't worry. We'll start over. We'll stay with Grandma for a while."

When my grandma returned with pictures of Malka and her family, we listened to her stories as we sat in her living room. I kicked my feet until my mother told me to stop.

"It's a miracle anyone is alive," my grandmother told us, referring to Malka's odyssey from Poland to Argentina. "Thank God they had an open visa policy and let them in." She unwrapped a doll cuddled in tissue paper from Avram's factory and handed it to me. "From Malka and Avram."

"Grandma, I love it," I told her. I stroked the elaborate embroidered dress. A doll with real hair eyelashes and eyes that blinked.

During dinner at my grandma's kitchen table my mother told us her plan. "Divorce means a long legal separation in the state of New York. I filed but unless I prove adultery it could take years. I want to get rid of the bum now."

"What's adultery?" I wanted to know.

"You ask too many questions," my mother said. "Mama, I want out of my marriage and the only way I can do it is to move to another state with less stringent laws. I could go to Reno for a few months, but who would watch Mimi? You're all alone in this big apartment. You won't be able to keep it, even if you could convince Isaac to give you more money. And I doubt he will. He's tighter than Dad. Why don't we sell the heavy furniture, pack up our summer clothes and move to Miami Beach?"

She set down her fork, her face puzzled. "Florida? Without anything? What about my friends? A *mashugana* idea."

My mother's words rushed out. "You'll make new friends. Listen Mama, we can cut expenses by getting a place together. The cost of living is less there. Mimi will love the sunshine and the ocean. We all need a fresh start. And, I don't know how long the money will last from the factory. Max and Isaac are fighting again. Rachel called and told me Max says Isaac is squirreling away money for bonuses that they're supposed to use for capital expenditures. Isaac says Max is padding the expense account. Rachel's making a life of her own in Syracuse as a nurse and she's not coming back. We should go."

My grandmother looked at me, her blue eyes absorbing the strange, idea of a new beginning.

"What do you say, Mama? Think about it. Mimi can go to school where it's clean and bright, not *schlep* on subways in a big, dingy city. Let's move in the summer."

Grandma's hand touched her throat. "So many changes. Your father gone. You, almost divorced. I don't know." She looked around. "What about my things?"

"We'll sell them and buy rattan. No more velvet and heavy drapes. We'll decorate with light, airy colors—maybe pink or turquoise or a white sofa. I hear the sun shines every day. No more winter coats, galoshes." My mother looked so hopeful.

"Let me sleep on it. I've barely unpacked from South America."

"Mama, I've got to get out of here," my mother's voice pleaded. "I don't want Will around and my job at the photo studio is a dead-end. I don't want to go without you, but I will if I have to. What have you got here anyway? Isaac and Max are only going to want to borrow money from your nest egg."

My grandmother's expression changed. The softness around her mouth curdled into an eggshell hard *O*. "It's not so much money. I need it for my old age. The boys have the business. Besides, I might want to have some more fun."

She picked up her fork and finished her dinner.

Chapter Three

Mimi

It didn't take long for Grandma to decide. At a family dinner at my Uncle Isaac's house my uncles started an argument over their ideas for expansion. Uncle Isaac thought hiring more sales people and going west was a good idea and Uncle Max thought moving manufacturing to the Bahamas would cut costs.

At the end of their argument Uncle Isaac yelled, "*Schvartzes* don't need slippers on the beach." He threw down his napkin and stomped from the room. Isabella made a tsk-tsk sound with her mouth, shaking her head. She stood up to clear dishes.

Max looked embarrassed. "Mama, can I talk with you?"

"Now?"

Max nodded his head.

She got up from the table, her plate filled with food. "Why do you and your brother have to fight? Cause an upset at every meal?"

"Let's go in here," he said guiding her into the den, a paneled room with a desk and shelves of books, boring books without pictures.

Later, I found out what he wanted when she spoke to my mother in the cab on the way home.

"The boys want me to put some money into the business." I watched my mother's mouth turn down. She looked out the window. "Okay, they need a boost. Nathan said you have to spend to make, although I never saw too much spending. Anyway, I'm giving them thirty thousand dollars. Then they have to leave me alone. That's it. I told Max, 'No more money.'" She reached over and touched my mother's knee. "Sarah, make the plans. Let's go to Florida." My grandmother sat back, her purse perched on her lap, looking straight ahead, as the taxi lurched through traffic.

I knew if I said nothing I could be privy to details of what was going on. I made myself small between the two of them.

"Mama, are you sure you want to do this? That's a lot of money. What are they doing with it?" My mother moved closer to me in the cab, her hand on the back of the seat in front of her as we stopped suddenly.

"What? Now you want to talk me out of it? They need to expand. More production, different equipment, I don't know. I don't have a head for business like your father. I want to get away from all this." Her gloved hand waved at the traffic, buildings, garbage piled on the street.

"No, it's a good idea. Give them a lump sum and then tell them you're done. Mimi and I will move in with you next week so we can begin to prepare and consolidate costs."

No one spoke until we dropped off my grandmother. My mother took my hand as we spread out in the back seat.

"Mimi, we're going to start a whole new life." She leaned her head back and sighed.

My mother and I left our flat near Lexington and 32nd Street when she returned from work on Friday night. We hadn't seen my father in weeks. My mother complained bitterly about money he owed her. With borrowed suitcases, we left our furniture behind in lieu of the last month's rent.

"Won't we need a sofa?" I asked staring at the faded flowers and the saggy seat.

"Yes, but we'll buy a new one. Let's say goodbye to Mrs. Malley and go to your grandmother's. We're starting over." Her chin jutted with a triumphant air. She held one suitcase under her arm and her camera cases in her hand.

"What about school?"

"Stop being such a worry wart." Her voice softened and I watched the line of her mouth soften. "You'll go to school wherever we live. Education is very important. I want you to be able to do some of the things I didn't. Like college."

"Are there good schools in Florida? My friends said Florida's swampland."

"Mimi, there are good schools everywhere. We'll probably stay in New York until you graduate from elementary." She paused to pull a hair off my face. I thought about how I wanted her to wear lipstick and rouge and do her nails like the other mommies.

That satisfied me for the moment. "What about the food in our refrigerator?" I worried about my milk and a few oranges.

"Leave it. We'll stay with Grandma while I save money and then it's off to the Sunshine State. Plenty of oranges there." She gave me a rare smile, which always made her face prettier, as she pulled my head toward her to kiss.

"What about Dad?" How was he going to find me?

She stopped, placing the suitcases by her side in the stairwell. "For a ten-year-old you ask a lot of questions. Our marriage is over. Have you seen your father in the last few weeks? The man's a drunk and doesn't care about us. If he wants to see you, he can come to Florida."

I marched behind her to the corner where we took a taxi to my grandmother's. I wasn't close to my dad, but I'd miss seeing him, those eyes, filled with questions. People said I looked like him. Mrs. Dreichspun whispered I looked like a *shiksa*. The photographs on our walls belonged to him. I never saw him take pictures. How did that part of him go away? Why couldn't I touch it?

My grandmother ushered us in with a fuss, offering food and drink, as though we were there for a holiday visit. My mother stayed down the hall. I took over Grandpa Nathan's sickroom. After he died, Aunt Rachel and Grandma cleaned it, but the antiseptic and medicinal smells remained, clinging to the drapes and seeping into the other rooms. His coughs still echoed in the apartment.

I'd never had my own room and I loved the space. My grandmother put up pink curtains to match my dust ruffle and bedspread. I loved my closet so much I straightened my few pairs of shoes every day.

I remember the day he passed away. I was playing with my tea set on the floor in his room. My mother called for my grandmother. When she came in to get him ready for the company, she touched her lips to his cool head. First, she shook him calling out his name. Then, hysterical, she sobbed over his body with grief.

My mother whisked me away, my tea party pieces flung into the corners of the room. After the ambulance left with his body, the apartment filled with people. I did my best to stay out of everyone's way, hiding under furniture to watch their legs. Relatives arrived, many who spoke with accents or in other languages. Neighbors draped the hallway and bathroom mirrors with black material. My mother took me home to stay with Mrs. Malley, who clucked over me.

My mother took a few days off from work to attend the funeral and sit *shiva*. My feelings were hurt that I wasn't allowed to attend.

We sat on low stools. People paid their respects with platters— *challah*, whitefish, bagels, chopped liver, *rugelach*, brisket. I never saw so much food. As plates emptied new ones appeared. Relatives brought presents and pinched my cheeks until they hurt.

"Eat, *shayna madeleh*, you're so thin." Then they'd corner my mother and say, "She's all skin and bones."

With my mother gone during the day and the school year over, I spent more time with my grandmother. She began her preparations for the move to Florida, cleaning out closets, wrapping dishes, even though she knew it would be awhile. I asked why I couldn't attend Grandpa's funeral.

"Funerals aren't for children. The rabbi spoke for a long time about what a giving man he was, devoting his free time to the Slonim Society." She snacked on crackers, the crumbs dropping onto the rug as she moved between the hall closet and an open box on her bed. She held up a satin dressing gown. "Think I'll need this in Florida?"

I shrugged my shoulders. "What's the Slonim Society?"

"Slonim was the name of Grandpa's town in Russia. The men formed a society to help each other, follow traditions. They even volunteered with the fire department. Many of them came to America and they formed a burial society." She noticed my questioning look. "They prepared others for their journey into the next world." An uncomfortable expression crossed her face. She made a clacking noise with her false teeth.

"What next world?" She didn't answer me. "He touched dead people?" My eyebrows arched in recognition and surprise.

"Yes, he washed their bodies and wrapped them in gauze so they'd be ready."

I made a face. "Ready for what? That's disgusting."

She shook her head, more crumbs falling as she held another cracker between her lips. "I don't want to talk about it."

"But I want to know. My mother didn't like him." I followed her back and forth.

"Your grandfather was a complex man, very religious. In his village called a *shetl*, the men helped one another."

"I still don't understand." I swung my legs from the chair. A small scab on my knee drew my attention and I began to pick.

"According to Jewish law there can't be any material benefit from the dead. It's a function of the community to dispose of the body."

I guess all kids are fascinated with gory things. "You mean bury him? He took care of them when they died and now they helped him?"

"Right. He was called a *mitassekim*, a person who performs sacred tasks. It's an honor."

That got me. "An honor?"

"When someone died, the entire community stopped work. Do you remember we sat *shiva* for a week to mourn?"

"Oh, so that's what all the visiting and food was about. Exactly what did he do with the dead bodies?"

"Must you ask so many questions?" My grandmother resigned herself to answering my questions and sat down on the bed.

"In the Jewish faith there has to be a cleansing for the body after death. One time a neighbor lady said something that led me to believe your grandfather wasn't where he said he was on Sundays. I told him I wanted to go with him to see what he was doing. So he took me with him."

"We took the subway to Brooklyn and then walked a few blocks to a corner building. A nice lobby and then I had to go down stairs. In the white-tiled basement the Slonim Society, all the men from the temple, stood around the dead man dressed in his best suit. *Gottenyu*, it wasn't someone I knew. I stayed along the wall. I could hardly breathe. When was I ever so close to a dead person? They gathered around, said a prayer and asked for forgiveness." She stopped to eat some sugarless candies from her housecoat pocket and offered me one.

I shook my head. They tasted like rainbow pieces of rubber. "Why?"

"They undressed the person then asked for forgiveness for any indignity or embarrassment." I wanted to interrupt her and ask about why he'd be embarrassed if he was already dead, but I knew she'd stop the story. I gave her a satisfied look. "They also said a prayer in Hebrew asking God to forgive any sins the man committed. They never spoke except for a prayer after they put on rubber gloves to wash the body, the water splashing the white tile floor." She broke her reverie to look at me. "It has to be done in a certain order, the head, then the right side before the left side. Mr. Dreichspun cleaned the toenails and fingernails with a large wooden toothpick."

"Yuk." Fascinated, I asked, "Why did they do it?"

"Nathan said the Bible told us what to do and we had to follow it. My family lived in the city and didn't follow these customs."

"The Bible told them to wash people?"

"Yes. Of course in biblical times they didn't have a steel table to lay the person out so they put the bodies on rocks or in a natural cave."

"Mallory's grandfather died and they waited a week before they had the funeral." Mallory, my best friend at PS 127, liked to laugh. I couldn't wait to tell her this strange story.

"Probably people came from out of town. We have to bury the body right away except if it's the Sabbath or *Yom Kippur*." She saw my perplexed look. Who made up all these rules? "It was hot in Palestine in ancient times when they figured all this out." I started to giggle.

"I don't want to talk about it anymore. Your Grandfather was always gone. Everything was more important than to be with his children. When I saw what he was doing, washing dead bodies, I was so angry. 'For this you leave me alone with the children on Sundays? For this you stay out 'til all hours?' I never screamed at him like that before."

"What did he do?" My mother pooh-poohed her stories as *bubbe meyses*, grandmother's tales. Did she make all this up? Washing dead people?

"He shrugged his shoulders and fell asleep. Enough already."

My grandmother, fed up with my questions, picked up a *Photoplay* magazine and disappeared into the bathroom.

Chapter Four

Mimi

Miami Beach, 1959

With my grandmother's blessings my mother flew to Miami, rented an apartment on the beach to establish residency and filed for divorce under the more liberal Florida laws. I never knew all the details because they kept secrets. If I asked questions, they'd change the subject, switch to broken Yiddish, or tell me it wasn't my business.

After six months my mother emerged a divorcée, which meant more whispering. Nice Jewish girls didn't get divorces, especially when they had a child.

Isabella and Rachel picked over most of the furniture. Isabella took my grandmother's rococo velvet sofa, the dining room set, end tables, and lamps. Greta said she didn't want any of it. Rachel traveled from upstate New York to say goodbye to us and made arrangements to have her childhood bed and dresser shipped to Syracuse. Only a few things came with us.

We journeyed to the Sunshine State with two trunks, five suitcases and too many boxes to count. One huge package contained my grandmother's fancy gold mirror. We brought pots and pans, dishes, linens and clothes.

After a twenty-four hour train ride, where my grandmother packed enough food in wax paper for the entire car, we arrived to eternal brightness, the light gleaming on white buildings, palm trees, and wide beaches. People walked around half-naked, their bathing suits barely covering leathery tanned bodies.

In August 1959 our three generations of women inhabited a two-bedroom garden apartment on Meridian Avenue, a square pink edifice with white balconies and a tile roof. Saint Augustine grass, its sturdy sun-loving blades shooting toward the sky, stretched across the lawn. A wrought-iron fence separated Beach Colony Apartments from the sidewalk. Exotic red, pink and double-yellow hibiscus bushes hugged the building. When I walked outside our first night to glance at the clear stars, I smelled the sweet perfume of night-blooming jasmine, a scent I associated with a new beginning.

Exploring our new digs excited me. A few times a week we ate at Wolfie's, a New York style deli peopled with oldsters who shuffled to their seats and gorged on the complimentary kosher pickles in metal bowls on the table. Our regular waitress, Trudy, an ossified transplant from Jersey who spoke in a brash manner kept her foot tapping while we made up our minds. No other kids. Just me between my mother and grandmother.

My mother enrolled me at Ida Fisher Junior High. I rode the bus, my lunch bag gripped in my hand. My saving grace was that I was taller than the other seventh graders so they left me alone. Most of the kids knew each other from elementary school. Some girls with glossy lipstick and pert conical breasts sat together chatting in the cafeteria, a camaraderie encouraged by propinquity and time.

No one spoke to me the first few weeks but I was used to being alone. Eventually, I found some other outcasts and we clung together like seaweed embedded in driftwood. With Michaela, whose father wanted a boy, Bella, from a broken home like mine, and David, a clarinet player with bad skin and braces, we formed our own clique. I looked for them every morning outside the large banyan tree that shaded the school lawn, its exposed roots twisted into seats for us. We shared copies of words from Elvis Presley songs we heard on WQAM, passing them around like the Lifesavers I hid under my tongue.

My teachers exuded sunny attitudes, especially Mrs. Greenblatt, who taught English. She introduced me to John Steinbeck through *The Pearl*. Later I tackled *The Grapes of Wrath* and devoured *East of Eden*. When I saw the movie with James Dean, I was smitten.

My mother wanted to take driving lessons as soon as we could afford a car. Until then, we walked, took a cab, or rode the bus. I didn't miss the dirty subways or trains, vagrants loitering with their leering looks. Everything in Miami Beach was clean and fresh.

We explored the new freedom in our own ways. My mother went to work at a classy photo studio on 41st Street called Bacharach's. Studio portraits for prominent society people hung in the window with fancy frames. Big difference from Patchelli's and his opera music and cologne. Old man Bacharach had a son who wrote songs and was trying to make it big in Hollywood. From what I could tell no one thought it would happen.

A few weekends we took buses to Coconut Grove, a haven for creative types. The artist colony on the bay side faced Dinner Key, its boat slips filled with expensive yachts and pleasure vessels. At Key Biscayne a few miles away, we'd drag Grandma to Crandon Park zoo with its wide beaches. She'd cover herself in tanning oil and wear a bathing suit with a matching cover-up. My mother told her she looked like she was going to lounge at a cabana instead of walk around a zoo, but she didn't care. Unlike the Bronx zoo, a vendor sold snow cones, palm trees shaded monkey cages, and coconuts littered the ground.

Later, on the beach, I watched a man with a screwdriver punch a hole in the soft end of a green and brown mottled coconut. He handed it to his raisin-brown little boy to drink with a straw. Afterward he ripped away the sides with a hammer. Brown tufts of hair held a ball. I moved closer. When he split it open, he offered me a piece of the pure white meat. At first I shook my head, but then I relented. First I touched the rubbery texture, then I smelled it. I had no idea raw coconut meat would be so delicious. I felt like Robinson Crusoe.

Grandma, thrilled by her new space, decided to live. Since Argentina she felt more in command of her world. First, she changed her wardrobe, spending hours shopping on Collins Avenue and returning with shopping bags filled with pastel dresses or shifts, some with parrots and palm trees. Next, she changed herself.

One afternoon as I studied math at our Formica kitchen table, she asked, "How do I look?"

I didn't turn around right away. She'd adapted to Florida by wearing wedgies with cork soles, clear plastic on top, her toes squooshed inside. She carried a bag with fake colored jewels on the front, the white plastic handle over her arm.

"Mamala, tell me. What do you think?"

I flung my arm over the back of the chair to twist myself around. Platinum blonde! My grandma's hair was short with a curl over her forehead and swept off her neck in the back.

I didn't know what to say, then stammered, "You look glamorous. Very Kim Novak." I knew that was her favorite movie star.

She pulled a small bag of cashews from her purse and popped a few in her mouth. "It's okay?"

I got up to hug her.

"Nathan would never let me do this." She looked in the ornate, totally out of place mirror that hung over the sofa, the rest of the room decorated in rattan.

"You look sensational," I said. And she did.

That wasn't my mother's response when she came home from work. "Mama, what have you done?"

My grandma paraded back and forth in front of us, glancing in the mirror.

"I needed a lift. I went to Lincoln Road and found a beauty shop." She touched the back of her hair near her neck as though it couldn't have possibly been hers. "Mimi says I resemble Kim Novak."

My mother gave me a chagrined look and started dinner.

A few months later my grandma announced she had joined Slenderella, a weight loss salon. "Mama, how much money did you give them?"

My grandmother, sheepish, said, "A deposit. Two hundred fifty dollars."

My mother repeated the amount. "For how many weeks?"

"I don't know," she said in a small voice. "I think a year."

"Where's the paper you signed?" My mother searched a drawer in the kitchen. The hum of the air conditioner in the front window drowned out the undercurrents of annoyance.

As Grandma looked in her purse for the contract, a fake ruby became unglued and dropped to the floor. My mother sat across from me at the kitchen table with her glasses, hair pulled back into a ponytail. She leaned down to pick up the ruby. She studied the contract for a few minutes, then pulled off her glasses and laid them on the table next to the ruby. "This is for a year. Do you realize you just spent two thousand dollars?"

"What?"

"Yes. Look."

My grandmother, who never read it, began to sniffle. "I just wanted to be thin." I got up and hugged her again.

My mother waited until Saturday to march into Slenderella.

She consulted an attorney, but it was an iron-clad agreement. "They're thieves. Mama, don't sign anything unless I read it first. Promise me. Okay?"

But Grandma went anyway and lost twenty-five pounds.

She still wore her pink corset, "mine undergarment" she called it, so her stomach appeared flat and her bosom pushed higher.

One late afternoon as I stretched out on the pink and turquoise flamingo print cushions of the sofa, my grandmother pranced into the room, twirling her skirt. When I inquired as to where she was going in a new candy-striped shirtwaist dress, she said, "Don't tell your mother, but I'm starting Arthur Murray. I want to learn how to dance." She leaned across me to check the mirror for lipstick on her teeth, kissed me goodbye on my head, and pranced out the door.

"Where did she go?" my mother wanted to know when she got home. I shrugged my shoulders.

Later, while I was in bed under the covers reading a book with a flashlight, I heard them arguing. I crept out of bed and put my ear to the door.

"You're going to use up all your money with this nonsense. Have you ever heard of a budget?"

"My whole life has been a budget. Enough."

"What if the boys cut back your funds? Maybe the factory isn't doing so great. You need to plan ahead. How much did you spend on dance lessons?"

"Not so much." My grandma's voice muffled as the window air conditioner rumbled.

"How much?"

"Twenty-five hundred."

"Mama, Mama."

"It's for a year. I'm going to learn the tango."

I knew my uncles sent Grandma a monthly allowance from

the slipper business. They opened another factory in Jersey City to manufacture pillows, abandoning the idea of slippers in the Bahamas. At first the checks were regular. Then they'd call to say the money was going to be late because of a crisis–a delayed shipment or a supplier who didn't pay or a plumbing problem at home. The irregularity of it made for instability. If Grandma received a check, we went to Wolfie's. If it was delayed, we ate hot dogs.

Our first winter without snow, we slept with the windows open. I kept waiting for the skies to cloud over with a mask of gray that never happened. Even when it rained the clear skies burst through the clouds, a flower exploding in lush foliage. Sometimes sun showers arrived where the sky leaked and the sun smiled through the drops, as though it couldn't make up its mind whether to laugh or cry. Afterward, the air smelled fresh and the clean dampness hung like suspended butterflies, the leaves an unreal green.

Isaac and Max and their families arrived in February and stayed at the Delano on Collins Avenue, a hotel with a nice pool adjacent to the white beach. Excited to see my cousins, I showed off my tan. The adults exclaimed over how tall I'd gotten and my uncles teased me about my new bra and budding breasts. My mother took a day off work and I played hooky so we could take them to them Parrot Jungle. At the end of the week on their last evening, they dropped a bomb at dinner in the hotel's restaurant.

Isaac began just as our seven-layer chocolate cake arrived with coffee for the adults. Ernie played with the candle wax of a short taper in front of him. Isabella and Greta excused themselves to the ladies room. My two uncles moved over and filled in the empty seats so they'd be across from my grandmother.

Max looked away, then cleared his throat. "Mama, we have to cut back. Business is not what we thought it was. It's not expensive here like it is in the city. We have to send a little less."

"What's a little less?"

"Don't worry. You'll live. You'll have money for extras." Max looked at my grandma's hair.

My grandmother looked uncomfortable at the thought of anything impeding her good time. "What are you talking? Business is good. Your father left a big factory. Less?" She dabbed the corners of her eyes with her cloth napkin.

Isaac and Max exchanged glances. Max, newly married to Greta, continued.

"Mom, this is the way it has to be. You can't get blood from a stone. The business is not doing well. People don't want leather slippers anymore. They buy cheap plastic ones. Throwaways. We even saw rubber ones at the big shoe show. Something new called thongs. We haven't been able to switch over easily with our equipment. Look, you won't starve. We're still going to send you an allowance. Just not as much." Isaac unwrapped a cigar and squashed the cellophane in his hand. Crinkling, it fell to the tablecloth. He sat back in his chair to light it.

My mother burst into the conversation, leaning forward into the group, her hands placed flat. Even in anger her face remained lovely. "How can you justify taking Mama's money?" she hissed, above the clink of glasses, the tinkle of a piano, and waiters reaching between us to fluff the napkins of the absent parties.

"Look, stay out of this. Unless, of course, you're living off Mama's allowance, too," said my Uncle Isaac. Max's face froze. He placed his hand on his brother's arm.

"Isaac, watch what you say. Remember, we made an agreement."

"What agreement?" my mother wanted to know.

My Uncle Isaac half-stood and leaned across the table. "To not offend you, you blood sucker."

"You can call me names, but it doesn't erase the fact that you've run Nathan's business into the ground."

"Listen, Miss Know-It-All, you were supposed to help keep her on a budget and we find out she's signed up for Slenderella and dancing lessons."

"Shaa. Quiet. People are looking," my grandmother said.

My uncles ignored her. "After all she's been through you think I'm going to tell her she can't have some fun?" My mother's face turned ugly, her mouth contorted in anger.

"Fun? You're worried about fun? We're fighting for our lives with this business, you ingrate."

"You . . ." My mother's words sputtered, her cheeks flushed with rage, as she took my grandmother's part. Before I knew it, she pushed back her chair that fell over as she stood up, grabbed my hand, and urged Grandma to follow her. With long strides, her arms swinging, she brushed by my aunts returning to the table. Other diners watched, their heads turning to follow us.

While we waited in the circular driveway outside the Delano for a cab I tried to fade into a concrete column. I hated embarrassing situations. My mother paced back and forth and my grandmother wept.

My mother fumed for hours while my grandmother sat on the sofa wringing her hands, an occasional squeaky sob punctuating the silence. I retreated to the bedroom with *The Old Man and the Sea*, my English assignment. The relatives returned to New York without saying goodbye.

Chapter Five

Mimi

If my uncles sent less money, I never noticed. My grandmother continued her dance lessons, often enlisting my help to lace up her corset. With her hands on her waist she'd push backward and hold her breath while I pulled in the back. She claimed it gave her an hour-glass figure. After she dressed she'd tip her L'Heure Bleue bottle onto her middle finger, dab the back of each ear, her wrists and cleavage and sashay out the door.

Months later as I slouched into a multi-color webbed aluminum chair outside our door with David and Michaela studying for final exams, my grandmother showed up in a big white shirt and pedal pushers, an elderly gentleman in tow. With a deep tan like a barbequed lobster, he sported a straw hat and a shirt that ballooned in the breeze, a riot of flapping hibiscus blossoms.

"Mimi, I want you should meet Alberto Roselli." My grandmother touched his arm and tilted her head toward him. I couldn't see her eyes behind her oversized sunglasses.

I nodded. He instructed me to call him Al. Michaela and David became absorbed in their notebooks. Embarrassed at my grandmother's flirtation I buried my head in my notebook.

"We met at Arthur Murray," my grandmother said, as though I needed to know that. She waited for my response. I was dumbfounded.

Al nodded, folding my grandmother's arm into his, gray hair exploding from the top of his shirt. In an Italian accent, he said, patting her hand, "Your grandmother is a wonderful dancer. Does a mean merengue."

She smiled at the compliment. "Al's staying for dinner," she said when they turned to go into the apartment. Michaela giggled, David did a fake cough, and I rolled my eyes.

When I went inside my grandmother and Al were sitting on the sofa holding hands. I never thought about her having a boyfriend. Apparently, neither did my mother.

The expression on her face exhibited more than surprise. I could tell from her look she wasn't happy about another person complicating our lives. A light sea breeze moved the white chiffon curtains in front of the jalousie windows.

"Mimi, help me get dinner together." I followed her into the kitchen, a small room with little counter space and no room for more than two people. "You start the salad," she said in a normal tone of voice. Then, she motioned me closer and asked, "Who the hell is he? She's got a suitor?"

I shrugged my shoulders. The world of adults was incomprehensible to me.

During our red snapper dinner we learned Al's son lived in Miami. He said, "My wife, may she rest in peace, came with me to America in the 1930s, before things got too bad in Milano. My son has a men's clothing store on Lincoln Road. I worked there a few days a week."

"Isn't Al a snappy dresser?" my grandmother asked us. I nodded yes. I silently swore I'd never go out with anyone who wore flowered shirts.

Within weeks Al became a fixture in our apartment. He lived a few blocks away, so he'd stroll in late morning, straw hat pushed back on his head to reveal a thinning pate, in bathing trunks, a striped towel under his arm, carrying a small cooler. "For the beach," he'd tell me while he waited for my grandmother to emerge from the bedroom in a wide-brimmed hat, sunglasses, and her wedgies. Once I caught them in the kitchen smooching, their arms entwined around each other. I didn't know old people kissed.

With school out I checked for snacks in our humming Frigidaire many times during the day. Even *American Bandstand* got boring. Besides salami, kosher pickles and tubs of cream cheese for Sunday morning bagels, Al's seltzer bottles leaned against bottles of my grandmother's insulin in the door. I only saw her give herself an injection once when I interrupted her in the bathroom. I don't know how she put a needle in her thigh every day but she did.

I searched among the strange fruits and vegetables my mother insisted we try. I loved mangoes, parrot-colored and delicious, even though they left strings between my teeth. Papayas, looked like mangoes on the inside with glossy black seeds, but tasted awful. My mother turned sticky sweet guavas into jam. She also bought kumquats, small, oval and orange, too sour to eat and okra, a vegetable that looked like miniature slimy Coke bottles. She defended her experimentation by saying, "We're living in a tropical place and have to sample what it has to offer." So we washed the skins, sliced it up, the pungent smells escaping and tried everything raw first. Once, miniscule fruit flies invaded. We sprayed until I coughed myself hoarse.

Our apartment became smaller. Eventually, my mother complained about a lack of privacy with Al hovering around all the time. "Why can't you watch TV at his place?" my mother wanted to know.

"What? And have the neighbors talk that I'm there alone with a man?"

My mother's mouth looked sarcastic, but her speech was respectful. "You're here alone with him. Besides, it doesn't matter.

We don't know anyone. Who's to disapprove?"

At the end of the summer my mother came home and announced she'd found a job taking pictures for *The Coconut Grove Express,* a small publication that covered city politics and high-profile people. She gave notice at Bacharach's, bought a used blue Ford with a few rusted spots that sat on the street, signed up for the long awaited driving lessons and prepared to venture into new territory. Al volunteered to take her to the lessons, which I thought was nice of him since he had to borrow his son's car.

By the time I started back to school after Labor Day in the muggy heat, my mother was driving across the Julia Tuttle Bridge and bringing home stories of a world inhabited by bohemians, artists, businessmen, and society ladies. With Al hanging around all the time, she stayed late at work. It wasn't that she didn't like him, although his accent drove me crazy, he was just in the way, his feet up on the coffee table sipping his seltzer, shirtless on the sofa.

On Saturdays, in the last ounce of Sabbath twilight, my grandmother and Al, his remaining hairs pouffed in the front by Brylcreem at her suggestion, left for a walk. She was happy. Al didn't have my grandfather's energy or drive. He lived on a fixed income doled out by his son, Burton, a portly man in his forties with sallow, pockmarked cheeks and a penchant for flowered shirts too.

One afternoon when my grandmother treated me to new patent leather school shoes from Mary Jane and a white pique dress from DiPinna's, we stopped at Burton's store to say hello. He greeted my grandmother and then left to wait on a customer. I don't know if he was pleased or not with their relationship, he never smiled much, but he didn't verbally object. By the time we walked home, the new shoes had given me blisters and I was limping.

"I must take you to Rome, the winding streets of Florence,

my birthplace in Milano. I haven't been back in years," Al told my grandmother as they sat on the sofa holding hands one afternoon.

She warned me not to ask about his past. "He's had a sad life, leaving Italy, losing his wife."

"You've had a sad life, too. You lost your husband and had to leave Poland." I paused before I asked, "What happened to your family? Why didn't you go back?" When I asked before, she ignored or shooed me away. This time, her blue-violet eyes stared at me.

"Mamala, I don't want to talk about it. Nathan came back and forth twelve times to get me. Finally, I arrived with your mother and Uncle Isaac in 1929. I never went back even though I tried. By the time I could make such a trip, it was too late. The Nazis killed everyone. No one was left except Malka who escaped to Argentina. I'm alone in the world."

"You have me and Mom," I said trying to cheer her. She looked away. "Why did the Nazis hate them? No one will tell me."

She touched my shoulder. "Sweetheart, I can't talk about it. Too upsetting for me. I'm sorry you haven't had a better education. Don't drag up the past. I just want to be happy now. Besides, your mother's still rebelling against your grandfather. She bristles every time I bring up his name."

"But, what was your mother like? I know I was named after her. What did your father do?" I had more questions, but she cut me off.

"I'm going to get some fresh air," she said and left fanning herself with a *Screenplay* movie magazine.

When my mother came home, I asked her about Nazis. "Really, Mimi, must we talk about his now? I just walked in the door." She pushed hair off her forehead with the back of her hand, the heat in the apartment stifling us, then busied herself tearing lettuce for a salad in the kitchen, her back to me. She took out strange fruits to add to it.

"Well, when? No one wants to tell me anything." I felt sulky, my bottom lip sinking. I sat on a chair and kicked my feet back and forth.

"Look, it's in the past and that's where we're leaving it. They murdered twelve million people, six million of them Jews. Your great-grandparents and the rest of the family were among them." She became impatient and reached for a cigarette, pulling a piece of tobacco from her lip. She turned to face me and pulled over a wooden stool re-covered in brown vinyl. The ash from her cigarette grew until it dropped on the floor.

"I don't understand why they killed them. And why won't anybody talk about it? And how come I don't go to Sunday school like David and Michaela?"

"Why are you confronting me with this today?" My mother's voice rose, irritated with my inquisitiveness.

"Because I want to know. There are too many secrets in this family. I can't talk about my father. You freeze up when I mention him. No one will tell me about grandma's family. Why aren't you teaching me anything about Judaism?" I felt relieved getting everything out. I pushed the cuticle on my thumb.

My mother placed her cigarette on the ashtray next to the washed vegetables. I watched the back of her, her shoulders stiffened in her blouse, her tan legs young-looking. "I'm not going to give you a history lesson. Go to the library and start reading about what happened to the Jews during World War Two in Europe. Research Germany, Austria, Poland. Our family was swept away like dust. It's painful for your grandmother to talk about it because she had such an idyllic life in Poland."

I interrupted her. "Why didn't she go back? Don't you remember anything?"

"She tried, but it didn't work out." Her tone softened. "I remember my grandparents and the apartment house we lived in. That life is gone forever. For all of us. Anyway, after the war, the Yiddish newspaper I worked for sent me to photograph the Displaced Persons camps. To record what happened. I stopped believing in God. I'm an atheist. If there's a God that could allow that level of human suffering to happen, then I don't want any part of him." She stopped abruptly, blinking. Her eyes, watery with memories or smoke, looked away from me.

"Can I see the photos you took?"

"I don't think they're appropriate for a child to look at. They're raw, upsetting."

"I'm almost fourteen years old. I want to see them." I felt like stamping my foot. The room felt claustrophobic, uncontrollable demons crowding me toward dark, windowless places. My mother's feet shifted in her ballerina flats.

The stool scraped the linoleum floor and her skirt twirled as she stood up. She took another drag from her cigarette, put it out in the ashtray and turned back to her food preparation.

The next morning, four leather bound albums lay among the clutter on the dresser I shared with my mother. I opened the one on top and saw her handwriting in blue ink on the inside cover. BERGEN-BELSEN, 1946." Before I was born. I flipped through the black and white photos encased in plastic pages, some accompanied by yellowed newspaper clippings with Hebrew writing. Sad, dirty faces, emaciated bodies, and lost dreams. Was this what was haunting this family?

Chapter Six

Mimi

Once again, my grandmother prepared for a long trip. Only, this time, she wasn't going alone. And, if she had any money worries, she didn't share them. My mother expressed concerned though.

"Mama, who's paying for such a grand escape? Al?"

"Don't fret, Sarah. I've taken care of everything." She continued to take folded nylon nightgowns out of her dresser drawer and stack them on the bed. I sat curled up on her pillows, peeling purple nail polish off my toes.

"Are you paying for this? Is Burton? Mama, who's footing the bill?"

"Sarah, stop it. You're spoiling my fun. I want to have a good time."

"I hope you know what you're doing."

For the most part I stayed out of the way, babysitting for a young couple with a chubby baby girl a few doors away. After passport photos, itineraries, telegrams to Al's friends, new luggage, and lots of clothes, she and Al, abuzz with excitement, left on an early Saturday in June for Rome. Burton, their chauffeur to the airport, honked for them in his aqua Cadillac convertible, a sour look on his face.

After they left, I realized how much I missed my sweet grandma with her thin band of tragedy, its invisible wrappings that made her fragile. My personal sounding board left on vacation for three months.

The school year drew to a close as a blanket of hot, sticky summer weather descended into every corner we inhabited. The dark recesses of my closet held living things, the stickiness seeping into damp shadows. Green mold sprouted in our shoes and shower. Swarming mosquitoes made evening walks impossible. My mother and I returned from a stroll to Burdines, my favorite department store, with raised red bumps on our arms and legs. Worse, palmetto bugs launched surprise attacks. One, the largest bug I had ever seen, scuttled across our kitchen floor. I jumped on the sofa shrieking for help and almost fainted when it lifted itself into flight to buzz near my head. What kind of a place was this that grew giant bugs and creeping mildew?

With my grandmother gallivanting and my mother working during the day, if I wasn't babysitting, I retreated into library books. I wanted to find answers to the upsetting pictures in my mother's albums. I searched through tomes about what happened to the Jews during World War II and viewed photographs that were worse than I could have imagined. When I tried to ask questions my mother refused to discuss the past. I began to comprehend her reluctance.

I picked up a paperback book at the bus station, the transcript of the monster Adolph Eichmann's trial in 1961 and subsequent hanging. At least he was dead. Israeli agents kidnapped him at work in Buenos Aires where he had been living as Ricardo Clement and flew him to Israel to stand trial. The world learned he was responsible for the death of millions in concentration camps.

It was the most depressing summer of my life. What I read shocked me. How could my family keep something so monumental from me? As a kid I didn't read the newspaper and neither did they. I thought about times my grandmother turned off the TV with a sigh and changed the subject.

I asked Michaela about Nazis and she said her neighbors had tattoos of numbers on their arms. I began to look at everyone's skin between the elbow and wrist in stores, at the library, even at the beach or bowling alley. Then I realized the couple with the Viennese accent at the small deli where we bought bagels, lox and cream cheese for Sunday morning brunch had numbers on their arm. No wonder they seemed so sad. Instead of breezing in and out I spent more time asking them about the weather, hoping for a confession about the past.

David said his grandparents, Holocaust survivors from Hungary, lost everything and everyone. I shared what I learned about Eichmann but he already knew.

"My *zayde* says Eichmann summoned Hungarian leaders to a meeting in forty-four to discuss a troop withdrawal. As soon as President von Horthy arrived, Hitler arrested him and sent Jews to the gas chambers in Auschwitz. My grandparents survived and started over in Cleveland as grocers."

"How did your grandpa escape?" I wanted to know. It seemed miraculous to me.

"His parents were taken away and he never saw them again, but he hid in damp basements for days, then escaped to the woods to join the partisans."

"Partisans?"

"Groups of people who lived in the forests and tried to rise up against their oppressors. Most were caught." He sighed and I could tell this was depressing him, too. "Eventually he was picked up and sent to a different camp and was liberated by the Russians. He met my grandma in a DP camp."

The pictures in my mother's albums haunted me. The aftermath. Where David's grandpa and grandma met. Those nice older people with silver hair? He told me his grandfather lectured to school children about why they shouldn't hate.

Bella knew more than anyone because she had been to Sunday school and *bat mitzvahed*. She knew Hebrew and *Kaddish*, the prayer for the dead. She loaned me books by survivors with testimonials.

At first, devastated at how tragic it all was, I then became angry that no one had shared any of it with me. After a while I couldn't read any more or look at horrible pictures. I wanted to escape.

When I confronted my mother, who worked long hours at the paper, she didn't want to discuss the past.

"Mimi, give me a break. I spend all day working and smiling at my boss," she told me kicking off her shoes as she settled in to watch her favorite show, *I Love Lucy*, with a TV dinner in an aluminum tray on a stack table.

"Lucy's funny," she said stuffing her mouth with shriveled peas.

The news of what had happened to my grandmother's parents and the rest of her family haunted me. Even if I didn't know them. I stopped sleeping through the night, waking at four a.m., sweaty with nightmares of Nazis chasing me. I'd turn my light on and read until my heart stopped racing, the thumping a reminder of storm trooper's boots and screams of people being taken away in the night.

If it hadn't been for my Grandpa Nathan insisting my grandmother come to America, none of us would have survived. My mother and Uncle Isaac would have been killed with a million other children. We'd all be dead. I wouldn't exist. I couldn't imagine the void created by the lack of our existence, yet I knew that's what happened to millions of other families. Destroyed dreams, lost lives, careers dashed, talents gone. An entire generation stopped in its tracks.

Finally, after I examined the facts dozens of times, a multiple mirror of monstrous images, and couldn't change the outcome, I put it away. Away into the recesses of my mind where I couldn't pick at it every day. Time to leave my nightmares of Nazis hunting me behind. Who would want to kill me? But who wanted to kill Miriam and Meyer? My friends were relieved when I shut down my paranoia. Fun for them was the beach or the air-conditioned bowling alley.

With a dozen postcards from Italy, England, and France on the front of our refrigerator, my grandmother let us know she'd be coming home as the summer drew to a close.

My grandmother and Al arrived a few weeks after Labor Day. Burton invited us to pick them up in his Cadillac. Pretty snazzy. I sat in the back, my arm stretched out on the turquoise seat with white piping, smiling at red lights, the sun sprinkling freckles on my skin. My mother looked uncomfortable next to Burton. After initial talk about the traffic, they were quiet on the ride over the MacArthur Causeway to the airport in Miami. Probably neither of them was thrilled about the romance between their parents.

At the airport my grandmother's platinum hair stood out in the crowd as we watched her through the glass window outside Customs. Even from afar her looks were striking. With a push though the doors and shopping bags on her arms, she rushed toward me. I was hugged with such enthusiasm I groaned. My mother hung back a little then reached to kiss her cheek. Al stood there holding my grandmother's cosmetic case, a satisfied smile on his face. Burton moved forward to embrace his dad.

"How ya' doin', Pop?" Burton said, patting Al on the back, a small sign of affection.

"Good. I'm good," Al said nodding as though he had to decide.

"Guess what we did?" My grandmother reached back to pull Al forward. Her accent made her sound like one of the Gabor sisters. As a self-conscious teenager I knew people were looking at our strange group. "We got married!" She thrust her hand forward, a diamond solitaire gleaming and behind it an elaborate gold band with a filigree of vines.

At first no one moved. I blinked in surprise. Then I reached for my grandmother and Al's hands. I started to jump up and down, yelling, "That's so exciting. Congratulations!"

Burton's mouth dropped open, his hangdog expression appalled.

My mother didn't smile. "Why didn't you let us know?" she asked my grandmother.

"Better we should surprise you. Al asked me and I said yes right away. A rabbi in Rome performed the ceremony in a small garden. His wife and daughters witnessed."

Burton, who remained frozen, cleared his throat. "Pop, why didn't'cha tell me?"

Al took an intense interest in his feet, his shoulders slumped forward. After a few moments he pulled his posture taller. Softly, he said, "At my age I don't have to ask permission."

"Where are you going to live?" my mother wanted to know.

"Come on. Let's get your luggage," Burton said, urging us along.

My grandmother spoke to my mother as they stepped onto the escalator that took us to the lower level. I stepped on behind them, the black steps rolling down, never stopping. "We haven't figured everything out yet, but it's silly to keep two places. I thought maybe we'd let go of his apartment and he could move into ours."

My mother's face fell. "What about us?"

"I thought maybe you and Mimi would get a place of your own, closer to your work. So you don't have to travel so far."

My face flushed. "Wait a minute. I can't switch schools when I'm so close to finishing." I felt like a pawn.

"Don't get excited." My grandmother tapped my mother's arm as we watched for their luggage. Al stood with his hands in his pockets. "Shaa, shaa, Sarah, give me a hug. It will all work out. Aren't you happy for me?" She looked at her ring again.

My mother smiled at her. "Whatever makes you happy, Mama, makes me happy." I could tell from her voice she wasn't happy at all. She grabbed my grandmother's valise and followed Burton's shuffle to the car. We made a strange parade under the melting sun.

"I brought you wonderful presents, a scarf for your mother and a carved cameo for you," my grandmother said to me over her shoulder as she and Al held hands.

Chapter Seven

Mimi

Miami Beach, 1964

After a great deal of discussion my grandmother and Al moved to his place and I moved into her bedroom. She wasn't happy about his plebian furniture, but we convinced her new drapes and a change of carpeting would bring it up to her standards. She also convinced him to give up his rubber-soled Hush Puppies and wear Italian sandals. Finally, I had a space of my own. I painted one wall purple, put up posters of the Beatles, set up a bookshelf and bought a beanbag chair with my babysitting money.

High school started and I felt like an adult.

The year before, while I was in ninth grade President Kennedy was assassinated before Thanksgiving vacation. My mother and I cried for hours, clinging to each other like two shipwrecked souls abandoned at sea. It sobered us and the nation. I spent hours in my room writing morose poems.

By the time tenth grade rolled around, I gave up trying to fit in with my contemporaries. I didn't have the right clothes, two parents or cute hair. The budget wasn't there for the clothes. My mother worked, I had no father to speak of and my grandmother had just married a guy who wore a gold chain and sat in the sun too much. My blonde hair, yellowed from the sun, frizzed around my face. No amount of hair spray helped humidity. Worse, in Florida learner's permits to drive were issued at fourteen and my mother wouldn't let me get one.

"Mimi, I'm not an advocate of children driving. They let fourteen-year-olds get married in Georgia. Does that make it right? Maybe next year."

I still hung out with Michaela and Bella, but we never had classes together. David got teased too much for being with a group of girls so he abandoned us for the tennis team. He looked cooler than we did in his whites and a racket over his shoulder. His pimples even started to clear up.

Finally, my depression turned to anger. Why did my mother leave my father and New York? She wrecked our lives. At least if I had stayed in the city I could have taken the subway, gone to museums, stolen into a matinee. I was pissed off at everyone, even my grandmother who seemed so happy in her new life with Al fussing over her. It made me want to throw up. And, I could see they were going through the rest of her money like a sieve.

In eleventh grade I wore the same black T-shirt for days at a time and lined my eyes with a black pencil. I also began to smoke, stealing cigarettes from my mother's Marlboro pack. At first they made me sick but I was determined. I thought I looked cool in the glass reflection of a window taking a drag. I hoarded matches in a shoebox in my bottom drawer, sneaking outside behind the laundry room to puff and think about how I ended up in this godforsaken hellhole of mildew and moths.

I avoided Bella and Michaela at lunchtime and hung with a group of misfits who shared cigarettes behind the gym. Bella had a boyfriend named Norman with a car so she dropped me anyway. What a nebbish. My friends bored me, my mother worked too many hours and I needed some excitement. Good girl was over.

1965. Hundreds of protesting Negroes were arrested in Selma, Alabama. The Reverend Dr. Martin Luther King directed the demonstration from his jail cell. George Wallace, the governor, a staunch segregationist, spouted hateful rhetoric. We didn't have any Negroes in our school, let alone living on Miami Beach. Maids had to be off the street by curfew. I hated living in the south.

My peer group didn't care about injustice. News to them was that Murph the Surf was arrested in Miami for stealing over $400,000 in gems, including the Star of India, the largest sapphire in the world, from The Museum of Natural History. Big deal.

In "my dark phase" I met up with Tony Fassouli, another transplanted New Yorker, who thought all the sunshine and clothes-horse kids were shit, too. He sat across the aisle from me in math and started sending me funny cartoon drawings of the teacher. At first I ignored him. Then I took a second look. Cute. In a *West Side Story* George Chakiris way.

He walked me to my next class, waited for me after gym. Next he offered me a ride. Better than the bus. I didn't think my mother would like the idea of me riding in a car with a boy so I didn't mention it.

Tony and I hung out together sharing cigarettes and homework assignments, although he didn't study much. A tall skinny kid with thick dark eyebrows and black eyes, his wavy black hair, cut sleek on the sides, ran straight across the back of his neck. Sometimes he'd comb it into a DA, just to see if any of the teachers would notice. With jeans slung low on his hips, his swaggering long legs shot out in front of him. He was the first guy I ever knew who didn't wear socks with his loafers. I thought he was the coolest guy who ever lived. I also think he thought I was faster than I was because of the way I dressed and my tough attitude. The truth was I knew nothing. Nothing.

The first time he kissed me we were in the back of the auditorium during lunch going over our Algebra II assignment. I was helping him. His hand grazed mine and a warm rush passed through me. With an extended look, he grabbed my hand, pulled me up and dragged me behind a pillar so someone entering wouldn't be able to see us. He boxed me in with his arms, leaning toward me. I felt his warm breath, his lips touching mine.

At first the kisses were gentle. My legs felt like melted butter. As his mouth searched mine, his tongue prying between my teeth, his hips began a grind. The movement felt so natural to me. With his long fingers reaching under my shirt, his hand explored my breast. They grabbed my nipple through my bra and another surge of warmth and wet spilled into my rapid breathing. I couldn't even make an effort to stop him. I felt as though my heart would break out of my chest. So this is what "turned on" meant.

Fear made me push him away before someone caught us. We stood inches apart, our rapid pants making me feel like we had completed an athletic event. He took my hand and we sat down again. He leaned toward my ear, his nose nuzzling me and said, "You're hot." I blushed, the redness inching from my neck to my face, a mask of flattered embarrassment.

Tony drove me home later that week and invited himself in so we could continue our love-fest on the sofa. Upright at first, soon our bodies stretched out, him on top of me. Before I realized how far things had gone, my blouse was bunched up under my head as a pillow, his kisses showered my breasts and hands danced in and out of the elastic on my underwear. My face burned from his unshaven chin.

I whispered to him through my heaving breaths, "You're not a virgin, are you?"

He propped himself up on his arm to look at me. He laughed with a sexy grin. He shook his head in disbelief. "Are you?"

I nodded yes. His eyebrows rose in surprise. "We can fix that."

What a set up for my mother to walk in on.

"What are you doing?" Her voice reached the upper registers as I grabbed for my shirt. "Who is this?"

I couldn't speak at first. "Tony. Tony Fassouli, my mother."

He scrambled to his feet, jeans lower than his underwear. "How do you do? Ma'am."

"Don't Ma'am me. Get out. What's that on my daughter's neck?"

My hand slapped the hickey, a red-purple present from yesterday's make-out session. Tony grabbed his shirt, slung it over his shoulder, waved goodbye to me, and sauntered for the door.

"What kind of *schberniks* are you hanging around with? Don't you know you can get pregnant? God forbid you end up in my situation."

"What situation?"

"Never mind." She waved me away, her brow in a deep crease. "I don't want to see him around here again. Do you understand?" She turned around, her back to me and then spoke again, her voice calmer. "Maybe we better see a gynecologist. I don't know if he'll give the pill to a teenager but I'm not taking any chances. That's all we'd need is another kid around here."

"I'm not going to get pregnant. We're not even doing it."

"Yet. I saw the way he looked at you. They all want it. I'm making an appointment for you." She stormed outside and leaned over the balcony, maybe to make sure he was really gone, and lit a cigarette.

I avoided him the next few weeks, but he was persistent. The last day of school before summer vacation, I waited for the bus long after most of the school had emptied out. I stayed to help my favorite teacher, Mrs. Sapp who taught honors English, pack up her books and clean her boards. Tony pulled up in his car and leaned his arm out the window. Two girls next to me giggled while they signed each other's yearbooks.

"How 'bout a ride?"

I shook my head.

"Come on. I won't bitecha'."

I looked down the street past dry cleaning stores, a soda hangout, and a doctor's office. No bus in sight. I looked out at the sky, clouds gathering in layers, a light drizzle leaving spots of rain on my library book. The girls next to me ran into a deli. I walked over to his car, a 1960 Oldsmobile with whitewall tires. Tony leaned across the leather bench seat and opened the passenger door for me with a grin.

We didn't say much the first five minutes. His Canoe cologne wafted past me. The rain came down harder while the windshield wipers swished in a rhythm. My heart, steady and scared, pumped. He drove through puddles at twenty miles an hour and he turned on the radio. Bob Dylan's scratchy voice wailed "Mister Tambourine Man." I preferred The Supremes and their new hit, "Stop! In the Name of Love," but Tony was singing along and I didn't think he'd like it if I switched radio stations. I relaxed and put my notebook on the floor. What was the big deal getting a ride? Better than getting drenched.

"See? I'm going to be a gentleman and take you home." The sky turned deep gray as the storm pelted the car in big, fat drops. Tony pulled over two blocks from our apartment into a side street overgrown with sea grape bushes and frangipani trees, their pink blossoms tossed in the wind. The engine came to a halt.

"Can't leave the radio on cause it'll run down the battery."

The windows fogged with our breath as we sat in the silence. The ominous sky soaked day into night, an inkblot of dampness and eerie light.

Tony reached his arm across the back of the seat to play with my shoulder and hair. "No, I really can't," I told him. "Besides, my mother doesn't want me near you."

"Why? I'm not such a bad guy. Why doesn't she like me?"

I gave him a look that said, "You're trouble."

He leaned back against the seat, his hands behind his head, moving his legs to my side. He pretended to doze. Outside it got darker in increments. No one was around in this weather. I looked at his profile, remembering what one of the cheerleaders, Maxie Rosen said as he sauntered down the hall. "A skinny Elvis, only hotter, huh?"

"So, can you and me get back together?" He looked toward me with hope in his eyes, the lashes longer than I remembered.

I didn't answer. I wasn't as enamored of him as I was the way he made me feel, a warm sensation rocking through my body, hungry for his kiss, his fingers.

Within minutes we advanced to where we left off on my couch. His praying mantis legs leaped into the back seat and he motioned me to join him. I looked out through the steamed window and couldn't see a thing. The deluge hadn't let up, a steady downpour of tropical rain, the inside windows fogged with our breath.

My panties slipped off easily beneath my khaki skirt. Tony reached for my hand and placed it on his cock. Hard and big. I was afraid to speak. How was it going to fit inside me? And what if I did something dumb? A streak of lightning illuminated us. A clap of thunder started a new round of thumping rain on the hood of the car. He moved on top of me. I felt a thrusting between my legs damp with my own wetness. It matched the syncopation of the rain. His fingers stroked my hair as he murmured, "Mimi, Mimi, my little Mimi." Tony separated into his own world, eyes closed, breathing hard, his mouth contorted. I looked to see where he was going. A guttural moan changed to a muted scream. His body went limp on mine, his heart pounding like a solo drummer.

"Tony? You okay?"

"Yeah, I'm fine. Wow, you're great. What a beauty." He looked at his watch. "Ohmigod. It's late. My brother needs the car and I've got to get you home."

Amid the flurry of re-positioning our clothes, wondering what to do with the gushy stuff, searching for a tissue, climbing into the front seat, I realized, I wasn't a virgin anymore. The glop of tissues I stuffed into the bottom of my purse spotted blood. A fleeting sadness swam by me that wasn't love, but I cheered myself with the thought that I had gotten rid of an albatross. A warm glow flowed to my cheeks. I was a woman.

A storm surge pounded the car as I slammed the door and ran for our apartment drenched with rain, sweat and a new love.

Chapter Eight

Mimi

I suppose I could have rebelled when my mother insisted Tony go away, but I decided I didn't want a boyfriend that much. He pushed me too fast and I began to panic. I felt smothered by his attention, his waiting for me a block from our apartment, wanting to know what I was doing. He followed me all summer. A few times I gave in and we coupled in the back seat of his car, but I wouldn't let him near my home. I made him use a rubber and he complained bitterly.

"It's like taking a shower with a raincoat on."

My mother thought he was trouble and she was right.

In the fall I saw him near my locker and told him we were breaking up.

"You're dumpin' me? You gotta be kidding." He leaned into me, his arms on either side of my head. He glanced down.

"Tony, I don't want a boyfriend right now."

He smirked at me. "I'm as good as it gets, baby."

His eyes, large and flirtatious, gave me the once over. Was I making a mistake? I ducked under his arm, my heart rattling. I hustled away, my books to my chest in an effort to quiet the thunder. No, he was too dumb. I didn't want to be doing his homework the rest of the year.

At first, he sulked, called my house a few times and then

hung up. Soon he found someone else. Besides, I didn't like the way the other girls whispered when I changed in the locker room. He sent me notes, but I crumpled them up. A boyfriend took too much time. My mother escorted me to the doctor anyway. I put the pills in my bottom drawer.

I stopped wearing eyeliner and joined my old friends in their pursuits. We made beach bonfires, scattering when the police showed up and spent hours at the bowling alley. Bella dumped Norman the Nebbish so she, Michaela and I went to watch David's tennis matches. We were in a different survival mode now. We just wanted to make it through the school year.

On Saturdays my mother scoured the rental section of *The Miami Herald*, relaxed in our rattan lounge chair covered with pink flamingoes. I thought she was just curious but it turned out she had a plan. My grandmother stopped by for a visit without Al one afternoon, a shopping bag on her arm.

"Al's working with Burton today," she told us adjusting her Merry Widow bra under her red and white Swiss polka-dotted dress with spaghetti straps. She opened the bag to show us her purchase, linen hand towels with embroidered pastel flowers made in China from one of the *tchotke* shops on Lincoln Road.

My mother made a face. "Mom, you told me you were going to stay out of those places." She turned over the towels, then moved into the kitchen to get ingredients for soup and pulled out a chair at the table.

I loved the tourist shops on Lincoln Road, their shelves displayed with cheap tape recorders, baroque crystal lamps, shellacked blowfish, beach towels, cameras made in Japan, statues of Chinese warriors painted gold, cellophane bags of baby starfish and conch shells, their pink lip waiting to be grasped to hear the sound of the sea. Treasures. All treasures.

"I've decided to move to the Grove," my mother announced chopping an onion. She wiped her eyes with the back of her hand.

I gathered a towel and sunglasses for the beach. Examining

myself in the full-length mirror behind the bathroom door, I pulled my elbows into my sides to create cleavage. My bathing suit, a black-and-white gingham two-piece with a ruffled top, made me feel twelve and look seven. I moved closer to pull at an angry pimple on my chin. Best to leave it alone.

My grandmother joined my mother at the kitchen table to chop celery and carrots for our community chicken soup.

"Al's had a sniffle for weeks. Wait. You're moving? How will I see you and Mimi?"

I spoke up. "I'm not going. I have friends here. It's not fair to make me start over again." I felt a panicky bile creep into my throat. A fury hammered in my head. Why did I have to be the one that adjusted to everyone's changes?

My mother, a cigarette hanging from her lip, handed me my mixture of Johnson's baby oil and iodine to get an even tan. She took another drag on her cigarette.

"Ladies, ladies, don't get excited. We can make it work. Mimi, you'll love it there. Lots of artist studios and guitar players. No wedgies," she said looking under the table at my grandmother's feet. "I'm looking for a place off the main drag. What if you stayed with Grandma and Al until you finished the school year? I'm working long hours and come home late. Spend the weekends with me. I'm not far. We can talk on the phone every day. Just like you do with Michaela and Bella."

"Sarah, you didn't ask me. You just announce this *mashugana* idea. What if Al doesn't like it?" My grandmother touched her throat. "We like our privacy."

Privacy? Did that mean they did it? I was grossed out.

"Mama, Al won't mind if you present it the right way. Take over my lease here so Mimi can keep her room. It's only for six months."

My grandmother got up to add her vegetables to the chicken boiling on the stove. She wiped her hands on a dishtowel.

"I don't know," she said, her eyes crinkled with worry.

I knew I didn't like being shuffled around, but I didn't know why exactly. Did I feel abandoned, like when my father took off? Or just embarrassed that I wasn't going to live with my father or mother? And who wanted to hang around with two old people who kissed all the time?

"Mama, your place is smaller and more expensive because you have a fancy address near Surfside. This place will cost you less and you'll have more room. And, Mimi won't have to change schools. Please?" My mother's voice begged almost to a whine.

Within two weeks my mother moved into one of seven available apartments on the second floor above The Coconut Grove Playhouse off Main Highway. The security guard who locked up every night lived in one. Another belonged to an activist lawyer. The rest were inhabited by schoolteachers who taught at Ransom-Everglades, the private school nearby and the last one was reserved for the star of whatever show was playing.

Unfortunately, parking evaporated when a show was in town. A metal outside door that opened with a passkey led to a semi-dark staircase, a bit creepy at night. We could sneak into the balcony to watch the shows, mixing with the crowd as though we had purchased tickets. I saw *The Owl and the Pussycat* starring Alan Alda, even got his autograph, and a revival of *Strange Interlude* by Eugene O'Neill, my mother's favorite playwright, with someone I never heard of named Geraldine Page, but whom my mother swooned over.

I didn't have any friends in the Grove and took to hanging out at the library on weekends, a contemporary structure of wooden beams. If my mother worked I went with her on assignments as photographer's assistant. She teamed with different reporters and seemed to get along with them, kibitzing back and forth without flirting. She'd never let any of the men assist her with her equipment. "I can hoist my own stuff," she told me. More than once I observed Sam or Derek's eyes take in her lean body and thick hair that sometimes fell over her face.

During one assignment, where the paper ran a series on the colored sections in town, my mother took her best photos. We started in the Grove at the Stirrup house built in 1897 on Charles and Main built by a Dr. Simpson. Derek, a fortyish guy in blue jeans with a pencil behind his ear—what a cliché—interviewed Simpson's granddaughter, Florida's first board-certified Negro pediatrician, taking notes in a spiral bound book. My mom also took pictures of the Mariah Brown house nearby, the oldest one in the Grove, built in 1890 of virgin pinewood by immigrants from Eleuthera.

From there we drove in Derek's dirty Jeep, my hands holding on to the bar across the empty roof in the back, to Brownsville on the other side of Miami. Georgette's Tea Room built in 1940 looked like an ordinary two-story apartment house to me. I listened as Derek interviewed the manager, Miss Elliot, an elegant dark woman with straightened hair piled on top of her head and big hoop earrings. I sat near a window air-conditioner that dripped condensation and drowned out parts of what she said.

Georgette's had been a hidden, lavishly furnished, hideaway for celebrities who weren't allowed to stay in the hotels where they performed, especially Billie Holiday who kept a permanent residence upstairs. I knew who she was because my mother played her blues records.

My mother snapped pictures of Miss Elliot and set up a tripod for the exterior of the building. Sweat stained her blouse, but she kept working. I had never seen my mother so happy and fulfilled. She thrived in a creative environment.

I, without much purpose, felt adrift. I went through the motions of finishing high school, but I didn't really belong. I didn't even attend my own prom. Tony went with a slutty-looking girl who wore heavy black eyeliner. My grandmother was in her own world with Al, the newlyweds snuggling in front of the TV to watch *Peyton Place* and *Red Skelton.*

Without warning, change enveloped us leaving behind sand crabs of trouble. Or *tsoris* as my grandmother would say. I graduated in '67 and made plans to attend Miami-Dade Community College. My grandmother offered to pay for my tuition. I used babysitting money to buy a dilapidated Ford and felt ready to begin anew, making plans to move in with my mother in the Grove.

A certified letter arrived from my uncles addressed to my grandmother. She rushed in crying and handed it to me.

Dear Mom,

So glad you're happy with your new husband, Al. We look forward to meeting him when we come to Florida next year.

There's no easy way to say this so I'm just going to state it. The business has run out of money. We had a small fire last year and the water damage from the fire hoses ruined a lot of stock. By the time we recovered from that the economy dipped. Seems people buy ready-made in department stores and we don't have those contracts. We can't send you a monthly allowance anymore. Max and I are going to sell the business and find jobs. At that time, we'll split the profits with you. If there are any after we pay the creditors. I'm sorry. Now that you and Al are married perhaps he can contribute to your upkeep.

Love,

Isaac

The reverberations of the bad news sailed around the plaster walls then bounced off the ceiling. My grandmother cried, cursed her fate and then slept. When my mother arrived she reprimanded my grandmother for spending her money on frivolities like Europe and dancing lessons and Slenderella.

"What? I shouldn't have fun?" My grandmother snapped her bathrobe around herself with a flourish and went to her room to cry. Al came in from his daily walk that he called his constitutional.

"I think you've had too much fun," my mother said under her breath.

Al shrugged his shoulders. "So I play the ponies or the dogs once in a while. My son gives me an allowance. I can't ask for more money. Business isn't so good with all the people moving to Fort Lauderdale to get away from the Cubans." He sat down and pushed his straw hat back on his head and wiped his shiny forehead.

My mother couldn't spare a dime. My tuition? It faded away, like my grandmother's perfume evaporating in the night breeze.

Chapter Nine

Mimi

Coconut Grove, 1967

If Miami Beach with its pastel hotel row became a haven for opportunists, tourists and elderly escapists, then Coconut Grove spelled cool and hip. Society matrons from the Woman's Club, wealthy professionals, professors from the University of Miami, scientists, authors and a group of studio artisans and musicians buried themselves in the verdant landscape. All acquiesced to the lazy and free lifestyle that found artists setting up easels on the sidewalk in front of galleries, kids without shoes in Kwik Chek, dressed down celebrities in sun glasses heading for yachts and ruffians panhandling near the outdoor cafes. Coconut Grove was the place to be seen.

Many of the pillars of the community inhabited 1940s estates, large stucco or coral rock homes that abutted the serene bay front or remained buried down winding streets like Ye Little Wood in a jungle of greenery. None of them were prepared for their sleepy town of free-thinkers to change.

A few blocks away on Charles Avenue, Miami's first Negroes established themselves in the 1920s. The descendants of Bahamian settlers and others who migrated to South Florida, many inhabited the homes their ancestors built. Known as "Colored Town" it was a part of the Grove, but I was struck at how different it was from its surroundings when we drove through it on Douglas Road. Unemployed men sitting outside stores, women in their maid uniforms waiting for the bus, children playing barefoot in mud, the steady movement of paper fans compensating for a lack of air-conditioning. Poor people with few opportunities.

I got a job in the Grove working at Lile's, a store that sold sundries. My mother thought it was great because I could get my birth control pills at a discount, but the truth was I didn't need them. I wasn't interested in going to bed with anyone. I wanted to get out and the only way was school. I figured it would take me a year to save up tuition to attend a four-year university in Gainesville like my friends. Once again, my life was on hold.

Hippies, anti-war protesters and folk singers began to gather in the park across from the library every evening. The pink-orange sun glistened on the water smearing hazy light over groups settling in for discussion and music. I stopped by when I finished work to make friends and check out the scene.

I tasted my first weed with Roy, a kid whose blond kinky hair fell into sausage-shaped curls. Sometimes I hung out with disaffected actors who painted their faces with peace signs and wore fringed vests. I loved the environmentalists who staged hug-ins with the trees.

Even though my mother had a job with an establishment newspaper, she started to take pictures for herself again. She loved shooting people more than scenery although she added some great sunsets to her portfolio. With an available darkroom she became inspired to shoot retired people feeding pigeons, disenfranchised Negroes in Liberty City, and weekenders enjoying their sailing vessels, canvas slapping in the wind. She also enjoyed documenting the gatherings of people who protested our government's involvement in Vietnam.

Utilizing another side of her creativity, she turned to tie-dying T-shirts with a rainbow of Rit dyes in our kitchen sink, rubber bands scattered about to make starburst designs. The small kitchen space became our lab, the bathroom our store. By the time we finished the sink was blue, the floor red and the counters green. The bathtub turned black and our hands stained purple. Some of the shirts turned out so great I sold them to the other kids.

My mother became passionate about the war. "Why are we sending our boys across the ocean to fight? We don't belong there," she told me over and over. As each issue of *Life* magazine showed up with graphic pictures on the cover, she'd become more vocal. One time I thought she might be jealous because she wasn't part of the action. "Why is it necessary to show us dead people? Can't they shoot the countryside and the villages we're wrecking?"

We both despised Lyndon Johnson and his war machine. We marched down Main Highway in a candlelight vigil chanting, "Hell no, we won't go" with eighteen-year-old boys.

After the sundown rally my mother introduced me to Steve, the organizer of the event who lived in one of the Playhouse apartments. Many of the participants, kids close to my age, brought their parents. "I want you to meet a guy with some moxie," she told me.

Steve was the first adult I knew who had long hair. Mostly it was my generation who used it as their badge of rebellion. He looked more like a renegade student than an activist lawyer.

"I just came from work," he told me, pulling the hair tucked behind his ears forward onto his face. Once the Prince Valiant haircut was in place he undid his tie and pushed it into his pocket. A T-shirt that hung over his shoulder went over his white long sleeved shirt, PEACE NOW scrawled across the front and a peace symbol on the back.

Steve gave me a warm handshake, then handed me flyers to pass out for a protest scheduled at the University of Miami the next night. "We'll wake up those rich kids," he told me. I turned and handed one to the first person who passed.

The event the next evening on the Hurricane's campus drew about fifty people, mostly students but a few professors with wire-rimmed glasses and hair below their collar. Not many compared to the events Steve was organizing in the Grove. Members of Students for a Democratic society, SDS, showed up with posters of dead Vietnamese, villagers shot in the back. One girl with red hair to her waist wore a T-shirt with revolutionary Che Guevara's picture.

We marched from the campus down Riviera Drive, toward Sunset Road and back again, attracting little attention except for a car of frat boys who threw oranges at us. My mother looked like one of the kids with her auburn hair braided, bell bottoms, and one of our tie-dyed shirts.

People who felt distress about the Vietnamese felt terrible about the treatment of black brethren, too, as they wanted to be called, and Native Americans. No more Negroes and Indians. Their cultures crept into ours. My mother wore an authentic beaded headband, the fringed end hanging down the side of her face and moccasins. She wished she could have grown an Afro.

When we finished at our gathering spot and stretched out on the dewy grass, I saw Steve look at my mother, his eyes lingering on her long legs in tight jeans. Then he reached for her hand and rolled onto his stomach to face her. She became self-conscious and turned away. Maybe because I was watching. I wanted her to have someone in her life. She had to be horny as hell by now.

During our drive back to the Grove through winding streets, the sky hidden from view by banyan trees, their massive root systems crunching the sidewalks, I said, "Mom, I think Steve likes you."

Her head whirled toward me, as though I stated something preposterous. "What? Oh. I don't have time for a man. Complicates things. And I want you to stay away from a relationship, too. At least until you finish college. Don't make the mistakes I did."

"What kind of mistakes did you make? Am I a mistake?"

We stopped at a red light, the color turning our faces a pretty shade of pink. "Mimi, of course not. I just picked someone for the wrong reasons." She looked away in discomfort. "Come here. Let me hug you." She reached across the seats.

I wasn't ready for that. "Mom, you need to loosen up a little. You oughta try some pot."

"What? Is that what you're getting into now? Mimi, drugs are absolutely the wrong way to go." Her hands gripped the steering wheel.

"Pot's not a drug. It's a plant. It would relax you. You wouldn't be so uptight."

"We have a good mother-daughter relationship and I don't want to spoil it. I don't want to hear another word about pot."

I squished lower in my seat and remained quiet the rest of the way home, watching cars with couples in them. With a road tour of Neil Simon's "Star Spangled Girl" playing, we circled the Playhouse in search of a parking space for a half an hour. I hadn't seen the show but had sailed past the star, Tony Perkins, in the hallway.

We passed cottages built fifty years ago with porous coral rock, simple family homes tucked into lush foliage, and huge estates, their wrought iron gates keeping out lookers, on acres of land that rolled to the sea wall and the water beyond. We ended up walking three blocks with our elbows linked just as the show broke, brushing past theatergoers in sequins and boas.

A few weeks later Steve called when my mother wasn't

there. He was organizing a big rally in the Grove to protest the U.S.'s biggest assault of the war. Twenty-five thousand men were committed to fight near the Cambodian border. President Johnson said the bombing of North Vietnam would continue. Steve, with passionate outrage, said it would be the biggest rally ever.

Flyers went up on telephone poles everywhere. I don't know how he worked with all his organizing. His practice mostly consisted of kids fighting their draft board, others with bogus medical deferments, and parents making arrangements to ship their kids to Canada.

David, my high school buddy, wrote to me from the University of Florida in Gainesville. His dorm mates panicked when they failed a test. If they flunked out, they were back in the draft pool. Big motivation to study.

The day of the march Roy, the neighborhood pothead, and a bunch of kids stopped in late morning at Lile's, the Grove's upscale drugstore, to tell me the crowds would be huge. People started filling up the park at lunchtime, where I ate my sandwich on a pigeon-decorated bench. A drop of rain fell onto my wax paper. I checked out the clouds rolling across the sky, packed up the rest of my meal and dashed back to the store, the drizzle sprinkling my shoulders. It dripped all day, amid a constant buzz of people rushing in to purchase necessities and hippies wanting a Coke.

Mr. Scully, the manager, a portly man whose twin brother was the pharmacist, became nervous when the store filled with too many people, especially kids. "These hippies shoplift, you know," he said out of the side of his mouth. "And they don't bathe either. They drive out my legitimate customers." I didn't argue. I needed the job.

Buses left to collect people at Miami-Dade Community College, then headed up to Broward County to gather more participants.

I couldn't wait to get out of there, dancing from foot to foot behind the counter, assisting a Coral Gables matron picking out a Revlon lipstick. She finally picked out Persian Melon. By four o'clock old man Scully decided to close early because the police were cordoning off the streets with sawhorses. I walked through puddles that soaked my sneakers to the apartment.

I waited for my mother stretched out on the sofa, thumbing through her copy of *The Bell Jar*. The back said the author, Sylvia Plath, was a poet who committed suicide. Really depressing.

My mother dashed in, anxious to change and head back out for the rally. Emerging from her bedroom, she said, "'Ya think I should go braless?"

I looked at her in her jeans and a black top, her hair in braids. "Huh?"

"No one's wearing bras anymore," she told me. She examined herself in the mirror near the door, slipped her bra straps out of the armholes of her blouse, unhooked the back, pulled the bra out from the bottom and turned her body to view each side. A macramé planter from a hook in the ceiling, overflowing with a spider plant, blocked half of her view.

"No bra. Come on. Let's go." She tossed the rejected bra on a chair as she stuffed her key into her pocket. I grabbed her camera bag.

The rain had stopped and a clean, fresh smell steamed from the sidewalks. The foliage glistened with raindrops, a variety of greens surreal in the crepuscular light.

My mother and I walked past art galleries, cafes, clothing boutiques, and Lile's toward the park adjacent to the bay, boats bobbing in their slips from the choppy water, her cameras swinging in their leather bag. She spoke about her job at the paper, how angry she was at our government for escalating the war and how happy she was that we left New York.

"Mimi, find what you're passionate about and you're life will work. Don't give it up for any man."

"But, don't you think you'll ever marry again?" I slowed down my pace.

"What for? I'm not having any more children and I can't imagine letting a man tell me what to do." She stopped walking under a streetlight that had just flicked on to illuminate her face. She shook her finger at me in jest. "Wait a minute. That doesn't mean you don't have to marry to have kids. We still come from a traditional background and this society frowns on illegitimate children. Why are you asking me this? You're too young to think about getting involved with someone, especially if they're the likes of Tony Fassouli."

I chilled with shame at the mention of Tony's name. How could I have ever kissed him, let alone gone all the way? We moved into single file to let others pass.

"Would you live with someone? Lots of people are doing that now. Michaela wrote she's moving in with her boyfriend at University of Georgia."

"Mimi." She stopped to turn and look at me. "Unless someone melts me to my knees I'm not getting involved. I want you to finish college. I'm probably getting a raise soon and it'll cover some of next year's expenses."

As the last vestiges of an orange-purple sky faded to pastels, we walked on to where clumps of people stood around under mangrove trees laden with Spanish moss, the ends of their cigarettes and candles dotting the darkness. A group of staid-looking people in button down oxford shirts, who looked out of place among the FREE LOVE signs, carried lanterns and flashlights. Bodies stretched out on blankets spread over damp grass. Others sat huddled in groups listening to a guitar player, singing along as they hugged their knees. Someone was imitating

Bob Dylan, singing "Like a Rolling Stone" in a raspy voice. Wet leaves scattered through the air, whipped by plodding feet. The sweet smell of marijuana wafted through the bay breeze.

Steve's voice from a bullhorn began to shout directions. "All war protesters line up on the sidewalk. We're going to be moving down Bayshore Drive and then turn back toward Dixie Highway. Hold your signs high and please extinguish all smoking materials." A twitter of laughter and fake coughing sprinkled through the group.

Buses arrived and a hundred more joined us dressed in jeans, headbands or floppy hats and outfits with beads and bells sewed on them. Someone lit a stick of incense and waved it through the crowd while a high sweet voice began to sing "All We Are Saying Is Give Peace a Chance." Air brakes of a bus parked along the side squealed and more people, many parents with their kids climbed off yelling, "Hey, hey, LBJ, how many kids didja kill today?" Stringy-haired students, guitars slung across their backs with multi-color woven straps, asked for signatures on a petition.

Steve stayed near the starting point and directed people into formation while my mother walked the sidelines to keep people from blocking the sidewalks. I shadowed her, carrying her bag. Occasionally, she'd stop to take a picture with the Nikon around her neck. The streetlights added an eerie glow. A cop approached Steve to check his permit. All in order.

The streets began to fill with observers, older people who clapped in support, couples, their arms slung around shoulders and little kids who ran alongside as though we were a happy parade instead of marching to protest war and death. A few solemn-faced men smoking cigarettes, wearing muscle T-shirts, jeans and yellow hardhats watched the preparations.

I don't remember exactly how it started, but the cops confronted a group of kids dressed in black chanting slogans. Later someone said they were passing weed, but I didn't believe it. Everyone knew that could jeopardize all of us. A girl named Zephyr who lived in the park, gave a burly cop in wraparound glasses the finger. Her protector, a skinny kid, his beard tied in a rubber band, pushed the cop when he began to yell at her. Other cops came to assist him. Nightsticks appeared and fists flew through the air. Zephyr and her gangly protector, dragged by their feet, were pushed into a police van.

A group of longhaired kids armed with slingshots and rocks took aim at the cops from behind a stand of pine trees, trunks sticky with sap and bark peeling away in layers, like the evening calmness we had envisioned. A black kid I knew from Overtown, wearing a dashiki, his Afro a halo around his head, threw a gasoline bomb into the street. The explosion, a bonfire of flames, scattered more people. Through the turmoil Steve's voice on his bullhorn kept repeating, "Please avoid confrontations. Let's show them peace."

Skeleton-masked protesters began smashing store windows, the tinkle of glass a delicate sound in the cacophony. I saw Lile's front window go and hands reach in to loot displays of suntan lotion, picture frames, and makeup. Police officers shouted to stop as guns exploded. Ray, purveyor of medicinal plants, ran lopsided across the street, then tripped and fell. I gasped, "He's been shot." But he picked himself up and began a scrambled action between two buildings. Screams and curse words clung in the air like the *slap slap slap slap* of the boats in the water.

When we saw we couldn't run past a cordon of police officers with linked arms, my mother grabbed me in the chaos and flung herself on top of my back never letting her hands off her cameras. I could barely breathe with her weight on me, the hard asphalt of the street gnarling into my bones. I squeezed my eyes shut. For a few minutes it was quiet. My mother shifted her weight to pull the

Nikon off.

Construction workers roamed with pieces of wood yelling epithets of, "Come here, you pansies. We're gonna kill the draft dodgers. Bunch of fairies." I heard cracks, cries of pain, panicked moans, calls for help.

Another crack. A whizzing sound. My mother's weight collapsed onto me, her fingers loosening their grip on her precious camera. A wetness streamed down my face. I touched my fingers to the gooey liquid as a flashlight glowed red on my hand. I struggled to push her off me. She rolled off to her side next to the curb filled with debris. Blood covered half her face, her left eye matted with it and hair. She touched her hand to her head.

"Mimi. I'm shot. Go. Take my camera." I could hardly hear her scratchy voice.

"Mommy, don't leave me." I knew my sobs made me incoherent. I scrambled to be upright, her blood sticky on my back.

I backed into a doorway as a young policeman strutted toward her. He pulled my mother up by the arm and began to drag her away. She shrieked for me to run, but I wanted to go with her. I knew she needed medical attention. She flung her arms around in protest.

"Get your filthy hands off me, you pig."

I stood behind him, frozen in fear, and watched his thick neck, a short boy's haircut fresh above his collar, his back taut in his blue uniform. When he knelt down my mother hit him in the chest. He wrestled with her, reaching for her wrists. He flipped her onto her back as she kicked, his knee holding her down. I saw him punch her in the eye. The click of the handcuffs sounded final. The shrill wail of an ambulance streamed closer. By the time I ran back to her, her body was limp, the camera bag kicked aside. The cop held a rag against her head.

"Calm down and everything will be okay. You've been shot,

lady. I'm just trying to apply pressure."

"She can't hear you. She's dead, you idiot," I screamed.

I grabbed the Nikon lying in the gutter and with little knowledge, I began to shoot my mom as two paramedics lifted her onto a stretcher. As she was being taken away, her words echoed in my head. "Advance the film forward. Turn on the flash." They closed the door. I jumped on the bumper and pounded on the door and yelled that I wanted to go with her. I saw her feet, the shoelaces of her untied sneakers, through the wired glass. Someone with strong hands pulled me off as the engine started.

Steve continued on the bullhorn in an effort to calm people down but it did little good. Spinning red lights joined sirens, sending a macabre chill through the air. The construction workers took off, tossing aside their clubs. Jagged strikes of lightning lit up the debacle followed by claps of thunder in rapid succession, a monster movie with bad weather and villains. Roy led a group, directing them like a conductor screaming, "Pigs, pigs, pigs." The cops, even more furious, began to reorganize.

I ran for Steve to tell him about my mother. While my torrent of words spilled forth, the sky opened up. The deluge of water shook the trees. A branch cracked, then fell onto the pine needle carpet of the park. Leaves scattered into the street. Lightning lit up the cops and kids, combatants in a silent black-and-white film. Once thunder rolled again heads split against wood in syncopation. Was God speaking and telling us to stop?

The thunderstorm brought most of the melee to an end. Kids ran for cover. The cops, water pouring from their helmets, covered their guns and ran for their cars. Sirens announced to those in the paddy wagons their journey to the police department had begun.

Sheets of rain cleansed my emotions. Lightning splayed the midnight-blue sky with streaks of yellow-white. I ran toward Lile's because my mother told me never to stand under a tree. I leaned against the white brick wall. Sobbing into my arm, I felt a hand on my shoulder.

"Hey, Mimi. We'll figure it out." Steve, drenched, too, had on a khaki canvas hat that kept the water from dripping in his eyes. I nodded, tears blending into my wet face.

"Do you have her cameras?" I patted the bag on my shoulder and with confidence I said, "I think I got some good shots."

"Come on, kid, I'm taking to you your Grandma's on Miami Beach. You're not staying down here by yourself. Then I'll come back and check on your mom.

"I think she's dead. She was shot. I saw them take her away."

The look on his face told me he loved her. "Shot doesn't mean dead. Do you know where they took her?"

I shook my head, too overcome to speak.

"They probably took her to Mercy Hospital."

"Or the morgue," I muttered to myself. "I want to go with you."

"Mimi, it may take hours until I find her. I have to go to the police station to make a statement. Who knows how long that'll take? Go home, get dry and I'll come back for you when I know more."

Part of me wanted to resist him but the other side said my grandma would be watching the eleven o'clock news. Scared and grief-stricken, Steve guided me as we splashed through puddles, fliers face down in the mud, sawhorses on their sides, red police lights reflecting on our stricken faces, toward his car.

My grandmother opened the door, her chenille bathrobe clutched to her bosom, fear on her face. "Mimi, you all right? Look at you. What happened? Who is this?" My grandmother stood back from the door. Al was asleep on the sofa wearing a paisley silk robe, the TV blaring news of the aborted march.

"I'm Steve Greenberg, a friend of your daughter's. May I come in?"

Chapter Ten

Mimi

Thank goodness my mother didn't die. She returned from Mercy hospital a few days later, her head bandaged in a gauze turban, a braid hanging down the left side of her face.

"The nurses fixed my hair. What's left of it," she told me with a weak smile.

A week later I went with her to the doctor. As he unwrapped the dressing, I gasped at the open red gash in the middle of her shaved scalp.

"You have a nasty flesh wound. Being grazed by a bullet is not something I recommend. Why don't you leave the activism to someone younger from now on?" he asked her. She grimaced as he touched her.

It took months to heal. Her auburn hair, clipped short and combed over the bald spot, started to even out. Unfortunately, the Grove paper let her go, labeling her a provocateur. Steve took on the case. With income from her photos of the march picked up by wire services, we got by. They appeared in national magazines like *Life* and *Newsweek*. The pictures I took of her on that night came out blurry.

Mid-June police officers killed an African-American robbery suspect and the city exploded in riots and fires. Even though my mother rested often, she accepted when AP called her to cover it.

I drove her to the street in Liberty City to shoot the aftermath of wreckage, looted buildings with smashed windows, graffiti and burned out cars.

Steve stayed close during my mother's recovery. By the time she felt a hundred percent they acted as a couple. With his apartment down the hall, they practically lived together. Weary of the parking situation I wasn't surprised when my mother told me they were moving to a funky house on Jasper Street. In the fall of '67 a few blocks from the Playhouse my mother and Steve set up housekeeping in a place with a carport for two cars and landscaping so overgrown with sea grape I could hardly see it.

Once the war ended with our humiliation and protesters in decline, Steve cut his hair, put on a suit and joined a prestigious downtown Miami law firm that handled immigration, although he hadn't sold out completely. If I stopped by on a weekend the house reeked of pot and he'd be wearing one of my mom's tie-dyed T-shirts, lounging in his jeans. Their place became a hub of liberal opinions, left-over hippies and avant-garde artists. The dilapidated guest house secreted in the back yard and shaded by date palms had a roof covered in purple passion flowers. It became an office and darkroom for my mother.

"I'm working on a black-and-white book about the sixties in South Florida," she told me.

After my mother's hair grew in she cut it into a short wedge, plucked her eyebrows, put on some lipstick and applied for a photography position at *The Miami Herald*, an award winning newspaper. They hired her! Hallelujah! She had her purpose back. Gauzy skirts and peasant blouses gave way to tailored pants suits. I checked the credits on the front page photographs and often her name appeared on the byline.

With some funding from Steve that September I joined my friends at University of Florida in Gainesville. I swore I'd pay him back. I went through on the trimester system so I caught up to my peers who had started a year earlier. As a journalism major I worked on the school paper, *The Gator*, and finally met like-minded kids--ones who talked about the earth, the downtrodden and the oppressed. Al said I was a bleeding heart liberal, but I thought I was just someone who cared. Steve and my mom said they were proud of me.

In 1970 during my internship at *The Miami Herald*, the city of Miami Beach planned a retrospective thirty-fifth anniversary memorial to honor victims of the Holocaust. My mother, asked to blow up a dozen of her most significant photographs from the DP camps, spent evenings and weekends in preparation. The mayor, the governor and other dignitaries from around the world accepted invitations to attend the event.

I bought a black sheath for the occasion.

Steve was out of town on business and my grandmother refused to come. "Too much sadness," she told me. "Why do I need to be upset?"

That evening after the speeches my mother met with survivors in the gallery for an hour. Some came with compliments about her photos, others wanted to tell their sad stories. Her weary eyes caught my attention across the room.

"Come on, Mimi. Let's get out of here." She gathered her purse and headed toward the door. She remained silent as we walked to the car. What else could be said about such tragedy?

I drove. "Want to stop and see Grandma? We're in the neighborhood."

"Sure," my mother said without enthusiasm.

My grandmother opened the door in her flowered housecoat with snaps down the front, her thick glasses refracting light. Her silver hair, the platinum long gone, was combed back from her face. She still had the habit of greasing herself with cold cream. I swiped her shiny cheek with mine and my mother did the same. We sat down on the familiar rattan furniture.

With a serious expression she said, "Mimi, Sarah, I just found out Al has the big *C*. Burton told me. Al never said a word. I knew something was wrong because he sleeps so much. I don't know how long he's got. Can you imagine? Me, the sick one with diabetes burying two husbands?"

My mother got up to hug her. I didn't know what to say. Al, an okay guy, made her happy. They danced together, traveled while the money lasted, ate at Wolfies, went to the movies. I glanced at the half dozen roses on the table he bought her every Friday afternoon for Shabbat. She reached in her pocket and dabbed her nose with an embroidered hankie.

"Anyway, I want to give you something," she said. She disappeared into her bedroom, opening and closing the door quietly because Al was sleeping. She returned with a small white cardboard box, yellowed with age, a small stain on top and two plastic newspaper bags.

"Mom, Mimi doesn't need any more of your stuff. She's in a small apartment." My mother got up to get a glass of water.

"Wait. This she'll want."

I loved my grandma but I didn't want the *tchotchkes* that she kept trying to pawn off on me.

I moved onto a tufted hassock to be knee-to-knee with her. Before she placed the box in my lap and gave me a nod to open it, she pulled the table lamp closer to us. I pried off the cover and gasped.

"What is it?" my mother called from the kitchen.

Nestled in the cotton was the most beautiful piece of jewelry I had ever seen. A double strand of white pearls gleamed at me, each one carefully couched between two knots, a large diamond leaf clasp holding the creation together, reflecting pastel colors.

I picked them up, the smooth, cool surfaces, liquid in my hands.

"Grandma, these are magnificent. Where did you get them?"

"From your grandpa on our anniversary. Many years ago. Put them on."

My mother came into the room and watched as I slipped the pearls over my head, lifting them so I could examine the clasp. "How come I've never seen them? Why haven't you worn them?"

Her shoulders did a short shrug and her head cocked to the side. "Who knows? Once I got to Florida I didn't think they belonged. When I met Al I put them in the vault at the bank. I want you to have them. They're from another life, another world that I lived long ago."

I stood in front of the gold-framed mirror over her sofa. They looked magnificent against my black dress. I pulled my hair off my neck and piled it on top of my head, twisting from side to side to catch the light angles. For a moment I looked pretty, my face reminiscent of sepia photographs of my grandmother in her twenties.

"Grandma, are you sure you want to give these pearls to me and not my mom?"

My mother's face looked worried. "Mimi's a responsible young woman but those are very valuable. I'm not sure it's a good idea."

My grandmother waved her hand. "Ach, your mother would never wear them. Maybe someday you'll have an occasion. You'll have a daughter. Pass them to her."

I hesitated before I asked the next question. "Mom, would you not wear them because you didn't like Grandpa Nathan?"

My mother looked sulky, arms folded across her chest. "Don't be ridiculous. They're not my style."

My grandmother, very still, her voice soft, said, "Maybe I should have left him. Such a *mashugana* with money and the children, but I was afraid. One time I thought I would go back to Poland, to my family." She reached forward and kissed my forehead. "If I had you wouldn't be here. Or your mama. I didn't know how to survive without a husband like women today. Sarah, I never told you but I envied you when you left your husband. Nathan was so strong, so decisive. Maybe it wasn't the best for my children. Maybe I was selfish, but I couldn't leave. Where would I go? After the war I couldn't even go back to Poland. Then he got sick. Ach. Now I worry about Al."

She paused and looked away, her eyes teary. I reached out to touch her hand. She looked at me through her thick pink glasses and began to speak again.

"Thanks God I had time with Al. Didn't I deserve a husband who adored me? Brought me roses. I don't know. Did I make the right choices? If Nathan hadn't insisted I come, I wouldn't have you, Mamala."

My throat clogged and I knew if I let go tears would pour. I got up to hug her.

She touched the pearls around my neck. "Besides, it's you who should have them."

"I'll always treasure them." I waited before I spoke again. "Why won't you ever talk about your life before you came to this country? What happened to your family?"

She handed me the plastic bags from the couch.

"What's this?" I asked.

My mother broke her silence. "Mother, don't give her all that crap. What's the point dredging up the past? Tonight was hard enough. The war's over. Everyone's gone. I'm through with survivor guilt. Let's rebuild."

I pulled out letters, some tied with thin strips of lavender ribbon, others held together with rubber bands. They fell into my lap. My grandmother watched while I took off the bindings and grazed through them, her eyes shifting behind her glasses.

Strange colored stamps, postmarks from Poland and Belgium, return addresses 21 BIELANSKA STREET written in elaborate handwriting with blue fountain pen ink, AMERYKA misspelled. All addressed to my grandmother, her name, PAULINA, written with a flourish, the final "a" ending in a long curl. Blue and white onionskin paper slippery to touch, a musty smell hiding the truths, slid through my fingers.

My mother leaned over and grabbed the papers on my lap in her hand. Waving them over her head, her face red with fury. "This is a waste of time. It ties you to the past. I'm going to throw them out." She tried to tear the pile in half but she couldn't. A few fell to the floor. She took one and the tearing sound cut through me. My grandmother began to cry. I jumped to my feet, a hazy feeling swallowing me.

"You can't do that. I want them. They're my history, too." I grabbed for the letters as my mother held them out of my reach.

She yelled into my face. "Get on with your life. Don't get stuck like everyone else in this family. Worthless pieces of paper." She stopped moving to tuck the bulk of them under her chin and tear another one into small pieces.

"No! Give them to me." I wrenched them from under my mother's neck and hid them behind my back. I heard my grandmother's weak cries.

My mother turned to my grandmother who sat folded into a sad heap on the sofa. "Oh, Mama, why did you do this? You'll have her living in the past like you." Then she turned to me. "Go ahead. Keep them. Waste your life looking backwards. I guarantee you'll find nothing. Nothing." And with that she left, slamming the door behind her.

I sat down next to my grandma who wiped her nose with a tissue from her pocket. She asked me, "What's wrong with her?"

"I think she's upset at looking at her own photographs tonight.

They triggered bad memories."

I got up and gathered the pieces on the floor and put them into one of the plastic bags.

My grandma dug in her pocket and handed me a small velvet bag. I emptied it onto my lap and two perfect diamonds fell out. "My father gave them to me in case. They're for your mother. I wish she hadn't run out like that."

Then she gave me the final package of letters, bound in a faded red satin ribbon, envelopes torn open, ragged edges folded down. The same handwriting from the other letters looked shaky. On the outside a round stamp appeared near the addresses. Chills skimmed up my spine and raised the hair on my neck. I recognized German words on the outer edge of the design and in the center an eagle with spread wings flew, its feet gripping a swastika.

"Grandma, what's this? Where did they come from?"

"It's all I have left of my parents, my three brothers, their wives and children, my cousins, aunts, uncles. Pieces of paper. Paper children who no longer speak."

I pulled out a few sheets. The handwriting crawled across the yellowed pages on both sides, unrecognizable to me, save the dates and places at the top. Warsaw, 1939. Brussels, 1940. Warsaw, 1942.

"What languages are these?" I didn't recognize the strange words.

"My mother wrote to me in Polish, my father in German, and sometimes Yiddish, my brother Carlo in French and a little English."

"Will you help me translate them?"

Her hand went to her chest as she shook her head. "Oh no. I couldn't do that. Relive the horrors all over again? No. The secrets are there for you to discover. I can't do it. Some day you'll have time. You tell my story, my life that turned out so different than

I thought, not made-to-order like my childhood dresses." She paused to turn out the light. "Did I ever tell you what the gypsies said to me when I was a young girl and they read my palm?"

Epilogue

Over the years, long after I had a scandalous affair with Bob, my editor at the paper, I wore my pearls on special occasions, a reminder of my sweet grandmother. She would have wanted me to follow my heart.

Ten years my senior, Bob left his wife and kid for me. Consumed with scarlet-woman guilt I knew I was a home wrecker. My mother told me to heed the consequences of starting a marriage based on someone else's hurt. It didn't stop us. Passionate about our work and each other we eloped to Key West for a moonlit justice-of-the -peace wedding after his divorce became final.

Money remained tight with alimony and child support, but eventually, his ex re-married and his son, Evan, let me befriend him. Evan adored the twins, who I insisted on naming Paula and Nate, although I hadn't followed much else in my religion, letting it get lost in my mother's atheism.

When they entered college years later and I finally had time to pull out my grandmother's letters, the ancient missives, still encased in their original plastic bags, held such mystery for me. I turned them over and over in my hands, then put them away.

When Al died my grandmother faded into a smaller version of herself. No more fancy clothes or makeup. Just stooped shoulders and thick glasses from her failing eyesight. She resigned herself to old age in a retirement apartment, shuffling with a shopping bag to the grocery store or the bank, making friends with the other widowed ladies.

According to her Cuban caretakers, one morning she mixed up her insulin injections. They found her in a diabetic coma. I rushed to Mount Sinai Hospital and sat by her bed for hours. My mother and Steve stopped by, too. Without gaining consciousness, she murmured unintelligible words, a repetitive litany of sounds strung together, lost pearls flung into time. As I sat with her, an unread magazine open on my lap, light streamed through the Venetian blinds from the afternoon sun. I watched her closed eyes twitch occasionally in her unlined face.

A plain-faced nurse's aide, pushing a cart, came in to turn my grandmother and change the sheets. She acknowledged me with a nod and set about her business, the pad of her rubber soled shoes making a muffled noise on the linoleum floor. She chattered at me about the weather, traffic.

"Wish I knew what she was saying," I said closing the magazine, not expecting a reply.

Overweight, in her forties, she grunted as she moved my grandmother to her side and slid fresh sheets beneath her. "She's speaking Polish."

"How do you know? Are you Polish?" I moved forward on my chair, the magazine fell to the floor. Her accent sounded like my grandmother's, v's for b's, no th's, even the cadence of her speech the same.

"Yes. I come from Gdansk and lived in Chicago cleaning hotels with my husband for ten years. We moved to Florida for the sunshine. Winters in Chicago are like Poland. Brrr." She continued to tuck in corners and swish sheets and blankets. Self-conscious at her own verbosity, she asked, as she motioned toward the limp body with her chin, "Where was she from?"

"Warsaw. Do you know what she's saying?"

The nurse's aide leaned her ear over my grandmother's face to listen, her head turned toward me. "She's talking to her mother and father. Says she's sorry for leaving them, that she'll be there soon." She stood up straight. "Make any sense to you?"

"I'm not sure." I picked up the magazine.

Five years later, after my mother and Steve were killed in a car accident on Sunset Road, slick with rain on a Saturday night, I played with the old letters in my grief. In our Grove cottage I sat by the coral rock fireplace wrapped in a sweater. The rare occasion of a cold snap made a cozy evening at home welcome. Bob sat across from me reading and smoking his pipe, the cherry wood smell mixing with the hickory logs. I had to know what was in these "paper children." Maybe answers for Paula, who wanted to be a writer and Nate, my future attorney. Or better yet, answers for me.

A few days later I met with Rabbi Lehrer at Temple Beth Israel. After I peeked into the peaceful holiness of the sanctuary, we sat in his office, light streaming through the windows behind him. Young and in shirtsleeves, a black skullcap on his crown, he seemed open and friendly as I handed him the letters.

"I know we have congregants, some of whom are Holocaust survivors, who speak these languages and would love to assist you in translating these letters," he told me. "My suggestion is to make copies. I'll put it in our bulletin and we'll get volunteers."

I agreed. It felt awkward to be there. I stood up to leave, my purse on my shoulder. He walked me through the door out to the front of the synagogue steps.

"Thank you for your help."

"Oh, no problem. I'm anxious to know what's in them, too. I love family history." And, with a smile, added, "We have almost five thousand years of living history. For most of that time we survived in countries among alien cultures and still preserved our identity. Maybe I can teach you some of our traditions and bring you back to your faith."

A surge of longing rocked me. I hesitated. "Maybe, Rabbi. Maybe you can."

Paper Children

As a child, I would often see her
She was, like her room, old and gray
Surrounded by words, like fallen birds
With thick accent, my grandma would say

These are my paper children
Torn from my family tree
Lost in the European cauldron
The only one remaining was me

It wasn't until many years later
That I knew I needed her to explain
So the next time I met her, when she picked up the letters
her eyes misted and her voice dusted with pain

These are my paper children
All that's left of my family
While they may be but a few of the millions
they were everything to me

Oh my god, I then understood, the blood left me
as my tears fell onto her memories
We cried and held on to each other
For the writing of our history

These are my paper children
torn from my family tree
lost in the European cauldron
the only one remaining was me

It's been many years since she joined the others
But I can see her face clear as the sun
I pray over the writings, like the candles I'm lighting
for her parents, husband, daughters, and son

Now I hold her paper children,
Like I hold my own kids close when they ask.
I teach them as they're building their future,
"Remember to honor our past."

Music and lyrics: © 2004 Barry Brooks

Family Album

Left - Meyer
Above - Paulina

Right - Miriam
Above - Meyer

Upper Left - Paulina and Carlo, Upper Right - Paulina's
Children, Below - Paulina's Family at the Spa

Above - Paulina, Nathan, Sarah
Below - Nathan's Family

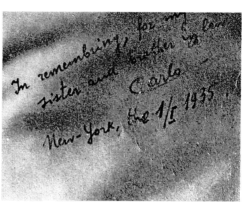

Left - Paulina,

Above - Carlo's inscription
on music book

Below - Meyer supervising
construction site

Paulina
1955

Acknowledgments

I utilized many history books about the Holocaust, but by far the most helpful research on post-Holocaust Europe was the symposium at Arizona State University in February of 2002, "Aftermath: An International Conference on European Jewry Immediately after the Shoah."

Broadway on the Bay by Carol Cohan was very helpful for information about the Coconut Grove Playhouse. The patience of Vanda Hawkins in translating piles of fragile letters was invaluable. Kim Appis has done a marvelous job of interior design and capturing the eras.

Thank you to all those who gave me suggestions in its formative stages: Judy Starbuck, Virginia Nosky and editor, Deb Ledford. Agent Cherry Weiner gave me the gift of believing this was a compelling story.

A special note of appreciation to songwriter, Barry Brooks, who penned the music and words to "Paper Children" as a tribute to my grandmother.

Special gratitude to Kathy L. Patrick, founder of the world's largest book club, for picking *Paper Children* as an Official Pulpwood Queen Book Club Selection for 2011. Her support has been invaluable.

My eternal love goes to those who have acknowledged my desire to write – Jessica for her editor's eye, Ara for encouragement and Skip, my love and support. And, finally, to my beautiful grandmother who sat and told me stories.

For multiple copies, educational discounts
or speaking engagements, contact:
www.marciafine.com
www.paperchildren.com
facebook.com/paperchildren
facebook.com/jeanrubin
http://jeanrubinblog.com
http://marciafinebooks

Reader's Guide for Paper Children

1. *Paper Children* is written from three different points of view. What ties the three generations together besides family? Who is the strongest?
2. What kind of issues do immigrants face in a new country? Are they the same or different than they were at the beginning of the twentieth century?
3. Paulina seems to be an "at effect" character. Where do her strengths lie?
4. Is Nathan a hero or an anti-hero? What is the irony in his saving a stranger's life? Was he responsible for his brothers, sisters and parents? How did they treat him?
5. Sarah is a rebellious young woman. How did her relationship with her parents foster this? Does she love her mother and father? Does she accept responsibility?
6. Mimi had to learn many of life's lessons herself. What was the most important one?
7. What roles do religion and tradition play in the lives of the main characters—Paulina, Nathan, Sarah, Mimi and Will? Are any of them conflicted about their own views?
8. What parallels do you see between life today and Paulina's life in Poland? What did Carlo mean to her?
9. In today's world many people are still displaced. What are the repercussions of the people who survived World War II and their stay in the Displaced Person's camps?
10. What are Nathan's views about capitalism, America and unions?
11. How did the Holocaust reverberate through the generations?
12. Why did Paulina wait so long to share the letters?

CPSIA information can be obtained
at www.ICGtesting.com
Printed in the USA
FFOW02n1905190318
45756715-46620FF